TORI

Book #2 of Glory

Dale Mayer

Book in this series:

Genesis

Tori

Celeste

Glory Trilogy

TORI
Beverly Dale Mayer
Valley Publishing Ltd.

ISBN-13: 978-1-988315-82-9
Print Edition

About This Book

Hurt and betrayed by the man she thought was the love of her life, Tori Chandler goes into hiding to heal from too many soul-deep hurts to deal with otherwise. But Devon has bigger reasons for seeking her out than giving her an apology that he'll be the first to admit she deserves—and then some. He needs her help to save the people in their town of Little Glory, trapped behind a strange energy pattern.

As an energy worker dedicated to preserving planet Glory's energy resource in its forests that all life is dependent upon, Tori isn't in the position to turn her back on those in need. She agrees to help Devon, only if he promises to stay out of her life for good once the job is done.

Devon gives Tori the promise she needs, without any intention of honoring it. He made a mistake that he regrets. Nevertheless, if Tori allows him back into her life for any reason, he aims to prove he can be everything she needs from now on.

The disruptive energy pattern found in too many places near Little Glory proves to be not only a cause for concern but also the start of something even more sinister. If so, that hints either Devon nor Tori, whether together or separated, or anyone else on the planet for that matter, will have a future.

Sign up to be notified of all Dale's releases here!
https://geni.us/DaleNews

CHAPTER 1

T ORI CHANDLER CHECKED her watch. Damn. She had
just two minutes to make a decision, if she wanted to
risk a trip to the bank. Her break was only fifteen minutes
long, and she didn't dare be late. Not with a new job and a
strict boss. She could always walk out of the bank, if the line
wasn't moving fast enough.

She needed the little cash she had for her rent. She had
to pay daily, until she had one month's worth saved up, and
she was already behind. Her landlord had caught her in the
hallway this morning and had given her an ultimatum.
Moving again wasn't an option. She needed that hideaway. It
was within walking distance to her new job and saved her
bus fare. That meant keeping her landlord happy until next
week, when she'd get her first paycheck from the health food
store. She'd already given him the last of her cash, and no
way would she use plastic. It was too traceable. She didn't
know if she was still on anyone's radar, but she just knew she
couldn't take the chance. She'd left in secret and had
planned to stay gone. Except for her sisters, nothing was left
for her back home.

In the past year, she still hadn't found another place to
call home. Pain and anger had sent her on this journey, and
now she was afraid she didn't know how to stop.

Moving a lot meant no accumulation of stuff. She had so

little to her name that, if her landlord dumped her belongings outside when he kicked her out, it would take no more than a single tote bag to pack them up.

This was her first chance to settle down in a long time. Now if she could just make it work.

"Tori, go for your break now," said Mary, her supervisor. "See you back in fifteen."

"Thanks." Tori smiled. "I'll just hop over to the bank."

Mary frowned. "Bad day for that. It's the last day of the month."

"And that's why I have to go." Tori gave her a bright smile. "Not to worry. If the line is too long, I'll just come back."

That brought a smile to Mary's face. "Good idea. You've been a model employee so far. You know how the owner feels about tardiness. Best not to push it."

Tori rolled her eyes at Mary's back, as the woman walked away; then Tori bolted for the front door. Did no one in this world understand that sometimes shit happened and had to be dealt with?

The bank was only a few businesses over in the big strip mall. Thankfully it was a small branch and served mostly locals. Regardless, it was still almost noon, and that meant there'd be a rush. As the building came into view, she saw no one else hurrying to get inside. That, at least, was a good sign. Tori pulled open one of the two glass doors and rushed inside.

A blissfully cool air-conditioned gust hit her, but she barely noticed. Her senses went on full alert.

All around here was an eerie silence. She stopped in her tracks and looked at the service counter. The tellers all stared at her, a mixture of fear and anger on their faces … and horror.

She straightened and realized that something was very, very wrong. Her instincts screamed at her to run. *Get the hell out of there.*

Then she heard it. *Click.* And something round and hard was shoved into her back.

"What a nice day for you to come to the bank." A gravelly voice spoke in her ear, accompanied by the smell of beer and stale pizza, mixed with the remnants of a sour belch that almost dropped her to her knees. "Welcome to the party."

Tori closed her eyes. Shit happened, all right.

But why did it always happen to her?

CHAPTER 2

POLITELY—THE ONLY WAY one should approach a man holding a gun—Tori said, "I wouldn't do that if I were you."

His croaking laugh made her wince. Yeah, he was so worried. Not.

She tried again. "Honestly. It will be fine if you just let me walk back out of here."

"Shut up." The sour breathy voice sounded pumped on Glory juice, a drug manufactured from the main flower named after the planet.

Damn, a juice junkie to boot. She really didn't need that. Glory juice made people hyper, excitable, and unpredictable. This situation was volatile enough without it.

Then again, so was her temper. And, damn it, she'd needed that cash.

The metal jabbed harder into her ribs. She winced, then snapped lightly, "Okay, but don't say I didn't warn you."

"Hey, get her over here. Stop messing around, man."

At the sound of the other man's voice, the gunman urged her forward. "Walk over to the tellers."

She whispered mentally, *Escort me to the front door. Let me out, and let me go. Escort me to the front door. Let me out, and let me go.*

"Hey, I said get moving." But his hand had turned her

around and now pushed her toward the front door.

She kept her smile inside and walked forward agreeably.

"Hey, Parks, what the hell are you doing?" cried out one of the other robbers. "I said, stop messing around."

As a precautionary measure, Tori whispered, *Ignore them. Open the front door, and let me out.*

The robber nudged her forward. "I said, move it."

Happy to comply and knowing time was running out, Tori walked faster and got to the front door. "Open it," he snarled. "Hurry up."

She quickly pulled open the door.

Behind her, the others started shouting. "Parks! What the hell?" A gunshot rang out, and her escort stiffened. She bolted through the doors. Shouts erupted behind her.

Outside, she raced to the left, toward the alleyway that would take her to a large parking lot at the back of the mall. She scanned the lot. Lots of small vehicles and nowhere for her to hide.

Except there.

She spotted two large delivery trucks, parked close together, the cab of each empty. She squeezed in between them and waited for her panicked breathing to calm down.

Tori saw no signs that she was being followed, yet neither could she discount it. She'd escaped. That meant the gunmen would have to make a fast decision. She could only hope that didn't mean a bullet for those left behind.

Shit. Shit. Shit.

She *so* didn't need this right now. She didn't dare head back to her job in this state, and neither could she leave those other poor people alone and helpless in the bank. She called the hotline. A computer answered, and she quickly gave the details and shut down her phone before it could be traced.

Thirty seconds was about the limit, and her call came in under that.

Hopefully that would be enough.

After several more bolstering deep breaths, she peered around the corner of the truck. The parking lot looked the same. She hadn't heard anyone approach, so chances were good she'd gotten away. She still had to get back to work though, and she really didn't want to be recognized. To that end, she slipped off her sweater and wrapped it around her waist, then quickly turned her long hair into a single braid down her back.

It was the best she could do in these circumstances. With a last glance at the time, she walked to the back-alley entrance of the shop and entered. Inside, she slapped her hand over her chest as she tried desperately to calm her breathing. So far, so good.

"Tori? Is that you?"

"Yes. I'm back. Just getting a drink of water." She did need water. She grabbed a glass and filled it from the bathroom sink. Feeling calmer, and hoping she was not as flustered looking as she felt, she plastered a smile on her face and walked out to the front of the store.

"Did you get through the bank lineup that fast?" asked Mary. A customer walked out of the store, a bag swinging on her arm.

"No. I saw the line from the outside and kept on walking."

"Told you."

"Yeah." Tori smiled. "Doesn't help me out now though."

"You need me to lend you a few bucks?" Mary lifted her cup of tea. "I have fifty on me."

Hope bloomed inside Tori's chest. She hated to do it, but she was desperate. "If you could, that would be … awesome."

When Mary handed over the money, the pressure in Tori's chest eased. This would get her past her landlord. At least, until she received the rest of her money.

The bank thing was a whole other story.

She wouldn't get out of that one as easily. Cameras were all over the place. The cops would be looking for her. And she had nothing she wanted to tell them. In fact, she had nothing she wanted to say to the police in any way.

But how to keep herself out of the line of fire?

She could run again. But she would get caught. Burnside wasn't very big. And she didn't have enough money to skip to another town farther away. Back to that whole *needing her paycheck* thing.

She might be able to bluff it.

But not likely.

At closing time, Tori raced through her closing procedure and, with Mary, locked up the store. She cast a look toward the bank but couldn't see anything different. It was so tempting to think she'd imagined it all. Yet she couldn't be so lucky. With a quick smile goodbye to Mary, Tori headed home.

At the end of her block, she stopped and checked out her surroundings. Nothing out of the ordinary. No one looking for her. No one even noticing her.

Just the way she wanted it.

She ran up the few stairs to her place and let herself in. Ground-floor apartments weren't her favorite, but they allowed for a fast escape. And she should know.

First things first, she put on the teakettle. "Jessie, I'm

home."

There was a brush and a scuffle of noise, and then, with the lightness that always amazed her, Jessie jumped onto her counter.

She sighed. "Jessie. Show yourself, please. Remember the rules."

Instantly her pet Polten, a red panda-raccoon hybrid common on Glory, showed up. In purple. "Purple? Really?"

He grinned. And showed his fangs.

She stared at him a moment, then shook her head. "Whatever."

With so many moves and energy changes over the last year, he'd changed colors a lot. Now his colors shifted, and his fangs grew apparently by whim.

Jessie chittered in response, then raced to the opposite side of her counter to jump across to her window. The woods were just outside. He knew it. She knew it. But he wouldn't go there until darkness fell. And then he probably wouldn't return until morning. She had no idea what he did overnight, but he'd been with her for as long as she could remember. He was more than her spirit pet—he was her best friend and her family.

Besides, not many friends understood about paranormal abilities here. A number of Earth-like planets had been selected for relocation of the human population after Earth started to die and needed emergency assistance—mainly requiring humans to get off the planet and to quit hurting it. In its entirety, the evacuation had taken years, but thankfully they'd had a program in place for decades prior. So, when it came to crunch time, they'd managed to get everyone safely off.

Glory had been one of the farthest and the less-tested

options. But many had opted to come here, and, over time, the planet had developed a decent population, with paranormal abilities popping up more and more. Tori could see a future when the energy workers would be more common in the general population.

In fact, given her current situation, Jessie was all she had. Here, at least.

Rummaging in the back of her fridge, Tori found the mostly empty bottle of Glory wine on the bottom shelf. "Gotcha." She dragged it out, popped the cork, and took it outside to the puny-size deck. She collapsed on her single chair and propped her feet up on the railing. She needed this. What a hell of a day. She took a long gulp from the bottle and leaned her head back.

Someone pounded on her door. She bolted upright and spun to stare in the direction of the entryway. Now who would be calling on her here? She groaned. Right, the landlord.

Grumpy, she stood and walked over to the front door, her fingers already fishing for the money in her pocket. Then the secondary thought struck her that maybe it wasn't her landlord. Considering what she'd witnessed today, the police might have found her. Keeping that thought in mind, she tiptoed quietly to the door, peered through the peephole, and froze.

No. It couldn't be.

The door shook with more knocking, as she stood here, her mind still trying to decide how life could hate her this much. Hadn't she been through enough today?

"Tori? Are you in there? We need to talk."

Talking with this man was the last thing Tori wanted to do. But it appeared that running hadn't gotten her anywhere.

Devon Wiltshire still found her.

That was his talent.

She'd done her best, and still he'd beaten her. She dropped her forehead on the door and silently whispered, *Go away. Turn around, and keep on walking.*

Sounds of footsteps could be heard on the other side of her door. They faded, then grew loud again.

"Tori, open up. I know you're there," Devon said, humor in his voice. "At least, now I do."

Tori pulled at her hair, wanting nothing more than to scream. Then resignedly she snorted in disgust. She opened the door to face her ex-fiancé.

CHAPTER 3

"D EVON. LONG TIME no see. And now that we've seen each other, feel free to turn around and leave." She peered around the doorway to see Devon's henchmen walking away. She smirked and shot him a look, before turning and walking back into her kitchen. He wouldn't leave. No way. Not now that he'd found her. She snagged the bottle of wine in her free hand and flopped down in her chair on the deck. She took a long swig of the cold liquid.

"Still drinking cheap wine, I see." Devon stood in the open patio door.

"Not being in the same financial category as you, I'd say that's a yes." And she tilted the bottle back and finished the last dregs. She put it on the cement and sighed. "What the hell do you want?"

"You."

She froze, and then a broken laugh slipped out. If she hadn't turned to make sure he was joking, she wouldn't have caught the hurt, as it flickered through his gaze. Him hurt? Hell, no. Now his pride might have been dented. … *That* she had no trouble believing. That went along with all the men in his family. Protectors. The whole long line of them.

And they had the skills to make that happen.

Unfortunately.

She turned away and stared out at the forest behind her

building. "Joke's over. What's the real reason?"

"I came to get you."

She waved her hand dismissively at him. "Sorry for the wasted trip, but I'm not going anywhere."

He stepped forward to lean over the deck wall, old paint peeling off with his movements.

Sourly she watched the chips fall and miss him completely. Figures. She'd be wearing those suckers if their positions were reversed. It had happened yesterday, when she'd leaned over in that same spot.

"Is this the best you could find?" he asked, exasperation mixed with mockery in his voice. "This place is a rent-by-the-hour flophouse."

Acid leeched from her own voice. "You should know."

He stiffened and turned on her. "No, I wouldn't." He glared at her. "A little trust would have been nice."

She didn't think it was possible, but his tone gave her the chills, and his words made her feel a little ashamed. Maybe he had changed. Then again, maybe not. "Ah, well, trust is a little hard to come by. You could ask your family for help." She crossed her arms over her chest and added in a deadly voice, "Oh wait. You already did that."

Devon stared above her head, a muscle in his long lean jaw twitching. "I'm sorry. I know Grandfather is a bit heavy-handed."

"Ya think?"

"He's protective."

She laughed and didn't bother answering. Devon was a poor relative to the wealthy Chancellors—poor being a relative term of course. He still had more money than she'd ever had. The Chancellors—powerful, male-dominated, and beyond wealthy—had been living and operating in this world as if they owned it.

In fact, she wouldn't be surprised to learn they'd somehow staked such a claim to the whole of planet Glory.

"Look. He didn't realize how important you are to me."

Present tense. Too bad. He'd had his chance. She'd forgotten what the original argument had been about. And what difference did it make? If Devon had been serious about her, he would have come after her a long time ago. A year ago. Not now.

Airily she said, "Whatever. So why are you here now?"

"To get you."

Now she was getting mad. She dropped her feet to the patio and stood, stepping right in front of him. "Obviously not. If you were here for me, then you'd have come months ago."

She saw the wince before he hid it.

"I ... We need you."

Her heart—held in suspension for that whisper of hope that he'd come for her because he couldn't live without her—fell. "Of course. It's a job, I suppose." She motioned to the world beyond the deck. "I have a job. And a life, thank you, and I'm allowed to be choosy about any clients I decide to take on."

"This"—he waved his arm at the cramped deck and the even smaller apartment—"is not living. You are hiding. How long do you think you can keep this up?"

"As long as I want. As long as I need to." She dropped back into her chair and closed her eyes. "It's been a shitty day. Go away."

"I know all about your shitty day. How do you think I found you?"

Well, doesn't that figure? All she'd wanted was a little

cash. The Chancellors did security in a big way. They'd probably seen the damn bank feed within an hour of the robbery.

"Why did you pick this hellhole?" he asked.

That did warrant a look around. She closed her eyes again and said, "It's not that bad." She took a deep breath of the clean air and added, "There is a lot to recommend it here."

"No resurgent energy is here. You can't recharge easily. Why? Why did you run here?"

She'd had enough, stating simply, "None of your business." There was a long silence, so long she finally opened her eyes to see Devon staring at her, his arms crossed over his chest.

"I'm not leaving without you."

"And that's where you're wrong." She glared at him. "I want you to leave my apartment. And I want you to leave now." Inside, she mentally repeated, *Leave now.*

A muscle pulsed in his stiff jaw. He hesitated.

She took two steps and stood toe to toe with him. She forced the word out of her throat. "Now."

His gaze hardened, even as his shoulders relaxed. "This isn't over." And he walked out of her apartment.

She followed behind him and threw the bolt home, locking him out.

Too bad she couldn't lock him out of her heart.

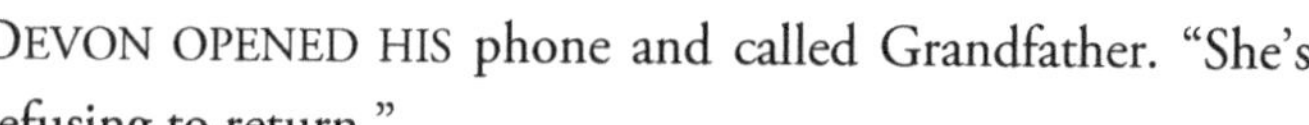

DEVON OPENED HIS phone and called Grandfather. "She's refusing to return."

"Doesn't matter what she wants. We need her. Pay her more."

"I didn't offer her any money. She's too proud."

"Ha. That was your first mistake. Go back and offer her money. She's destitute. Look at the way she's living."

"If she's living that way, it's for a reason."

"Yeah, because she doesn't know how to make a living in the normal world. She's an energy worker. They have to work energy. Nothing else in their life will go right, unless she follows her destiny."

Devon groaned under his breath. He'd been listening to this destiny stuff for decades. "She doesn't want to come back with me. I told you to send someone else."

"Well, she's your fiancée. So it's only right it should be you." Grandfather's voice sharpened. "Now listen good. You get her back here by tomorrow, and I don't care how. We need her here. People's lives are depending on it."

And Grandfather hung up. A voice next to Devon gave him pause.

"I heard most of that from over here."

Of course he did. Devon glared at his next-youngest brother.

"I don't know why we even use phones. The old man could just yell, and everyone between here and the other side of the planet would know what he wanted." With a laugh, Karl sauntered closer. "So, what will you say to her?"

"I have no idea. She won't open the door a second time."

That earned him a wicked grin. "Since when did locked doors keep us out?"

He studied his brother's cheeky face. "Are you suggesting we kidnap her?"

Karl stared at the trees around them. "With her abilities, not much we can do about forcing her. Look at the bank scenario. Look at the crew you took to her place. Hell, they're in the vehicle right now, shaking off her autosuggestion. She's potent, bro. And, without her cooperation, we'll have to knock her out and kidnap her."

Devon hated to consider the idea but had to admit, it had been sitting just out of his consciousness. "She'll hate me."

"No," his brother corrected. "She'll understand. Eventually."

And that would be too long. Devon had waited a year to come after her. Twelve long months to get it into her head that she really didn't want to be alone. That he really was her choice of a mate. Twelve long months of waiting. A whole damn year of hoping that she'd come to him.

Instead she'd chosen to live like this rather than be around him. He wondered if the hurt would ever go away.

As much as he admired her guts and determination, he saw how her energy was less than it had been. Either she couldn't recharge as easily as she could before or the town was draining her faster than she'd expected. And she had no partner to help with the recharging.

And, in Tori's case, she needed to recharge more than most.

So how had she survived for so long?

And how the hell would he get her home in time to help the people who were in trouble? The clock was ticking …

"Why is she the only one? Surely Grandfather could have found another one with her talents?"

"She's the one with the affinity to the woods, remember? Not even Genesis can do it alone. She said Tori was needed." Karl sighed. "Did you explain the problem to her?" Karl asked Devon.

"No." He stared at his brother helplessly. "I didn't know how. After she said, *No way*, I got angry and then …" He shrugged. "I guess I said the wrong thing because, the next thing I know, she ordered me to get the hell out of her apartment."

"And you left?" Karl raised both hands and gave a hard laugh.

"And I left."

Karl stared, then his lips twitched. "You realize you let your guard down, and she autosuggested you, right?"

Devon stared at his brother. "No, she wouldn't. She couldn't." At least she never had before. As he thought back on his lack of resistance, not even *thinking* to resist, he closed his eyes and groaned. "Damn it. She so did."

CHAPTER 4

TORI SHOULDN'T HAVE used her abilities on Devon. She felt guilty about that. Well, okay, only a teeny bit guilty. He did deserve it. What was she supposed to do, just pack up her stuff and leave with him? Because he said so? Those days were long gone.

The air was cool, as she came out of her two-minute shower. The apartment was tiny, but, after the day's events, her energy was drained. Damn, she was tired. At least she had a place of her own. And that was so much better than the alternative. Leaving her window open a few inches for Jessie, who she hadn't seen since Devon left, she crawled into bed.

Her mind teemed with the things Devon had said. And all that he hadn't. Something about people needing her help. She let out a skeptical snort. So not likely. She generally got people into trouble—not out of it.

She rolled over and fell asleep.

***

MUCH LATER, TORI woke. Something was off. Lying quietly in her bed, she listened to the sounds rustling outside in the forest. Many people avoided the woods. Unlike Tori, they didn't have an affinity to the woodlands. She did. And she could recharge almost anywhere, as long as she had Jessie.

If she were separated from Jessie for a long time period, she would have to find another solution. One option would be to go to the woodlands. Or back home, where the energies of the meridians crossing the planet soothed her energy, instead of aggravating it. Some people managed to spend their entire lives in towns like the one she was currently in. In that case, their systems adapted.

In Tori's case, she had never adapted.

But she needed to get the hell away, and this latest town had seemed to be a good option. With Jessie, she'd been fine. The others didn't know about Jessie, or, for some like Devon, hadn't wanted to know.

The thing was, his grandfather had seen Jessie but wouldn't back up Tori's claims. Then again, none of it mattered.

She and Jessie had been together for a long time. She'd be damned if some grumpy old man had the power to ruin that.

She sighed and punched her pillow. She hated waking in the night. She needed sleep. Especially with the recharging issues.

A whisper of something wrong crossed her consciousness.

Someone, … something, … was in the apartment.

"Jessie?" she called out in the barest of whispers. But she saw no sign of him.

She pushed aside the blankets and went to stand, when a strong hand clapped a cloth over her mouth, and a strange energy bolt hit her sleep center, knocking her out.

The last thing she remembered was Jessie's worried chirp.

Then she heard nothing more.

⚛︎

"DAMN IT. I should have stayed in the room with her."

"You think she would have preferred waking up with you there?" Karl laughed. "I don't think so."

"Maybe not, but she'd be over her anger by now." He stared around the dining room in the main house of his grandfather's huge estate. Big enough for the gatherings of the whole family, including all the extended family. Right now though, only a few of them were here.

Grandfather needed Tori's help.

They all did.

But she wouldn't want anything to do with Grandfather or Devon at this stage. He twisted his mug around moodily.

"When will you let her out of her room?" Karl asked Devon.

He glanced toward the stairs, leading to the room where Tori had been locked in, and frowned. "I was hoping she'd sleep longer. She doesn't look well."

"She's fighting the energy of that damn town." Karl shook his head. "Why would she go there?" He stood and walked to the sideboard, where he filled a plate with eggs and potatoes. "She could have stayed here and enjoyed the wealth."

Devon frowned and narrowed his eyebrows, glaring at Karl's back.

At the awkward silence, Karl swung around. "Shit. That was cold. I am so sorry."

"Don't be." Devon stood and moved toward the hall-way. "You're right. She made her choice."

As he reached the stairway, he realized he still had no idea why she'd made the choice she did.

Well, not exactly.

Yet he still wanted to know why she'd walked out and had stomped on his heart to get free.

CHAPTER 5

S HE LET HER eyelids drift closed. Weakness invaded her body, as though she hadn't recharged. That brought her eyelids open again. Why wasn't she recharging?

Then she realized she had, in a way, overcharged, but slowly, … very slowly. "Jessie?"

Gentle chattering near her head reassured her that her friend and spirit pet was here with her.

"What's going on?"

He chittered, and his presence blinked on and off.

She frowned. Normally, if they were alone, Jessie stayed visible. That he was flashing on and off like a neon bulb concerned her. In fact, she realized something was incredibly wrong.

As she sat up, the blankets fell down. She still wore her camisole and shorts, but the blankets weren't hers. Nor was the bed. In fact, as she searched the gloomy darkness, she realized that she didn't recognize the room itself.

Where the hell was she?

She cast her mind back. Devon. Had he kidnapped her? He'd been adamant about her returning with him. And it would be so typical of him to ignore her wishes and to steal her away in the dark of night.

Damn. She threw back the blanket and walked to the small adjacent room, grateful to find it was a bathroom. A bag was on the floor by the small table. She opened it to find her clothes and personal articles. And, from the look of the contents, it was all of them.

She sat back, her anger building quickly.

So he came to ask for her help, and, when she was less than delighted to see him, he kidnapped her and stole her away. Had Grandfather told him to not return without her?

That would have stuck in the old man's craw. She had never gotten along with him. Nor he with her.

That didn't stop the hurt, fueling her temper into full-blown anger.

How could Devon do that to her?

She moved to the door and tried to open it, with no success. She wasn't surprised. If she'd been kidnapped, no way they'd leave the door wide open for her.

Exhaling loudly, she decided the next best thing to do was shower. After a quick wash, she changed into jeans and a T-shirt from her bag and checked out the window. It wasn't locked, so she pushed it open and scanned her surroundings. Trees, bushes, and the gleam of water in the distance. She didn't recognize the area. Still, she recognized the energy.

And that wasn't good. It was morning, so she could be a long way from home.

At the word *home*, she gave a broken laugh. She didn't have a home. Not really. Everything had blown apart when her granny had died. Tori's personal life had blown up soon afterward. She'd walked out the next day. She'd thought she'd been building a future with Devon, until she realized that dream had been just as unattainable as the other things in life she'd dreamed of having.

It wasn't fair.

But so what? She was all about goals. She'd been making

them since forever and doing a fine job of reaching them. Until Devon had derailed her life.

Now she reassessed. She had her bag and the little she owned. Of course she had no money, and wouldn't Mary hate that Tori didn't show up to work today or pay back the borrowed money? Then again, Mary would just get it from Tori's incoming paycheck. Now she had to run again, with no money. Savagely she closed the zipper and approached the locked door.

Suddenly Tori realized that she was in big trouble. Only she wasn't the sticking-around kind to see what that meant.

DEVON APPROACHED TORI'S door with caution. Dealing with an energy talent meant one needed to be wary at all times. The fact that she was female and probably angry and spitting like a werecat meant that, right now, she would be extremely dangerous.

And her anger would be directed at him.

He knocked on her door. "Tori, are you wake?"

No answer.

He checked his watch. It was nine in the morning. She should be awake. Chances were, she was stewing in anger. He debated unlocking the door and going in and checking on her but took the coward's way out. "I'll come back in a bit."

As he turned to walk away, he found Grandfather standing at the end of the hallway, glaring at him.

"Well, you brought her home again. Why the devil isn't she in the forest helping our people?"

"She's not awake yet," Devon offered.

His grandfather snorted. "That girl always could sleep a

good day away." He turned on his heel, sending his parting shot. "Wake her up. People are hurting."

Devon stared after him. He could understand the old man's frustration. Time was ebbing away. But an uncooperative Tori would not help.

Still, time was a factor. Resolute, he returned and knocked on her door—hard. "Tori. It's morning. Time to wake up."

He leaned in to hear her response, but there wasn't one.

He closed his eyes. She couldn't escape that room. No way. The window was locked, and they were on the second floor. But his heart said she'd gone.

The key to the lock was stashed atop the doorframe. He quickly unlocked the door and pushed it open. "Tori? Are you here?" He flicked on the lights. Her bedding was tossed to the side, and there was no sign of her. Or her bag.

Shit.

He raced to the bathroom to double-check, but the small opulent room was empty. The window, however, was open.

Fresh air blew his way, and his heart pounded, as he leaned over the glass to peer out. What if her broken body was there, lying on the ground below?

But he saw no sign of her.

"Damn it." He scanned the edge of the property at the tree line. How far of a head start did she have? Surely she hadn't had time to go far?

The bushes shifted and rippled off to the left. Locking his gaze on the area, he waited for the movement to catch his eye. There. Running through the trees. He grabbed his phone and called security.

"She's heading to the north side of the property."

Jackson, head of security, responded. "Got it."

"Remember. Keep your ears plugged." He hated to say more but in this case … "Consider her armed and dangerous."

"Will do."

Devon ended the call and raced out to join the others in the search. He met his brother Karl at the bottom of the stairs. "She's escaped," he said tersely. Barely registering Karl's shocked surprise, Devon bolted past him out to the backyard. Footsteps pounded behind him. "How is that possible?" Karl asked. "She should barely be able to move."

"I have no idea. She was always a surprise."

"And apparently had more talents than she let on," Karl said, just a hint of humor in his voice. "Just think. She kept some things hidden from Grandfather. No wonder he didn't like her."

"Why do you say that? He was always polite to her." Devon hated the inference that he might have missed something. "I know they weren't overly friendly …"

His brother laughed. "You've never seen him for who he really is. There was more than dislike between them. The animosity nearly glowed from his eyes the one time I saw it clearly revealed."

They'd reached the shrubbery, and Devon dashed forward, knocking aside the branches. A path was farther in, but he couldn't count on her using it. Not if she knew she was being pursued.

And who was he kidding? This was Tori—no way she couldn't know.

CHAPTER 6

TORI RACED AS fast as she could through the forest. Her heart pounded, and, at the speed she was going, she was certain her feet had wings. She was almost high on the energy of the place. She'd been gone from it for so long that she was like an addict, getting a fix for the first time after a long drought. She wanted to laugh, and she wanted to cry. Her emotions were all over the place. Staying focused was hard, but she knew Devon wouldn't give her much longer to sleep. He would be knocking on her door in no time.

In fact, her senses said he was already out looking for her.

Damn. She'd hoped to have more of a head start.

The path turned left. She turned right and barreled into the bushes, heading to the woods. She could hide in the woods. They could never touch her there.

The safety of the woods loomed.

Behind her she heard shouting, dogs barking. Damn it.

She was flying strong, but this wasn't her usual entrance to the sacred forest, and she didn't know the shortcuts. Faster and faster, she flew, until she hit a solid wall.

A hard muscled chest. As she tried to catch her breath, she realized it was Devon. Somehow he'd managed to get ahead of her.

"Easy."

"How did you get here?" she gasped, when she could. Other men came running up behind them, as the dogs surrounded them, milling around excitedly. Tori put down a hand and whispered to the canines, "Calm down, guys. It's all right."

All the dogs immediately eased back, tails wagging and shoving their noses against her.

"How do you do that?" Devon asked. Then shook his head in exasperation. "That's not the issue right now."

"No? Then how about why you kidnapped me? Are you above the law, Devon? You think you can break into a lady's apartment in the middle of the night and steal her away? Can't you get a girlfriend on your own, without knocking her out and stuffing her in your car?"

She sensed the shock in the men who surrounded them, studiously ignoring her accusations. "But then you're part of the Chancellor clan. And the law doesn't apply to you, right?" She wove as much disgust as she could into her voice, which was hard when she was still trying to catch her breath.

He stared up at the sky and closed his eyes. "Always after the dramatic moment, aren't you?"

This time she didn't have to work up her bitterness. "I have a damn good reason to be upset."

He dropped those stunning blue eyes to gaze into hers. "Yes, you do. And I apologize for the way we were forced to bring you here."

"We?" she pounced. "Don't tell me. Your brother in crime helped?"

He pinched the bridge of his nose. "We need your help. Desperately."

The noise around them stilled. As if they were finally getting to the crux of the matter.

She waited.

"Lives are at stake. We have a large group of locals caught behind an energy field in the forest. We don't know if they are alive or dead. We've tried to make contact but haven't had any luck."

She frowned. "You have lots of energy workers on your staff."

He nodded. "And we've brought in specialists. So far, no one can get through the barrier."

That was odd. His family's company was known for their skilled workers. Someone should have been able to help. Unless … "Where in the forest?"

He stared at someone standing behind her. She turned around to see his grandfather. She snorted. "I'm so out of here."

She went to brush past him when Grandfather reached out and grabbed her.

She stopped and stared at the hand gripping her forearm. "Let go of me. Now," she added, her voice soft and silky. And dangerous as hell.

Grandfather dropped his hand. "Look. This isn't about your petty problems with my family. This has to do with innocent people."

"Well, that leaves you out of the picture," she muttered. "Did you tell these people that that area of the forest is dangerous? As in very dangerous?"

"Everywhere in the forest is dangerous. This is no different."

"This is very different," she exclaimed. "Most of the forest is workable. The back corner is a dead zone. You know that."

He glared down at her. "Most people think that's a

myth. There's no proof that any actual danger is there. So what if a field has closed? Open it. What's the big deal?"

"I imagine it's a really big deal if you had to kidnap me," she spat.

"Look, Tori," Devon spoke. "We're just asking you to help these people. No matter what you think of us, they don't deserve this."

And that was the first truth she could relate to. These people worked for Grandfather's company, and that just made them people in need of a paycheck. Not the assholes she was worked up about. Surrounded by some of those same towering males made it hard to breathe, let alone think.

This was another truth she couldn't ignore. As much as she hated the thought of helping Grandfather, she couldn't let these people suffer.

Her shoulders slumped. She turned slowly to look at Devon.

He gazed at her silently, waiting.

She'd waited for so long, when her life was intertwined with him. Always waiting for him. To call. To show up. To be there for her.

And she knew what she had to do.

She raised her gaze and looked at him directly. "Take me to them."

It took over twenty minutes to get into the vehicles, and another half hour to make it to where they could park the vehicles at the edge of the woods.

She could have been here in half the time if she'd been left alone. Of course, if she'd come here last night, this would all be over.

Damn it.

At the edge of the woods, she stood with Devon's men

gathered around her. She gave her body a much-needed couple minutes to adjust. The energy on this side was warm and electrifying. It grew darker the deeper one went in. Of course that added to the thrill.

It was also part of the problem. Everyone went into the woods for varying reasons. Everyone benefited from the forest energy.

Some more than others.

Early morning sunlight was her favorite time of day, and she was honored to be standing at the edge of the forest on this beautiful morning. She inhaled the fresh air, then took a second breath. She closed her eyes and tilted her head back, letting her face bask in the sun.

"What does she think this is, a holiday?" someone behind her muttered.

On most days, she would have commented. Today, she didn't want to mar the state of balance she was trying to get into. This side of the forest was a piece of cake.

The other side was a whole different story.

And she needed to be prepared.

"Are you ready?" Devon spoke from behind her.

She never moved. Inside, she had to ask herself the same question. On the other hand, she was here, so what the hell. "Absolutely."

"Follow me then." Devon stepped onto the wide path.

After a moment, she did. The other men surrounded her, presumably to stop her from running off again. They didn't have to worry. Once she realized people were seriously in need of her help, she was there for them.

After she'd done what she needed to do, then they should worry.

But, by then, she'd be gone.

"Thank you." A soft voice caught her ear. One of the men walking beside her watched to make sure no one else was paying him any attention, then said in a low voice, "My sister is one of those stuck."

She glanced at him sideways. "How long?"

"Over thirty-six hours now."

That would take its toll. "I'm sorry for her."

"They've tried everything."

She almost sneered. Devon's grandfather would have tried everything cheap first. He could have done the right thing off the bat. Then again, he could have come to her.

Oh, wait, he had sent Devon instead.

So not her favorite person.

"I know you didn't want to help, but they need you. No one else can get in." The man's voice broke at the end.

"I'm happy to help *them*," she said wryly. "It's this family I don't want anything to do with." She didn't have to clarify who the family was. Everyone knew.

"That's too bad. You were missed." Then, as if he was afraid that he'd gone too far and had said too much, he sped up and passed her to walk beside one of the other security men. Each wore blasters. That gave Tori pause. What kind of trouble were they expecting?

The only danger here that she was worried about were the energy fields and what they were trying to hold back.

Last time she'd been to the far end, there'd been little to blast and all kinds of reasons to run.

Just what had happened to the area in the last year? Moodily she studied the foliage, as they hiked through the woods. The flora was more brown than green, the vibrancy tired and used up, like a single mom in desperate need of an afternoon to herself. The forest in this section looked in desperate need of the energy that others had come here to absorb. She'd been so overwhelmed by her sense of homecoming that she'd not initially noticed.

And, for that, she was very sorry. She sent out beams of green joy to the plants around her. The woods needed to be given back what had been taken; she assumed the people around her had forgotten that part.

She frowned as her energy was sucked up immediately. Just what was going on here?

"What's the matter?" Devon asked. "You look"—he shrugged, as if he couldn't come up with the right word—"sad."

"I am." She added, "And angry and disappointed and working my way toward outraged." She swept her arms wide open. "What have you done to the woods?"

He narrowed his gaze at her. "You weren't here. You have no idea the toll this last year has had on the region." He motioned at the devastation. "Because of the damage, Grandfather was trying to find alternative uses for the land."

She gasped. "What? There can't be alternatives. This is sacred forest."

"A dying sacred forest."

"Anyone here could see that the forest is suffering, that there's been no energy given back to the region. It's been sucked out and left dry." She was starting to steam. "It's the basic laws of energy."

"We know that. We've worked hard to rectify the problem. And, when we couldn't find any solutions, a team came in to see what else could be done."

"And apparently none of it has worked," she snapped. She didn't have to worry about the forest being developed, no matter what Grandfather had in his crafty old brain. The forest would never tolerate it. "When I left, it was stunningly beautiful. Healing energy abounded, and life for the forest was healthy and vibrant."

"And then the storms happened. And the electrical impulses changed the nature of the energy here. And things have only gotten worse."

Storms? What storms? She hadn't heard anything about them. "You brought in specialists, I presume."

He nodded. "Of course. We didn't want the forest to just die on us. It needs our help, but we're out of ideas," he added shortly. "Have you talked to your sister, Genesis? Caught up on the problems she's been having with the pools?"

"Genesis?" Damn. No, she hadn't, and that was on her. Problems with the pools? So not good. Everything here was connected. If one area was damaged, it affected the other areas as well.

"As for Grandfather, are you saying he can't do something?" She couldn't help the sarcasm. That old man had made her life hell. She wouldn't forget it. Ever.

"It's not so simple. We've got a team working on this around the clock."

She shook her head. "With all that brainpower, you guys can't open this energy wall?"

"You haven't seen it." And, with that, he stormed ahead.

Now that she'd pissed everyone off, she walked alone. And maybe that was okay too. It gave her a chance to study the area, the energy that waffled instead of rolled across the ground in waves. It was sick.

And that hurt. She'd spent a lot of glorious time here. The air would normally lift her hair up with all the static, and she would have danced and laughed. Instead, depression settled on her shoulders, from the lack of positive energy. There was only negativity. Pain. Hurt.

The dominant emotion was sadness.

Why would the energy have that emotion? What could make it turn from joy into this? Except an inability to return to its own self. The energy here lived in a state of vibrancy. It loved that, and it always returned to that state—when it could.

And that's where the problem was.

It was damaged and couldn't rectify the problem on its own.

So why had the specialists not found a way to resolve the energy imbalance?

It shouldn't be that hard.

An hour later, she was on the verge of tears. The closer they walked to the back quadrant of the woods, the worse the plant life. Here in places, she'd seen plants withering, some on the edge of death. She couldn't believe it. The sun didn't reach deep inside, and somehow the creek appeared to be draining dry. At one point, she'd stepped off the path and walked to the creek edge. Devon had pulled her back without an explanation.

They continued on. Every step she took physically hurt. But she kept quiet and marched forward. There needed to be answers. And she'd be damned if she wasn't the one who would get them. She owed these woods a lot. And she'd given back a fair bit, but she could do more—and do it she would.

A shout went up in front of her.

Devon bolted forward. Tori stayed back, as the group surged ahead of her. She could have taken off on them, and they wouldn't have noticed. But that wouldn't get those trapped people out of here. As she came through the last few trees to the large open field, she stopped.

There was no large open field.

Only a gnarly knotted wall of something.

Something she'd yet to see. Was this what was hurting the forest? It was natural in a sense. The energy resonated from deep inside the twisted wood, but it didn't have a wholesome healthiness.

Then again, none of the forest did anymore.

As she approached, the men stepped back to watch. Through the branches, she spied a large group of people milling around. Each face watched her in hope. "Why were they in there?"

"None of your business," Grandfather snapped.

She turned to face him. "You did this? You're responsible for these poor people being in danger?" Her voice rose uncontrollably. She couldn't believe his duplicity. He'd already had lots of examples of that, but she hadn't expected this.

"What I did, I did for the community. Do you think this forest is going to heal itself?" Defensive, angry that anyone had dared to question him, and defiant at having his actions doubted, he stood up straight and looked down on her. And he was big; all the males in the family were.

A year ago she would have been intimidated. Somewhere along the line, she'd grown a spine. Or a pair of balls, as Devon's brother Karl had often said.

As it was, a crowd gathered around her on both sides of the jam.

She would have called it a fence, but it was a hell of a mess to downgrade to something so small. This was a huge problem. "Wow, you must have really pissed off Mother

Nature," she said out loud.

Part of her couldn't wait to dive into this, while another part of her wanted to run in the other direction.

This was big. Really big.

Grandfather was up against something he couldn't handle. He'd thrown everything he could at this problem.

Now he needed Tori's help.

If only she knew what to do.

As she deliberately turned her back on Grandfather, her gaze caught sight of the guard who'd spoken to her earlier. He swallowed, stared at her hopefully, and then shifted his gaze to avoid being caught.

She understood. They were all under orders. Some had personal stakes in this. And some of them were in danger of losing their loved ones.

Trying to block out the men watching her, she turned to the massive barrier and closed her eyes. She tilted her head back and opened her arms wide.

Behind her, the men shifted restlessly.

Across from the other side of the barrier, she heard murmurs. Whispers. Questions.

"What is she doing?"

"Why is she standing like that?"

"Isn't she supposed to help?"

Tori blocked them out of her mind, letting them sink into the white noise of the background as her authentic self stepped forward. When her balance was solid, she opened her eyelids.

In front of her, the gnarly tree mess had shifted into a seething mass of energy, twisting and knotting into a tighter morass that shimmered with a dark effervescence. Energy had a neutral base. People were the ones who attributed emotions to it, right or wrong, good or evil.

In truth, it could be anything. It took its properties from the area surrounding it.

And the people.

There was more to it, and she would need to spend a few minutes pondering the implication—but not now.

She didn't know if she could get through this, but it would take everything she had to try.

And she had to focus.

Taking a deep breath, she studied the energy patterns. In reality, she was nothing more than a locksmith. An energetic locksmith.

Patterns dominated nature. One could find them in every area of life.

In this case, as she studied the patterns in front of her, she realized that it wasn't one pattern but several. All working in and around each other. Twisting through themselves. Reinforcing one another.

Tension coiled in each of the patterns. Mentally she reached out and snipped one coil. It zinged backward, as the tension on the two sides lessened, and they sprang back, causing the whole mess to rock in response.

People cried out. Some backed away. Others ran closer.

She let her subconscious work, as she studied the pattern and picked out the next strand to cut. Again, with the tension released, the whole morass shifted and rocked, but it didn't fight back.

And that was what she needed to know.

Without having to worry about the energy attacking her in defense, she could do what she needed to do faster.

She got down to work. She cut and separated and unwound energy strands. She worked on the outside, revealing the layers underneath. She lost track of time, as she released more and more strands from their ever-tightening web.

She felt the tension in her own body build, as she worked longer and harder. Sweat collected on her forehead, and she would have loved to take a break but didn't dare take the chance.

Just because she was tiring, that didn't mean the energy was. It could easily regrow if she stopped.

That it had gotten so big was amazing ... and scary.

She worked steadily for maybe hours but was probably only one. She paused and reassessed. The left strand, once released, should ease back the tension on the other side. She reached out and snipped it. Instantly the bulk of the remaining strands fell back, and the energy pulsing around her dropped. Her hair fell back down to her shoulders.

She gave a long shuddering sigh of relief, then stepped forward and opened the energy gate.

Cool air rushed forward, and the large group of people rushed out.

Tori collapsed to her knees and bowed her head.

Now she was tired.

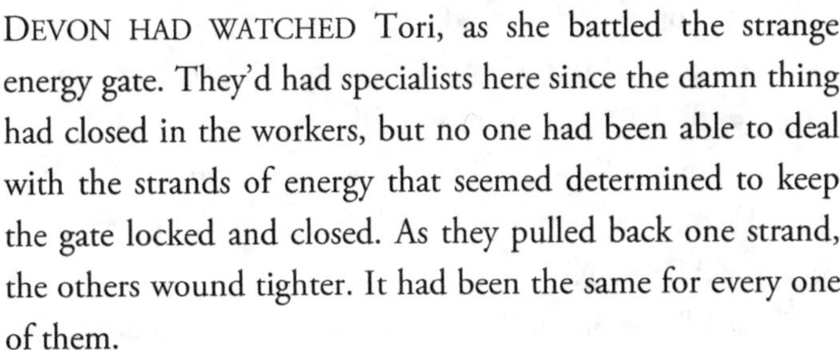

DEVON HAD WATCHED Tori, as she battled the strange energy gate. They'd had specialists here since the damn thing had closed in the workers, but no one had been able to deal with the strands of energy that seemed determined to keep the gate locked and closed. As they pulled back one strand, the others wound tighter. It had been the same for every one of them.

Until Tori.

The strands had separated at her order, cut when she

snipped them, and the tension eased as she cut strand after strand. Until the whole mass had collapsed in a big *whoosh*.

And still, she'd been physically able to step forward and open the gate.

She'd also done it in less than two hours. Grandfather had said she couldn't open it, and the specialists had said it would take days.

As always, she'd surprised them.

Or maybe shocked them.

He watched the trapped group, rushing to freedom, speaking to Tori on their way.

"Oh, thank God."

"Thank you, miss. Oh, thank you."

He lost sight of Tori, as the people raced past. He smiled as he watched the hugs and joyful exchanges. One of the workers turned around, a big smile on her face, as she seemed to gulp in the clean air on this side of the barrier. Her gaze landed on his grandfather. Her smile dropped away, and she backed up slightly. Puzzled, Devon studied his grandfather's face. Grandfather smiled, speaking animatedly with someone—one of the scientists. Both were waving their hands and seemed to be in good moods. So why the reaction?

Then someone screamed.

Devon raced to the sound, fighting his way through the crowd to find Tori in the heart of the group.

"She just collapsed." The woman was crying. "That's so sad. She came to help us, and it's been too much for her. I hope she'll be okay."

"Jesus." Devon raced to Tori. She'd fallen facedown, her head turned, but her arms were down by her sides. She hadn't tried to break her fall.

He reached out and stroked her hair off her face.

"Is she still alive?" The same woman bent closer. "She did so much for us …"

"She's alive. She's just exhausted."

He rolled her over gently. "Tori, can you hear me?"

She moaned.

"Easy, Tori. Wake up. Easy."

She opened her eyelids, her eyes pale blue, her gaze unfocused, struggling to understand. Her lips twisted in a frown.

And that broke his heart. When he'd met her, all she did was smile. Her face always shone, bright and cheerful.

He'd fallen in love with that vivacious woman.

And something had gone so very wrong.

He knew he was in the wrong. That he was responsible for wiping that joy out of her life, that smile off her face. He knew that, and the guilt ate away at him. He still loved her.

But he'd done a piss-poor job of showing her.

Now she hated him.

And he couldn't blame her.

But he slipped his arms around her body and lifted her tiny frame, hating that she seemed so frail. … Still, she was back in his arms. And that's where she belonged. He couldn't be happier.

She'd lost a lot of weight in the last year. Too much weight. The three sisters were all small, but Tori had slipped well past lean.

Carrying her carefully, he fell into step as the last of the group moved ahead of him. He hadn't taken a dozen steps when Stan approached him. "I can carry her, if you need a break."

Surprised, Devon ignored his brother's snicker from beside him. "I'm fine, but thanks for the offer."

"All right. Just let me know if you change your mind." He stepped back a few paces. "She let my sister out of that nightmare. I want to make sure she's taken care of."

Devon nodded in understanding. "I'll make sure she's fine."

"You do that." He cleared his throat. "And take care of her good." He shot him a stern look, "If you know what I mean." And then he damn-near ran away.

"What the hell was that about?" Devon came to a halt, watching Stan hurry off.

"Everyone knows," his brother said.

Devon stared at Karl. "Knows what?"

"That you broke her heart."

CHAPTER 7

W AKING UP SLOWLY, Tori stayed quiet, enjoying the
comforting feeling of being carried in Devon's arms.
Of course it would be him. He'd always been protective.

Even when furious with her, he would never let anyone
else hurt her.

Too bad he didn't find hurting her himself a problem.

She was jostled against his chest, as they moved down
the path. The rich smell told her where they were going—
back to the cars. She'd opened the knots of energy in the
forest, and then she'd dropped to her knees to catch her
breath, and, after that, she remembered nothing else.

She must have passed out.

It had taken an incredible amount of energy.

Thankfully she'd managed to get the job done. She
couldn't imagine what those poor people had gone through.
She didn't blame them because Grandfather was obstinate
and lacked the basics of good leadership. He had no problem
stepping on people to make his foundation a little more
secure. There was no competition for him, and there hadn't
been for decades; he'd either bought out—or forced out—
everyone who could be a problem for him.

Her nostrils twitched, as she sniffed the air around them.
It had a fresh smell again, as if the land was waking from a
long sleep. It should never have slept in the first place. She

wanted to know how it had. And why.

These were not easy questions, especially when she wouldn't be privy to any of Grandfather's company's information. But that didn't mean she couldn't come back here and see for herself. Or better yet, go to the sacred caves below this part of the forest. She could drive to some of them, then hike in farther. But she had no wheels, and she dared not ask anyone else to go with her.

She would contact her sisters. They could go together.

"How are you feeling?"

The rumble from his chest rolled out, long and clear. The sound fascinated her to the extent that she almost forgot the question. "I'm fine." She struggled to get down onto her own two feet. He tightened his arms around her, but she wanted to stand on her own.

"Stop struggling. I'll drop you."

"That's the point. I want to walk."

He stopped and glared down at her, letting her down. "You could just rest up and heal. There's no reason to always prove that you're strong enough."

Instantly her back went up. She shifted, carefully adjusting her balance, and stepped back from him. "I have nothing to prove." She turned and walked away. She hated the glare burning into her back, but she hated that damn pity more. His long-enduring sigh had her spinning around, almost spitting with frustration. "Stop that."

He gave her a mocking look. "Stop what?"

"Stop pretending that I'm being a difficult person." She closed her eyelids briefly, then spun around and kept walking. No point in arguing. Best to ignore him.

"You're always cranky when low on energy."

Her back stiffened, but she refused to comment.

"See? Any other time, you'd have tossed back a laugh and said something about me deserving it."

She frowned. Surely not.

"Now you're tired and cranky and just want to walk away from me. Like you always do."

Was that a bitter hurt in his tone? If anyone had walked away, it had been him. Sure, she'd physically walked but emotionally? He'd already left a long time earlier.

Silence reigned as they walked through the forest. Darkness should have been on them, but, as the forest responded to the freeing of its most prized energy, the colors zigged and zagged around her in a continuous ripple. The colors were warm and vibrant and beautiful. She was used to seeing this region full of responsive color. Although this appeared more exuberant than she'd expected. It was normal. Already healing.

And beautiful.

She couldn't help smiling, as the rays wafted around her legs—touching, freeing, healing the forest floor under her feet.

"You did that. You should be very proud."

He really didn't get it, did he? She shook her head. "Pride has nothing to do with it. I'm happy to have helped the forest, but what it's really done is made me very angry at the damage happening in the first place."

✦

"IT WASN'T YOUR doing," Devon said quietly.

"No, it wasn't," Tori agreed. "But then whose was it?"

"Why does there have to be someone to blame?"

"Because this wasn't natural. The forest was defending itself. But against what? Why did it feel so threatened that it tried to stop those people from leaving?"

"You think the forest was trying to protect itself?" His voice rose incredulously. He looked around in disbelief.

She glanced over at him. "Of course. What did you think it was doing?"

He didn't have an answer. He stared at her. Was she serious? Then he glanced around at the trees beside them. "That makes no sense whatsoever."

"Really? And why is that?"

"Because no one was doing anything to hurt it." He shook his head. "We all need this forest. All our systems recharge with the energy it produces. Why would anyone hurt it?"

"Are you so close to the issue that you can't see the most basic of problems?" This time she shook her head. "You're no fool, Devon," she said, her voice accusatory. She picked up her feet, almost flying forward in her frustration. She called back, "You know all the puzzle pieces. You figure it out."

She disappeared around a curve and under the brush, letting herself go deeper into the forest. And away from him. Damn. He was good with puzzle pieces. It was his specialty. Or it had been—when his abilities had been healthy.

"Tori?" he called out. "Where are you?"

She didn't answer.

Of course she let the forest do it for her.

And it gave him the response she'd expected.

Silence.

CHAPTER 8

"**T**ORI," DEVON CALLED out. "Answer me, please." Heavy footsteps pounded behind her.

She stopped, her head spinning, and bent over, breathing heavily. Damn it. Why wasn't she booking it out of here? The man had broken her heart. He couldn't be trusted. She knew that. But apparently she hadn't learned anything.

"Thank you." He approached slowly, cautiously.

And so he should. She had some serious issues burning inside her. She wanted to claw his face apart, but, at the same time, she wanted to jump his bones. She'd tried the latter and had walked away with a broken heart, which made the former choice her only option, but that wouldn't end well either. He was bigger, stronger, and way nicer than she was. He'd let her claw him up.

And that would just piss her off more.

"Look. I know you're pissed at me. I get that. I also understand you can't wait to get the hell away from me, but please, let's get you out of the forest safely first."

That didn't even deserve a response, but she couldn't resist. "You think I need *you* to get out of here?"

He shook his head. "Not the way you mean. I know you don't. This was always your backyard." He straightened and stretched out his arms, rotating them gently. "I was thinking about how much effort that energy knot took to untie. That you might be tired, and I don't want you to collapse out here and have no one around to help you."

"I'm tired but not that tired." She scowled at him. "And what do you care?" Okay, so that came out a little more bitterly than she'd expected. And, from the look in his eyes, he'd heard it.

He opened his mouth to say something, then snapped it shut.

"Yeah, don't bother." She turned to study her surroundings. The parking lot was just off to the left, another ten or twenty minutes ahead, but she wanted to go to the other side, where she might get some answers. She'd need to ditch Devon first.

"Forget it."

She turned to study him, under a hooded gaze. "Forget what?"

"Your plans. Whatever they are."

The bushes beside her jostled, sending the leaves bouncing up and down. She studied the undergrowth, then smiled. Jessie. "I wondered where you'd gotten to."

He scampered up onto her shoulder and made himself comfortable. He nuzzled against her neck, making her laugh, and caught Devon's gaze. Oh, right. He had never believed her about Jessie. He couldn't see Jessie, and, therefore, he didn't exist.

Some things never changed.

Whatever.

"I'll see my own way back." She turned to walk to the parking lot. "I've had about as much of your help as I can stomach."

AND AGAIN TORI walked away from Devon.

He fell in behind her. "Too bad. I brought you here. I'll take you home."

"Right, you'll take me all the way home." She scoffed. "The hell you will. Too bad no law is here anymore. You'd be doing time for kidnapping."

"There is law around here. And, yes, you could probably get me in a lot of trouble, if you chose to go that route."

"What a joke." She shrugged. "Grandfather *is* the law in these parts. And, as he probably told you to retrieve me, he certainly won't punish you for doing the job he gave you."

Damn. Now he was his grandfather's lackey in her eyes. It appeared that way on the surface, but there were extenuating circumstances. He and Grandfather had gone a few rounds after she'd left him. Too late to save his relationship with Tori, but it had been necessary to put Grandfather in his place. He studied her. "Surely you can see what kind of emergency we had here?"

"And? What did you do to cause this in the first place? All I did was fix the symptom. The original problem is still out there. It's dangerous, and it's still damaging the forest."

"Are you sure?" he asked cautiously, spinning to look back the way they'd come. "It looks normal again."

"Well, it isn't. And you should know that. You used to be able to read energy. What happened that you can't?"

He stuffed his hands moodily in his pockets. What to tell her? "No idea. From one day to the next, it stopped."

And had left him feeling bereft. Lost. And, as that'd been at the time she'd walked away, he'd been a mess. It had taken him every day since then to come to terms with it.

She parked her hands on her hips and stared at him, one finger tapping away, as if matching the tempo of her thoughts.

He kicked the ground and looked around. They were alone; everyone else had been all too happy to escape. Even his brother had left them alone. Then again, maybe that wasn't so surprising. His brother hadn't been a huge supporter of his engagement to Tori, but Karl had been outspoken since it had broken off. Telling Devon to wait. Tori would be back. She'd realize what she'd missed out on soon enough.

Only Tori didn't get the message.

Or, if she did, she didn't seem to give a damn. And Devon had realized belatedly how vast a mistake he'd made.

Karl had even changed his tune. Telling him to go after her before it was too late. But it was too late. Devon had left it too long, and any excuse he could come up with sounded lame.

Then this had happened, and he'd jumped at the chance.

And he'd been heavy-handed about it.

He couldn't find his rhythm with her, since meeting her again. Before, they'd always finished each other's sentences, thinking the same thing at the same time. Always. What they'd had together had been special. Incredibly special.

Until he'd lost it all. He'd been a fool.

"What are you thinking?"

Tori tapped him on the shoulder. Damn. He'd totally zoned out on her. He shrugged her hand away. "Nothing." He motioned to the remaining vehicle. "Can I drive you somewhere?"

She raised her eyebrow, shouldered her bag, and shook her head. "No. I'll get myself home."

Walking away was the hardest thing he'd ever done. He

knew she could look after herself, but he'd brought her here against her will, locked her in a room overnight, and dragged her out into the dead zone of the woods.

He stopped in his tracks. He couldn't leave her here alone. "I know you want to get rid of me, but I won't leave you here alone."

Those deep mysterious eyes of hers stared at him. Into him. At the person he was deep inside. Searching, asking, and then, as she relaxed, finding the answer she needed.

"Fine. You can drop me off downtown."

He raised one brow but said, "Let's go."

Silently, hesitatingly, she opened the door and slid in.

"Anywhere in particular downtown?"

She gave him a quick glance. "At the coffee shop. If it's still there."

Memories hit him. Hard. Long evenings talking over special coffees in take-out cups, sitting up on the rooftop garden overlooking the city. They might have had some arguments, but coffee had always been their meeting ground, and the coffee shop had been their meeting place.

Ten minutes later, he pulled up outside the long outdoor seating area of the local coffee shop and parked.

She opened the door, then seemed to hesitate.

He leaned forward, hoping.

With a bright smile, she said, "Thanks."

And she got out, shutting the door and walking away. Again.

CHAPTER 9

S HE FORCED HERSELF to stare straight ahead, keeping one foot in front of the other, instead of turning to look back at him. What she really wanted was to turn around, get back into that vehicle, and ask him why he hadn't come after her a year ago.

Everyone knew the two of them were perfect together.

And, if everyone was correct, how did he not know?

Behind her, she heard the vehicle drive away, taking her dreams along with it. Inside, she stopped and looked around.

And smiled, recognizing the feeling.

This felt like home.

"Tori?" Then came a rush of footsteps, followed by a loud cry of joy. "It is you!"

And she was engulfed.

"Ah, Vienna—"

Vienna sniffled. "Oh my, I was so afraid I'd never see you again."

"I'm here. Honest." But it was hard to talk when her face was buried in Vienna's wealth of black ringlets. Both the same age, the two women had been friends since forever. While she'd been wooed by Devon, Vienna had been wooed by his brother Karl.

When Tori had bolted, there'd still been stars in Vienna's eyes.

The Chancellor family was *the* family in town, and no one married into the family without Grandfather's permission.

She pulled back and studied her best friend, who beamed back. Vienna had always been the local beauty; Tori hadn't had a chance beside her. But Vienna was as nice inside as she was beautiful outside, and so they'd been best friends in spite of it all.

"When did you get back?" Vienna asked, bubbling over with enthusiasm. She wrapped her arm around Tori's shoulders. "Come and sit down. I'll get you a coffee."

Quickly Tori was seated in the back corner of the shop, and a huge cup of frothy hot liquid was placed in front of her. She settled in her chair and sighed happily. It was good to be back.

"Now tell me." Vienna arrived with her own cup. "Robbi is letting me take my break now. It's not busy anyway." Vienna pinned her with a look. "What is going on?"

Tori smiled and played with the handle of her coffee cup. "It's a little hard to explain."

"It always is."

"First, let me ask you a question. Are you still going out with Karl?"

A shadow whispered through her friend's face. Her lips quirked, but she shook her head. "No. We broke up after you left town."

"Ah, jeez. I'm sorry, Vienna. You two were good together."

"As good as you and Devon, *huh*?"

Not much she could say to that.

"Let's get back to you, and the really important question—are you staying?"

"I came back to help out with the far corner of the forest."

Vienna gasped. "Oh my. That was such a terrible nightmare. Everyone is talking about it. But I didn't realize everyone was talking about you."

"Yeah, there will be lots of talk for a while." She winced. She didn't want to be at the center of more gossip.

Vienna laughed. "I think it was more about Grandfather bringing you back to deal with it. The news spread all over town within minutes of the group being rescued."

"Figures. I'll contact my sisters, but …" Tori leaned forward. "Can I crash at your place, if I need to?"

Tori needed to contact Genesis, but her sister's apartment was too small for the two of them, only room for half a person on a good day. As for her younger sister, Celeste, Tori had no idea what was happening with her. Tori herself had been trying to figure out what to do when Devon had showed up.

A beautiful grin rippled across Vienna's face. "I wouldn't hear of anything else."

The next question was a little harder. "Can I also borrow your car?"

Vienna's brows shot up. "What's going on?"

"I don't want to say. … If you don't know, then you can't get in trouble."

Vienna shook her head, her long hair rolling from side to side. "What's this all about? Are you in trouble?"

Tori glanced around carefully, but all the other patrons appeared to be busy talking to each other. At least, she hoped they were. "No, I'm not. But I need to check out something, and I need a car to get there."

"Then I'm going with you."

"And that you can't do, sorry." Tori sat back and watched the troubled look settle on her friend's beautiful features. "I have to do this. I helped fix things today, but it was only a temporary solution. It'll all revert back again, unless I can figure out what's going on."

"You're going underground?" gasped Vienna. "Not alone?"

"I'm limited to those who can come with me."

"Take Devon."

Tori snorted. "He's the last person I'm taking."

"How about Karl?" Vienna peered over her huge mug, her gaze worried. "You can't go alone. It's too dangerous. You know that."

Now *that* she had an answer for. "I won't be alone." Her grin widened, and she leaned forward. "Jessie is with me."

Vienna shifted in her chair, her eyes darting from one side to the other. "Where is he? The last time I saw him, that critter was stealing the cake right off my plate."

Tori laughed. "You should have shared in the first place. He loves cake. Especially chocolate cake." Her friend harrumphed and didn't relax again, not after Jessie's name had come up. "So can I borrow your car, please?"

After a long considering look, Vienna said, "As long as you come back. No getting hurt, no running again."

"Not with your car at least." Tori laughed. "Thanks. I appreciate it." She stood.

"What?" Vienna looked up at her in shock. "You're going now?"

With a look outside at the sun high in the sky, Tori said, "The sooner, the better. I don't know how long it will take."

"Oh. Okay." Vienna pulled her keys from her pocket and put them on the table. She stood and hugged Tori.

"Please be careful. I just found you again. I don't want to lose you so fast."

With a reassurance she didn't feel, Tori hugged her best friend back. "I'll be careful."

AFTER TORI HAD climbed out of his car, Devon made it down one block before he pulled the big SUV off to the side. "Damn it, Tori."

When his phone rang, he checked the ID. It was Karl. "What?"

"Where are you?"

"Sitting in the car downtown. Why?"

"Grandfather wants to see you. And he wants Tori back here."

Devon leaned his head against the headrest. "I let Tori leave."

"What?" Karl's shocked voice rasped through the phone. "*Uh-oh.* Grandfather won't like that."

"Then he should have said something about it before-hand."

"He still wants to see you. Now."

"I'll be there in ten."

"Good," Karl said. "And heads-up, find a decent excuse for letting her go." His brother disconnected the call.

Devon sat here, deep in thought. He didn't need a damn excuse. Tori was not a prisoner. They'd treated her like crap, and she'd still helped out. If she wanted her freedom and space from them, who could blame her?

Grandfather for one.

Ten minutes later, Devon stood in front of Grandfather and watched silently as the older man paced the office in front of him.

"You had no right to let her go. We needed to talk to her."

"*I* had no right?" Devon dropped his voice to barely a whisper but hardened it in warning.

"Don't you get uppity with me." Grandfather stepped forward. "You're the one who kidnapped her."

"On your orders."

His grandfather snorted. "And, if you could do that, why not this?"

"Because I wanted her back here where she belongs." He watched Grandfather's face turn red. "And, no, I won't retrieve her for you."

Grandfather stepped back. "Then I'll find someone else who can."

"She's not our prisoner."

"Says who?" Grandfather walked to his chair behind the huge desk. "Get her back."

Not good. Devon knew he'd finally hit that crossroad that had been on the horizon for a long time. A crossroad Devon had worried about, had thought on, and had hated, knowing the day would soon be on him. But now that it was here, … he was relieved.

He studied his grandfather's angry face for a moment and shook his head. "No." Then he turned and walked out of the room.

As he walked across the long hallway and entered the stairwell, he felt lighter and relieved. Finally. He almost made it to the bottom floor alone, when he heard someone calling out behind him. "Devon, wait up."

His brother. Figured. Devon hadn't even seen him in the room. Probably standing behind him in Grandfather's office, behind the door for an easy exit.

"Devon, stop," Karl said, as he reached Devon's side.

"If you want to talk to me, keep up." Devon pushed open the double door and stepped out into the fresh air. He halted, tilted his face to the late-afternoon sun, and took a deep breath. It felt so good that he took a second one. He felt Karl's curious gaze on him. Devon chuckled and said, "I should have done that a long time ago."

"Maybe." Karl stared at him cautiously. "But now what?"

"I'll do what I've always wanted to do."

"*Um,* … you're kidding, right?"

"No. Not in the least."

His brother stepped in front of him. "Look. Don't do anything rash. Find Tori, ask her to come back and speak with Grandfather, and all will be well."

"No. I will find her, but I won't ask her to speak with him." With a determined smile, he added, "I'm not sure I'll speak to him myself."

"I know you're mad. I understand that."

"No, I'm not mad. I'm actually relieved." He slapped his brother on the shoulder. "Not to worry. I'm good. In fact, I'm really good." He headed back to his vehicle, stopped, and laughed. "I guess I'm walking." He turned to his brother and tossed the keys to Grandfather's SUV to him. "I'll finally get to drive my truck." He flashed Karl a big grin. "See you later."

CHAPTER 10

TORI PULLED VIENNA'S car onto the highway and headed in the direction of the north end of the forest. She had a forty-minute drive ahead, and the sun was at the very beginning of its descent. It was a stunningly beautiful afternoon.

To be honest, Tori had to admit she'd missed living here. Her whole life history was here. The small house she'd been raised in, her two sisters, the friends she'd had growing up, and her aging grandmother, who'd loved her and had sacrificed everything to give Tori a decent life. But more than anything, her grandmother, the last stargazer of her line, had shown Tori that her abilities were to be honed and used, not shunned, as so many others believed.

She'd thought Devon, with his own developing abilities, had understood. But he hadn't, not really. Because he hadn't been able to see Jessie. Jessie was one of the joys and one of the heartaches of Tori's life.

According to her grandmother, Tori's perfect partner would be able to see Jessie.

In a cruel twist of fate, Grandfather had seen her spirit pet, and Devon hadn't. Tori's lips twisted at the irony. Of course Grandfather, when broached about the subject in front of Devon, had denied it all. And that stuck yet another "crazy" feather in her cap. To top it off, instead of believing her, Devon had believed Grandfather.

Such was her life.

The highway was empty and, in some ways, terribly lonely.

As though she'd summoned him, Jessie appeared in the seat beside her. "Hey, Jessie. How are you?"

Jessie chattered in that wonderful conversational way he had, as if he understood. Her granny had said he did, and maybe she was right about that too.

Maybe it was Tori's own limited growth holding her back. If she had one-tenth of the talent her granny had, Tori would be happy. Granny had been amazing. But she'd passed on before Tori had finished her training. It had damn-near broken her heart.

But she'd survived, the same way she'd survived so much before. And that thought just led her into a depressing circle back to Devon.

He'd damn-near broken her too.

But she'd run and had rebuilt her life. Maybe it wasn't that great a life yet, but it had potential. And that's all she'd needed: potential. You could do anything once you had that. Her relationship with Devon *had* potential. Hell, *he* still had potential. But not with her.

She needed to head over to Genesis's place and catch up. Genesis might know what was going on in the forest. So, first, Tori had to take a quick look herself.

The parking lot turnoff was up ahead. The sun had dropped behind the mountain, sending eerie lighting across the sky. Beautiful and strange at the same time. She pulled into the lot and drove to the far end.

She knew where she was going, but some things had changed in the year she'd been gone. Large construction trailers were ahead of her. No lights, no vehicles, and apparently no people.

Great about the people. Bad about the machinery.

Jessie sat up and stared, then started to bounce in excitement.

She smiled. "Yes. We're almost home."

She parked the car beside the trailers and got out. Jessie raced around the grass and the trailers, checking out the latest additions to his world. This was his playground. It meant nothing that the people of the city had forgotten his ownership.

Without him and her, people couldn't survive.

But she'd had no idea that leaving could cause this kind of harm.

"I'm so sorry, Granny. I didn't know."

A warm breeze wound itself down the hillside, twisting through the huge mix of old-growth trees. This forest dated back hundreds of years, an ecosystem all on its own.

And it was damaged. Her heart ached, as she studied the large brown slash in the earth in front of the trailers. What were the men doing here? The bits and pieces that she could see didn't indicate exactly what they were doing. Or trying to do.

DEVON WALKED DOWN Main Street, picking up his pace the closer he got to the coffee shop. She could still be there. He pushed open the door and searched the room, ignoring all the knowing looks from the other patrons. They would have lots of new gossip to work on soon, once word spread about him walking out of Grandfather's office. Still, he'd never felt better.

He saw no sign of Tori. He frowned and made his way to the back of the restaurant. Vienna stood off to one side, speaking with a customer. Aware of the rising buzz of sound, she turned around to look and caught sight of him. He nodded to the front door.

She frowned, realizing he wouldn't go away, and walked over to talk with him. "What can I do for you?"

"Where did Tori go?"

Vienna raised an eyebrow. "What makes you think she was here?"

"I dropped her off here."

Vienna's lips tilted downward at the corners. "And?"

"Come on, please. Just tell me where she went."

"No. Not after what you did to her."

Damn. He should have expected that. "We needed her help."

Vienna shot him the evil eye and went on the offensive. He actually found himself backing up as her long finger poked him in the chest. "Did you ever think about asking her to help?"

"I did," he said defensively.

"In such a way that she understood how bad the situation was?" Vienna asked incredulously.

He felt the heat rise up his neck. "Maybe she was a little too shocked at seeing me to listen. In fact, she shut me off when she heard me coming." He glared at her. "She also sent my men walking away."

Vienna's lips quirked in a faint smile; then the humor of the situation brought her into a full-blown laugh. "Oh, that's great. And she could only have done that if she considered herself to be in danger—or was pissed off."

Devon glanced around and realized the whole restaurant had tuned into the conversation. "Okay. I have a few things to make up to her." He held out his hands. "I can't do that if I can't find her."

"I think she has a right to hide if she wants to."

"Maybe, but I can't apologize when she won't talk to me."

"You could try groveling." She sent him an overly bright smile.

He wouldn't get any help from this quarter. "Right. Thanks anyway." With a frustrated look around the room, he turned and stalked back outside. He stood here and wondered what the hell his next step should be, besides going home and grabbing his wheels.

"Devon?"

He spun around to see Eddie, the owner of the restaurant, lugging a couple garbage bags to his bins. "Hey, Eddie."

"I heard Vienna and Tori talking about the forest and going underground—"

Oh shit. Please, no.

Eddie winced, then lifted his arms and dropped them again. "Honestly I didn't hear that much, but …"

"She doesn't have wheels." Devon pondered the situation aloud.

Eddie cleared his throat. "I'm pretty sure Vienna will be walking home tonight." He turned around and headed to the back of the restaurant. "Please, don't tell anyone that I told you."

"So why did you tell me?"

Eddie stopped, as he was about to go around the wall. He glanced over his shoulder. "'Cause I know what it's like to love and lose and to know it was brought about by my own stupidity."

Ouch.

Devon opened his mouth to make some sort of retort, but Eddie had left. That was probably a good thing. First things first, Devon needed to get going.

He checked the hour.

And must get going fast.

Once on the road, Devon let the truck run free. For the last few years, he'd been at Grandfather's beck and call, day and night. Devon was a trained investigator, but Grandfather had paid for Devon's college tuition. Then he'd called in the favor once Devon had graduated. It wasn't what he'd planned to do with his life, but Grandfather had his own plans. And it was hard to go against family. Especially when everyone in the family worked for the family business.

Grandfather had taken over his company from his father. He'd been driven to turn the business into an empire. Somewhere along the way, he'd gotten so hard, he forgot how to be human.

And somewhere along the way, Devon had given up his own dreams.

As he thought about it, he realized he'd given into Grandfather's demands and had given up his dreams at the same time that Tori had walked out of his life, taking his future with him.

As a result, he'd buried himself in work. And became one of Grandfather's right-hand men.

"Great," he muttered to himself. "I'm broke, don't have a place of my own, and I'm not gainfully employed. So what else could go wrong?" Immediately he wished he could take those words back. Changes were happening, he could tell, and it was up to him to stay afloat.

It took longer to get to the parking lot than he remembered. He pulled in to find Vienna's car at the far end, beside the construction trailers. What were those doing here?

He'd heard rumors, but, along with Grandfather's odd behavior a few days ago, Devon had no idea what was going on. Grandfather appeared to be back to normal again. Shaking his head, Devon walked to Vienna's car and realized it was locked but still warm. So she'd not been here long.

No way to follow her tracks. He knew several entrances into the caves but had no idea which entrance she would have used. He randomly selected a wider beaten-down path. He took a long, careful look at the machines as he passed them. Something very fishy was going on.

The walk wasn't easy in good light, but, in poor light, it was downright treacherous. He had great night vision, and that was his saving grace. However, it would be so much better if his own abilities were fully functioning. He would have no problem navigating so much of the world if his heightened senses were cooperating.

He frowned, hating the loss. He also realized that his subsequent behavior was partly due to the loss of his abilities. He hadn't been himself since that loss. At the time, he'd somewhat blamed Tori, thinking she had left with his abilities. But what if the loss of his abilities had led to the loss of Tori?

Like a blind man, he'd lost his sight. Hadn't known what to do because his instincts were off.

And he'd stayed that way for the last twelve months, until he'd gone after her. But he'd gone on Grandfather's orders—after a year of waffling, a year of attempting to follow his instincts—because they weren't there to follow.

Bringing Tori home might have just saved him.

He hadn't done well by her, and he wasn't sure how much of that was the new Devon versus the old, but he was glad that she was in his life again.

He could make it up to her.

He would make it up to her.

He just needed the chance.

CHAPTER II

TORI STUDIED THE forest as she walked, her soul stretching in joy. She was where she belonged. It had devastated her to leave, but, thinking it was her only option, she'd run.

As far and as fast as she could.

For all the good it did. Devon had found her anyway.

Now, if only he had come because *he* wanted to, not at Grandfather's orders.

She couldn't necessarily hold that against Devon, but neither did he get brownie points.

And maybe that was the way it should be. She'd sworn off chocolate a year ago.

She wasn't about to break that rule for him.

Why should he step back into her life and act normal, when her whole life had been tossed into the wind? And the way he'd brought her back wasn't exactly moonlight and roses. He'd kidnapped her.

But you were needed, whispered a voice in her head. And she'd helped. She would have felt terrible if those people had died because she had escaped before she'd known.

So, in a way, she was grateful for having been there to help and to be given a chance to find out what was happening to her forest.

And that meant she had to be grateful that she was here on hand. And even grateful that Devon had brought her back.

In spite of all he'd done to her, in spite of all that Grandfather had done to her, in spite of everything, she'd saved those people. She had come back now to figure out what had happened to the forest.

But helping those people today made her feel good, as if her life had purpose, something she'd been missing for the last year. Growing up with Granny, being who she was, it was imperative that the triplets do energy work to keep their systems balanced. While on the run, Tori's energy work had been just to stay alive. And she'd not done so well, burning through her resources at an alarming rate. She'd dropped weight she didn't have to lose.

She'd always been lean and now? ... Medical school skeletons had nothing on her.

The sun was setting, as she crested over the last field and saw the huge trees waving in the wind. Lord, they were beautiful. She had an affinity for all plants, but the woods and the forests, especially the sacred forests, held a special place in her heart.

She was a caretaker who'd shirked her duty. And for a man, no less. Or rather, in order to avoid a man. Granny wouldn't be pleased. Yet, as a stargazer, Tori had known so much before it had happened. Tori had tried to throw charts, as had both her sisters. Genesis had a real talent but didn't like the answers. Tori's charts had contradicted each other, and Granny had said that was the struggle that Tori would go through herself.

She'd never understood that.

Celeste appeared to have inherited the largest of the stargazer talent. But she'd had no joy in the job. Tori had wanted to do well, but she hadn't the patience. Hell, Tori had patience for very little.

At least back then.

Now she had no idea. She'd changed.

Living on the edge, away from all she'd loved, … trying to stay under the radar, out of sight of Devon and all those he worked with. She'd almost succeeded. Until the robbery.

Sigh.

Life just couldn't be that easy, could it? Not for her. Her sisters seemed to have it all together. But not Tori. She was a mess. The one who'd walked into a bank, looking for her last fifty bucks, and got caught up in a bank robbery. Celeste would never have let something so messy happen. Genesis, being so nice, probably would have helped the bank robbers, while scolding them the whole time.

No, life was just messy for Tori.

She trampled through the woods, hearing the dry grass underneath. Devon had said something about the pools being affected, but it would still take time for the woods to be affected as well. The damage would creep from the water to the land, and nobody seemed to know what was going on.

But Tori knew. She stared at the dry prune-like branches of the shrubbery around her, the sheer lack of flowers despite the time of year, and realized the problem was way bigger than she'd first imagined. The knotted energy in the woods, locking those poor people in place, was huge—but the core problem was even bigger.

She could only imagine what it would be like if Devon were here to help her. But instead of his needing her help, she worried that she might need his help instead.

He'd always been great at problem solving. Honestly, she would have thought he could've handled that knot mess himself. But he didn't do energy the same way she did. He read energy. Read the answers to the puzzles that people were keeping secret. He couldn't do it for everything, couldn't do it all the time. But he did it enough that most people stopped to listen when he spoke.

Jessie raced toward her, his voice loud and excited, as he chattered away happily.

No. Not possible. Surely Jessie had made a mistake.

She spun around and realized, no—he hadn't. Devon. "Hell," she said. "I've changed, so why hasn't my world changed? How damn difficult can it be?"

<hr>

"IN WHAT WAY are you different?" Devon stared at her. He heard her frustration but also the doubt in her voice. The disgust.

Still, he was different too, and it was up to him to show her. Since she wouldn't—or couldn't—answer him, he spoke up again. "I walked away from Grandfather today. Walked away from everything he represented."

A tiny gasp whispered on the breeze.

He knew that must have shocked her. Devon's world was all about Grandfather, and Devon had walked away.

No one else had done that yet. Except Connor. But his wasn't as close of a family tie. Besides, Grandfather had wanted Connor gone. Only Grandfather hadn't expected Connor to join the other side. In this town, there were only two sides. Grandfather's side and the rest of the world. Devon guessed he'd just changed sides too.

After a moment she asked, "How did he take it?"

Devon wanted to laugh, but it was hard to find humor in the situation. "Shock. Disbelief and anger." At the contemplative silence, he felt emboldened.

"What will you do now?" she asked, with interest.

He laughed drily. "I came after you."

"Why?" *Ah.* The million-dollar question. And he waited

a little too long to answer. She snorted. "Right."

"I don't know, Tori," he said honestly. "It was instinctive. As if having finally made the *right* decision, I could maybe put my life back on the *right* track."

"*Right* decision?"

Soft now, her voice sent shivers down his spine. He studied her under half-closed lids, leaning against the big tree they had stopped by. "Yes," he finally admitted to himself. "Today was the right decision. The decision I should have made a year ago."

"I didn't want you to walk away from everything in your life."

"I know that."

"I just wanted you to be there for me."

"Grandfather turned on you because I loved you." Devon paused, his voice husky and thick. He cleared his throat. "It's impossible to see when you are in the middle of the scenario you're trying to look at." What could he say but the truth?

"True. But you had a chance to sort out your priorities, and … you did."

Dangerous territory. He searched for something less likely to set them off in the wrong direction. "I couldn't believe it when I found you. I had searched for so long, and then yesterday I saw the bank video feed."

"Damn. I suppose that robbery was patched to Grandfather?"

"Not right away, but, with the anomaly of that strange woman being escorted out of the bank for no reason, then of course it was. He has fingers into all anomalies related to the paranormal security system for the planet. You're definitely an anomaly. You know that. All anomalies run through the Center."

"I hadn't expected to end up in a bank robbery that day. And to think that's all it took to have my world come crashing down around me."

"Or maybe it was to bring it back in line. When you walked away, things changed."

"Not enough."

"No. Maybe not. But a lot has changed again. Although I'm not exactly a great prospect with no job."

"That never mattered."

He smiled. "No. With you, it never did. But I was raised to excel. When I lost my abilities, I needed that focus. I think I would have gone nuts without that drive. When you left, I wondered if my talent had left with you."

She stared at him, at his honesty, in shock.

"It had been changing in the weeks before you left," he continued, staring at a spot just behind her. "When you were finally gone, Grandfather tried to tell me how much better off I was. That you hadn't understood me. I never believed him, but, with you gone, it was easier to slide into the path he had planned out for me."

Letting her head fall back, and, with the setting sun bathing her tired face, she considered the old man and the iron fist he ruled with. "He's been ruling for a long time. He's also power-hungry, selfish, and has no concern for the environment around him."

"That's not true," Devon protested. "He wanted you here to help out his people."

She snorted at that. "Sure he did, but why did he send those people into such a dangerous situation as it was?"

"You could just as easily blame me for that. I was working security."

She stared at him. "You sent those people in there?"

He flushed. "I had no idea it was that bad. None of us did."

CHAPTER 12

"AND THAT'S JUST wrong. How could any of you—you in particular—not know?" she asked in shock. And saw the truth in his face. "Because you have none of your senses working, do you? You haven't just lost *some* of them. You've lost all of them."

The pain that whispered across his face made her want to stop digging, leaving him to keep his pain buried deep. But she couldn't. This was too important.

"Didn't you realize the forest was dying?"

"No," he said. "Not until I realized these people were in trouble. I hadn't been there in months."

"It didn't get that way overnight," she exclaimed. "It's been months in the making. Probably the whole year I've been gone, in fact."

"Did you ever consider that the forest started to die after you left it? After you, a vital energy worker, a vital connection to that forest, left?"

Silence. Slowly she said, "I hadn't considered such a thing. It would have to be a coincidence surely?"

He peered deep into her eyes. "Why? Are you so unaware of your power?"

"But I'm not the only one here," she cried out, not liking his suggestion.

"*Ah.* You don't know."

She tilted her head, a horrible sense of foreboding filling her. "What don't I know?"

"Your sister. Matt, the head of the Paranormal Council. The Portmans. The black rocks and the damage to the pools?"

She stared at him in dismay. "I haven't connected with my sister yet."

"Too bad. That's where you need to start. If you want to figure this all out, that is."

Crap. She stared at the forest around them. Her body felt better. Moved better. The adjustment had been natural, easy. Her energy system, charging system, had gratefully shifted back to its normal state. She'd been raised here, so the sense of homecoming was real.

The energy swarmed around her.

"Then let's go find my sister." She had said it naturally, then caught herself. Why had she included him in that discussion?

She needed to see her sister on her own. It had been a year. A long year. Now, insecurity wove through her at the thought. She needed to apologize to Genesis. And she had no intention of doing that with an audience. She also had to find her first. Was she at her apartment or at Granny's place? The latter definitely wasn't a place to take Devon.

"It's late." She turned back the way she'd come and started walking. "I need to get going."

Devon fell into step beside her. "To Genesis? Do you know where she is?"

"No, I'll start with her shop first—if it's still open. Then her apartment is just around the corner."

"Makes sense. She's probably got everything fixed up and back to normal again."

Her stomach sinking, Tori couldn't help stopping in her tracks to ask, "What happened?"

"Her shop and apartment were broken into several times."

Her stomach hit rock bottom. Genesis was the gentlest of the three of them. "Why would anyone do that? She would never hurt a soul."

"It had to do with the same mess. I think it's all good now." He shrugged. "Maybe even better. I've heard through the grapevine that business is brisk at her shop."

Tori wasn't sure if that was a good thing or not. Genesis liked her little place, but she was not a people person, so Tori didn't know how her sister was reconciling those two elements. "I need to see her."

"Yes, you do," Devon said, his tone sober. "She's needed you."

Tori stared at him suspiciously. "What else do you know?"

He shrugged. "I've heard things. She went head-to-head with Grandfather, and, although she had Connor and Matt at her side, she didn't have an easy time of it."

"Shit." Tori spun around to reorient herself. She was having trouble trusting her gut. Where could Genesis be? They were closer to the cottage, but Tori wouldn't bring Devon there. She had mentioned the cottage in the past but had never taken him there. And she didn't want to now. "Can you call her shop and see if she's there?"

Devon gave her a weird look, but he pulled his phone from his pocket. "If you know her number, I can."

She quickly rattled the number off the top of her head and hoped it was the right one. A year was a long time, and, as she was learning, it was too long. Why had she always assumed that Genesis could handle anything? No one could handle everything. Celeste was supposed to stay around too. Only Celeste had disappeared around the same time as Tori had. Damn.

"It's ringing, but there's no answer."

She nodded. "Please try her apartment."

"I could, but I doubt she's there."

With a sinking heart, she stared at him. She closed her eyes and swallowed. "Crap." The guilt was piling up, weighing more heavily with each passing minute. "I'm sorry I wasn't here for her."

"Maybe that was a good thing because Connor was." And something in his tone of voice made her stare at him suspiciously. Devon smiled at her. "They might make it now."

Good for her sister. But not for Tori. She would not go back in time. No sirree. Devon had made his mistakes, and he could damn well live with them. She wasn't signing up for more pain. Especially not of the Devon variety. Just for good measure, she said, "Maybe I'll find someone now that I'm home again."

Silence.

She ignored him. "Did you try calling her apartment?"

"The number?" he snapped out. "What is it?"

She rattled it off. And heard the ringing as it droned on and on. "Shit. So where is she?"

"You could try her cell phone," he said.

"I don't have the number."

"Okay," he said slowly, giving her a long look. "I am trying hard to not ask why, when you obviously know the other numbers."

"She got a new one, and I don't have it, okay?" Of

course she should have it. It was her sister. And she didn't need the reminder that she had been less concerned with what was going on with Genesis—her stable commonsense sister—whose life always worked out. And who apparently had her life thrown into upheaval when Tori hadn't been around.

Damn.

"Why don't I call Connor?"

Devon was already dialing, while she watched. She couldn't imagine that Devon and Connor were friends. Then again, they were both part of Grandfather's organization.

"Connor, I have Tori here, and she's looking for her sister."

Devon smiled and turned to look at Tori, as he spoke into the cell phone. "Sure, we'll do that."

She glared at him. "There's no *we* in any of this."

Ending the call, he snagged her arm and walked her back to the parking lot. "Sure there is. We've been invited over to Connor's place. They're cooking dinner, and there's enough for the four of us."

"There is no *four of us*. There is no *two of us*, remember?"

"Nope, sure don't." Cheerfully, in fact. Way too cheerfully. He led her back to the car. "Think about it. Something shitty is going on, and you need to hear all that Genesis has been through, before we can do anything to stop the harmful effects on the forest."

The bushes whacked her on the legs, as she tried to walk beside Devon. He had her hand in a tight grip and wasn't letting her pull away. And trying to walk beside him wasn't working either. She tried to step around him, and another bush hit her in the leg. "Stop pulling on me like that."

He let her go, waited until she walked up beside him,

and slung her arm through his.

"I can't get lost down here."

"The woods are dense."

"And I do know my way around." She couldn't keep her exasperation out of her voice. Surely he'd remembered at least that much about her. In a way, his lack of understanding of her skills hurt.

Then he did it.

"Sorry, I was actually thinking of myself," he said humbly. "You can get out of here, but I doubt I could."

Oh. She cleared her throat. "Sure you could. Or aren't you still going to be an investigator? Along with your puzzle-solving abilities, you'd be phenomenal."

"I'm done already."

There was a comfortable silence as she contemplated that. "Are you really going to quit working for Grandfather?"

"I'm not going to quit—I already have. You're the one who doesn't seem to accept that fact."

"Ha. I remember what you said. I'm just not sure I believe it."

"It's a done deal."

"Until he stops anyone else from hiring you. You'll have to move to another city or maybe even another planet." Pangs of loss started in her belly, and she hated them. She'd done without the damn man for over a year. She wasn't about to get sucked into that belief that he was there for her. Not again.

"I doubt Matt would buckle to that kind of pressure." Devon's voice turned thoughtful. "I should talk to him about the possibility."

She snorted. "Are we talking about Celeste's Matt? The Matt who took her pet and ditched her?"

"I don't know anything about that, never even knew she had a pet, and I doubt Matt would have ditched her over that. Celeste has a temper too, you know."

"Ha, mine is likely worse."

"You think I don't know that?" At her disgruntled look, he laughed. "It is damn good to see you again, Tori. No one else has quite the same color, the same flavor to their personality. You make everything brighter. Happier for me."

"Right. So much so that you were dying to come after me and bring me back."

"No." He shook his head. "Not at all. I wanted to haul you back as soon as you left. But all those cool heads around me ordered me to wait. To let you cool off. To let you see what a fool you'd bee—" Devon bent over, gasping in surprise.

Tori brandished her fist again, ready to throw another punch. "You did not just say that!"

His grin was on the pained side. "You wouldn't let me finish—and what was that about Celeste having a temper?" He held up his hand in a sign of acquiescence. "Okay, I was going to say, … let you see what a fool you'd been, but instead …" He paused and backed up a step, eyeing her warily. "… Instead I realized I was the fool for listening."

She lowered her hand, absentmindedly rubbing her knuckles. She hadn't really hit him, not hard. The shock of his words had her staring down at her hand, her mind roiling in confusion. "You … made a mistake?" Tori repeated, frowning. She would have died of joy if he'd said that to her before. She'd desperately hoped he would chase after her but had known he wouldn't. He'd been too stubborn. Too uncaring. She'd accused him of just that same thing before she'd left.

To be fair, the words had flown out of her mouth in a fit of temper and without a second thought. That was to her detriment. She'd been working on that. Apparently not hard enough.

"I'm sorry. I shouldn't have smacked you."

He grinned. "You didn't hurt me. I was just kidding."

She narrowed her gaze and pinned him to the spot. "About all of it?"

Instantly the humor in the air bottomed out, and he became serious. "No. Not all of it. I am sorry. For being an idiot. For not having come after you. For not having seen how upset you were."

It was hard to see any deceit in his gaze. He'd always been upfront with her before, but there was still that one problem that she hadn't understood. Now was the time to ask him about it.

She opened her mouth.

Crack!

In the next instant, Tori was lying on the ground, Devon on top of her.

"*Shh*," he whispered. "That was a gun."

"No way. There shouldn't be anyone here in the first place, and carrying guns around this uncontrollable energy is just asking for trouble." She glared at him. "Get off—"

And he kissed her. Hard. And then soft. Then everything in between.

Passion had always been like that between them. At the first touch of their lips, they'd been ripping clothes off each other.

He pulled back, her body already mourning the loss, her nerves humming along with joy, then crying out in regret.

"That was always the best way to shut you up," he muttered. "Listen to me. Someone is here. No way that was an accident, so the shot was meant for us."

"Oh, shit."

Jessie bounded toward them, jumping from one leg to the other in agitation. "What's the matter, Jessie?" She studied his antics for a few moments. "Not one man. Jessie says there are three of them."

That same damn odd silence she remembered from before was there again between them.

She groaned. "Whatever your personal beliefs about Jessie, do not doubt that he is here and telling us the truth. According to him, the men are walking toward us."

Devon rose into a crouch and sidled toward the thick brush beside them, peering through gaps in the foliage. He motioned with his arm for her to join him.

She scrambled to his side and tried to see who was approaching. Three men. All strangers.

Or maybe not. One of them turned to look at something, and she caught a glimpse of his profile. "That's the man from the bank robbery."

"I think it's all three of them."

She drummed her fingers on the ground, trying to think. "Why would they be here?"

"For you. Because of what you did. Either they want revenge or they want you to help them with their next robbery. That would be my guess." He looked down at her. "Can you send all three away?"

She stared at him, understanding what he was asking her to do. She peered through the shrubbery to take another look. "They're after me, and they know about my ability. Look at them. They have their ears covered."

The men were all wearing hats and earmuffs.

"That won't help them, will it?"

She shook her head. "Unless they are made of a special material."

"Try it anyway. If we can get one of them to walk away, that would help."

Knowing it would be beyond difficult, she closed her eyelids and focused.

Turn around, and go back the way you came from. It's a nice day. Turn around, and go for a long walk back the way you came from.

She kept her eyelids closed, sinking into the energy.

"It's not working," Devon whispered. "They aren't doing anything."

Shit. She reached deeper inside, strengthening her thoughts. *Take off your earmuffs, and turn around. Take off your earmuffs, and turn around.*

"*Um …*"

She tried to ignore Devon, but a part of her was listening to see if she was making any progress. *Take off the earmuffs. Take off the earmuffs.*

"You're doing it! They're taking off their headgear," he whispered.

She directed the energy outward even harder. *Turn around and walk away. Turn around. Walk back the way you came. Turn around. Turn around.*

"They've turned around and are heading back through the forest."

Tori sighed with relief and sagged in place. She would need a moment to recuperate. That took more out of her than she'd expected. It was no real surprise though. She had to direct these men to abandon something they were very tightly focused on accomplishing. If they'd simply been standing idle and talking to each other, it would have been easier. And, she thought with a wince, moving three of them had actually been physically painful.

"Are they still moving away?" she asked, after a few moments.

"They appear to be, but they're slowing down."

"Not good. Time to run."

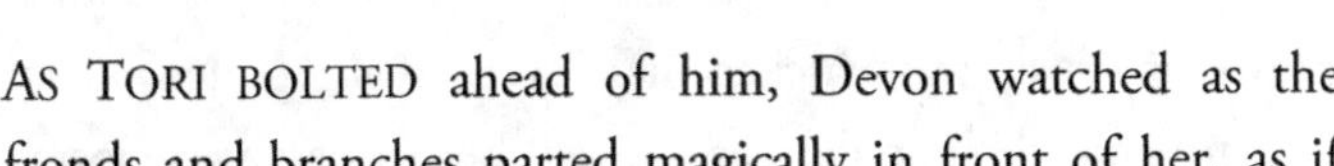

AS TORI BOLTED ahead of him, Devon watched as the fronds and branches parted magically in front of her, as if exposing a hidden pathway.

And maybe there was, but he hadn't seen one before. Then again, things happened around Tori and her sisters. They'd been called oddballs in town and at school. But, no matter what anyone said, they were definitely skilled in the paranormal.

He'd been stunned to see all three of those men take off their headgear and turn around and walk away. Devon would love to do something similar. But this flat-out run through the thick undergrowth of the woods, yet nothing touching her—well, that was damn-near magical.

A tree branch whacked him in the face, bringing his attention back to the forest around him. He glared at the offending limb as he pushed it aside and then suddenly realized that he'd fallen behind. Were the trees reaching out to slow him down and to hit him of their own volition? Or was it possible that Tori was directing the branches to do this? He did find that hard to believe though. Perhaps the most logical reason was that he let the space between the two of them widen to the point that her magical pathway was closing before he got there.

To test his hypothesis, he let the distance widen even more and realized it didn't really matter.

Because, however it was happening, the path was definitely closing. At the same time, he realized that Tori was moving so far ahead that he was in danger of losing track of her. He raced to catch up.

And tripped. Pain slammed into him.

Shit.

He struggled to his feet and picked up the pace, only now the brush was thicker than ever. She'd pulled so far forward that the energy that allowed her to pass was closing behind her, and, therefore, in front of him.

Keeping them apart.

He couldn't see her in front of him, nor could he hear her. He didn't know if he should keep struggling forward. He was damn sure they hadn't come this way in the first place, wondering if he should try a different direction. He realized with a sinking heart that he was likely lost.

CHAPTER 13

TORI RAN, HER mind focused on getting away and staying hidden. She had some idea what those men wanted, but she wasn't willing to stick around and have them confirm her fears. In fact, she would be happy to never see them again.

What the hell was going on in her forest? She'd been gone a year, but apparently a year was plenty long enough for all kinds of change.

Like Devon. Had he really said he'd been a fool for letting her leave?

She shook her head, her feet slowing. The energy of the forest kept her flagging reserves up, but no doubt she'd drained more than she should have by sending away those men simultaneously. And that should not be. She should be recharged now. Instead she sensed some reversal happening here.

Not good. She slowed, her hand pressing against her ribs and the stitch in her side. She'd always been a good runner, but apparently she wasn't as fit as she had been before either.

Or ... was it possible that the forest was pulling energy from her? Draining her?

She turned to look behind her and noted no sign of Devon. *Shit.*

She doubted she'd outrun him. Had he fallen behind or been hurt? Or maybe even shot? Surely not. She would have heard the sound of gunshots. Wouldn't she?

But her stomach churned at the possibility. Jogging back the way she'd traveled, she waved her arm, asking the woods to open the path wider so that she could see in front of her, see where Devon was. She would never get lost in this forest, but it would be easy for Devon, especially if he'd fallen behind. And she couldn't just leave him …

Up ahead, she heard faint noises. Instantly she closed the branches around her and peered through. Jessie chattered quietly at her side. She looked down at him. "Is it Devon?"

More chitters.

"Go see, please."

Instantly Jessie disappeared from sight and worked his way through the branches, climbing up the trunk of a particularly tall tree and bouncing excitedly on a branch.

"Good. It's him, right?"

At the louder chitters, she said, "Can you bring him to me?" It was a futile question because she knew Devon couldn't see Jessie, but Tori was beyond exhausted. Worried that her strategy wouldn't work, she dug deep inside to find even the tiniest spark of energy and forced herself to follow behind.

Putting one foot in front of the other, she trudged after Jessie. The branches shifted and eased back as she walked. If she had more energy, she could open a wider pathway again, but now it was just enough for her to keep walking. She mentally called out to Devon, hoping to help him. *Just pick up and follow Jessie back to me. He's in front of you. Trust him. Follow him. Follow Jessie to me.*

And there Devon was. She grinned weakly.

At the same moment, Devon spotted her, and relief broke out across his face. "There you are." He looked around. "Not sure how I found you, but I'm damn glad I did."

And then she realized how bad his situation could have been. "Sorry. I didn't notice you weren't behind me earlier. I would have gotten back sooner."

He shrugged. "I'm just glad you came back." He reached out a hand. "Can we walk from here?"

"I hope so. I'm tired," she admitted, taking his hand. As soon as his fingers closed around hers, she felt better. Calmer. More in control. She'd been so worried. Trying to change her focus, she asked, "Any sign of the men?"

He shook his head. "Are you kidding? If I couldn't follow you, I doubt they could."

She laughed softly. "Well, thank heavens for small mercies. The bad news is that I just reacted and ran to safety and didn't run toward the parking lot."

Weariness settled on his lean face. "That means we have a way to go. We'd better get moving. It's darker out here than I'd like."

She turned in a slow circle, orienting herself. "What time is it?"

"It's been just over an hour and half since we called Connor."

She winced. "Not good. They must be worried about us by now."

"I'm trying to get reception, but there's none so far."

"No, there won't be out here." She contemplated the issue. They had two choices, and neither appealed to her. "We're at least an hour away from the vehicles."

"Really? That far?" He looked around. "And, if that's the case, is there a closer exit where we can get picked up?"

"No." She groaned. "I just ran blindly, looking for safety, and the forest gave me a direct path to it."

From the look on Devon's face, she knew he didn't understand. "I'm only a few minutes from my ... our cottage," she quickly corrected. "That's what I meant about safety."

"A cottage?" he asked in surprise. "I think you mentioned something about it, but I didn't question you before. How do you have a cottage?"

"Granny."

That stopped him. Then again, Granny's name was enough to stop most conversations with the locals.

"She had a cottage here?"

"Yes, this was our real home. She kept a small place in town for the days we had school, but, other than that, we lived here."

"This far away?" He turned and looked at the thick woods. "How can you possibly know where we are?"

"The woods are always thicker and larger here at the edge of the cabin—to keep the location safe."

"And we can go there?"

"We might have to." She studied the evening sky. As much as she didn't want to take him to her special home, it wouldn't be long before the angry clouds overhead released their fury, and no way they could make it to the vehicles without a hell of a good soaking.

Raindrops started to fall.

"There's no help for it. We'll go sit out the storm. We can always wait until the worst has passed, then come back via the caves. I can reach the caves from here."

"None of this makes any sense, but, if you've got a place for us to stay warm and dry," he said, "now would be the time."

"Follow me," she yelled, as the wind picked up. She stopped as her hand was grabbed again.

"That didn't work so well last time."

She nodded and held his hand, leading him through the woods. By now she couldn't see anything, but it didn't matter. Her energy was like a homing device, and these woods were hers.

Her energy knew exactly where to go and how to get there.

Without warning, they entered a small clearing. Tori stopped suddenly at Devon's exclamation. The cottage stood in front of her.

Tears formed in her eyes, the stinging sensation a reminder of that last long, lonely year. She could have just come here to heal. That's what the place was for, and, in the past, it had always done a wonderful job. So why hadn't she done that? Why had she run from everyone?

Especially when everyone she loved was here.

"Is this it?" he asked doubtfully.

She tried to look at the cottage through his eyes. The building was small, deceptively small, and, with the rain sheeting down on them, and no lights on, it seemed to be a deserted shed than her childhood home.

"Yes," she whispered, "this is it." She walked to the front door and mentally unlocked the security, noting the extra layer of protection that someone—Genesis, most likely—had put on it. Truth be told, that scared Tori more than anything else she'd heard about Genesis's problems because this? … Well, this was proof.

And it was all too real. And damn scary.

How bad had this last year been? Had Tori come close to losing her eldest sister? She stepped just inside the doorway and flicked on the lights, noticing that her hand shook. Jessie raced inside, grinning from ear to ear. So many happy days had been spent here with the multiple spirit pets that Granny had adopted. Pets that had been lost or hadn't found owners or had come and gone to the spirit world but hung close to Granny. She'd been special. Hell, she'd been damn special.

And Tori missed her something awful.

That was why, she realized. That was why she'd run as far away as possible, instead of coming here. She couldn't stand the memories of her loss. Hated the pain. Knew it would only get worse as she and Devon split and as her world, past and present, broke completely apart.

So it was definitely not a good place to be. She'd wanted to return here, but the memories had hurt. Genesis was dealing with her own crisis, and, in a way, that had hurt Tori too—both because her sister was beautiful inside and out, and Tori hated to see Genesis in pain, but also because it meant that Tori hadn't been there for Genesis. Same for Celeste.

Tori had believed she could remove some of the problems from her shoulders as well as her sisters', so she'd turned and run. And kept on running. She hadn't had a plan any time in the last year, other than to find a way to keep moving forward.

Gentle chitters woke her up to the presence of a very worried Jessie at her side. He'd missed this place too. She'd also taken him from his home and all he'd loved. Damn.

Now something different filled his voice. Something that really scared Tori. She squatted beside him. "What's the matter, Jessie?"

He reached out a hand toward Devon, behind her.

She turned and gasped.

Devon swayed on his feet, his body in shock and ready to collapse beside her. "Devon? What's the matter?"

His glassy stare met hers, but he couldn't seem to formulate an answer.

All business now, she tugged him inside and quickly closed and locked the door. "Don't try to talk. Let's get you to the pool. Come this way." Urging him every step of the way and half helping to support him, she took him to the small room at the back of the kitchen. Pushing open the door, she tugged him forward. "Just a little farther. You can do this. You're almost there."

He followed her, one foot shuffling in front of the other. She managed to get him up against the stone edge, noting with relief that the water appeared crystal clear and eager for someone to work on. Hell, she'd love to dive in herself. She turned her attention back to the big man at her side. "Devon, I don't know what happened to you, but this is a healing pool."

His gaze turned to the pool, then back to her.

"Do you understand?" Her fingers were already busy undoing his shirt buttons.

"Yes," he whispered.

"Thank God. We need to get you out of these clothes." She tugged the shirt off his shoulders from the front, then moved around behind him and froze.

Blood dripped in a wide sluggish trickle from the long slashing wound across his back.

"Devon, you've been shot."

SHOT? NO. NOT possible. No one was around to shoot him. Besides, why would anyone? Devon hadn't done anything.

Only his back burned with fire. His muscles refused to work, and, somewhere along this last stretch of a path, he could barely keep his feet moving forward.

Shot?

He barely understood that Tori was taking off his clothes. How many times had he dreamed of her doing just that this past year? But now she spoke about a healing pool.

Healing pool? Here? How was that possible? But the evidence was before him. And that blew him away. The water was so clear and so blue and so beautiful that he felt his very soul reaching for it. Crying out for it. Needing it in a way he couldn't begin to understand, but his body was already on the move. He took one step, then another.

"*Uh*, hang on, Devon. We need to get the rest of your clothes off."

"Hurts," he mumbled.

"I know it hurts." Her voice gentled. "At least kick off your shoes. Let's sit you down on the side here."

The next thing he knew, he sat at the water's edge. It was so close. But not close enough.

Following his instincts and ignoring Tori, he fell backward.

She yelped.

And then he heard no more as the water—warm, caring, eager water—closed over his head, and he sank to the bottom of the pool. Just as he began to feel the need to breathe, the warm, gentle pressure of the water lifted him up for a deep gulp of air, then let him sink deeper below.

His arms lay outstretched, and the water soaked into his jeans and socks and covered his skin in the wonderful sensation of liquid healing.

The fire in his back burned hot and loud for a brief moment but was immediately chased away with the cooling waves of goodness. He groaned, the waters lifting him up higher and higher. Just as he needed to breathe again, he broke through the surface, and this time he floated.

His mind filled with colors and weird sounds. Not painful but not comfortable either.

He wished there were just peace inside.

And then he knew no more.

CHAPTER 14

TORI WATCHED DEVON bob in the water in exasperation. "Just a little more time and I could have gotten the
socks off too but never mind. Do you always go swimming
fully dressed?" She stood with her hands on her hips at the
edge of the pool and watched the healing waters take care of
him.

Jessie chattered excitedly at her side. She nodded. "Go
for it."

Jessie dove in.

She laughed as he twisted and splashed and swam, like
an otter with a newfound toy. Of course, after a year away, it
was a newfound toy again. This pool was his pool. It had
always been here, ready and available for everyone in the
family to use—and those from outside who came searching
for it. She remembered a few times when Granny had let a
stranger or two into the pools. It had been such a rare
occasion that they all knew there must be a special reason
when it did happen.

Their pool was powerful. It worked at a different level
than the ones in the caves. Those pools operated equally
well, but this one was just ... different.

And she was damn grateful it was here.

She chastised herself for not seeing Devon had been
hurt. That explained his getting lost. Devon was alpha in

every sense of the word, and he would never need help to find his way around. He was a problem solver. He had abilities—but not strong ones, as she recalled—or maybe she just hadn't thought so back then. Now that he'd lost them, she wondered if the pool could help restore at least a small part of them.

Stranger things had been known to happen.

As he appeared to be doing fine now in the loving embrace of the healing waters, she turned and picked up the shirt she'd managed to get off him before he'd fallen in. There was a small hole under his arm and beside his ribs. Thankfully the bullet had apparently struck at such an angle as to have grazed his back instead of entering his chest wall. A bad burn but nowhere near as damaging as it could have been.

Thank God.

She felt exhaustion setting in, more from the shock of seeing how close a call Devon had escaped versus her being worn out physically. She collapsed into a small chair beside the pool's edge. It had been so close. She'd led him for miles in the woods, while he'd been bleeding like a stuck pig behind her, and she hadn't noticed.

She closed her eyes and gave herself a good talking to. They were here now, and they were safe. The pool could fix him.

But could it fix her? She'd have to wait and see. The pool was focusing on him right now. She would go in later.

After one last glance at Devon, Tori pushed out of the chair and headed back into the cottage proper, reacquainting herself with her home. The atmosphere was different. It was still peaceful, but she noted an odor of turbulence. An air of trouble having been here and gone. She really wished she'd made it to Genesis's place and had had a chance to talk to her.

Tori had missed so much. She really hadn't meant to. In fact, she had been so lost this past year that she could barely focus on anything but surviving.

She rummaged through the kitchen cupboards, wondering if there was anything to eat. They'd always kept supplies on hand. Aha! It looked as though Genesis had restocked recently or had been in the habit of coming here a lot, as supplies were aplenty. After some contemplation, Tori thought she could pull together a pasta dish quickly and easily enough. Devon would wake up hungry.

And, if she didn't feed one appetite, the other would come to life. Knowing how combustible they were along that line already, she was happy to find something here to cook for him instead. Besides, she rationalized to herself, her own stomach was growling. She'd been hungry a lot this last year. For all her best efforts, living alone under the radar hadn't been easy. She was happy she'd done as well as she had, but it hadn't been good for her.

She hated to admit it, but she'd been a bit on the spoiled side, using her position as the middle child to get things she wanted. Not that a few minutes on either side of the triplet's birth time should have made a difference, but Tori had used it to her advantage and had carved out a middle child spot for herself.

If her sisters had something Tori wanted or her sisters looked to be getting more than Tori, she wasn't above using that middle child argument to take advantage. That had been a while ago, and thankfully she didn't think she'd been such a brat in the last several years, but it hurt to look back and to see the things she'd done or hadn't done as a reflection of who she was now. She'd learned a lot over the past year.

She'd figured Genesis had had it easy, but it didn't sound like that from what Devon was sharing. Knowing Genesis, she would have made the best of her situation, but that didn't mean she'd had it easy. She'd been the one left behind, dealing with the memories and the pain and the loss. With both Tori and Celeste walking away, Genesis had been completely alone.

And that would have been rough. Not to mention, she would have had to deal with the townsfolk and their judgment. The attitudes and smirks of those who looked at them and who laughed behind their backs.

Granny had been hated by some, feared by many, and revered by others. Tori had no idea what the hell had gone on while she'd been gone, but she was determined to find out.

With water on to boil, she checked out her old bedroom. It was the largest in the house, something she'd fought for growing up. Staring at the room from the doorway, she realized how much she missed this place. She had the biggest bed—an old metal one with a lumpy mattress. She threw herself on top and stretched out.

Oh Lord, even her back screamed for joy. This was exactly where she needed to be right now. Squirming comfortably on the coverlet her grandmother had made for her, Tori studied the posters that filled her walls, posters of the places and the people she'd hoped one day to visit and to meet. A writer. An herbalist who'd created a wonderful concoction to help people sleep. A chef who'd made a fantastic cheesecake using pokee flowers.

They were just random thoughts she'd pulled out of her head, while growing up here. But that was her. Random. She was good at a lot of things. She was great at none.

Sigh.

Her sister Genesis did fantastic star charts, even though she didn't believe she could. She didn't like the results, and that said a lot about her accuracy—as in, she was accurate, but often hated seeing the truths. Genesis couldn't handle the interpretation of the star charts. Tori was better at interpreting the charts, but she still lacked much of the patience required to throw them as perfectly as they needed to be drawn. She did enjoy working on them though. It was too bad that the world laughed at the damn things, so Tori had often argued against practicing her skills. Now she realized it was a talent to be honed. To be used. To be honored.

Their baby sister Celeste was talented. And yet had zero self-confidence. She was also magical with animals and often said she should have been a spirit pet and not a human. Her goal in life would be to turn into one.

Not a good goal. Tori didn't know if one person could be a spirit pet for another person, but, if it were possible, then Celeste would do it. But she tended to spend too much time with her spirit pets and avoided her human counterparts. She'd been a basket of uncertainty. Only Matt had ever seemed to ground her.

Sad to think that Celeste and Matt didn't make it.

Were Connor and Genesis good together, or was that just Devon's imagination? Too often one person settled in a relationship—and Tori didn't want that person to be Genesis. Her eldest sister was all heart. Tori was spitfire material. And she had no idea what she deserved.

She'd done enough spitting for a lifetime. She still couldn't believe she had Devon back in her life. Nor could she believe that they were both here in the cottage. Struggling to her feet, she made her way to the pool room again.

Devon now floated on his back, completely at peace, as the water gently lulled him to sleep. Jessie swam under him.

She grinned. Oh, if only Devon could see himself now.

It was a stupid thing that not everyone could see spirit pets. They were such wonderful creatures. But only those with paranormal abilities, and people who the animals trusted, could see these spirit pets. Devon fit one category but not the other. And there were very few paranormals on Glory. She wondered about paranormal abilities on all the other planets. There should be some kind of increased development in paranormals. There was here. And the greater the increase, the easier Tori's life would be.

She could never tell others about her abilities. Most of the people she knew didn't have any. Some of those who didn't have them hated those who did. She didn't know if that hatred was sparked by jealousy or something else entirely—like fear.

Fear made sense. People were afraid of what they didn't understand.

And rather than face the fear, or learn enough to not be afraid, they'd shunned it all instead.

And that meant shunning Tori. And her sisters. And Granny.

It made it difficult to find good friends and even harder to find boyfriends. Then again, having Granny in their lives had made it a nonstarter to begin with. All three sisters had been in the same boat, and it had helped them to stay close. They'd loved their granny. They owed her a lot, and they'd been loved in return. You couldn't ask for more. Granny had sacrificed a lot to keep the triplets together. Tori knew it, and she appreciated it. She also missed the old lady.

Tears formed in the corners of her eyes. She sniffled and checked on the pot she'd put on to boil. She added the pasta and set the table. She figured that the pool would kick Devon out soon, and she wanted the food to be ready at the right time. The refrigerator was almost empty of perishables, so Genesis hadn't been here in the last few days. But Tori found some butter and hard cheese to grate over the pasta.

Other than spices, she didn't have much else to add. She remembered the herb garden she'd planted before she went away. She walked outside to take a look and found chives growing in wild abandon. Delighted, she snipped off a hefty handful and carried it inside. At the door, she turned and studied the strange air outside. The cottage was protected, but an electrical storm was going on out there. Very weird. She'd seen a few before but had never been comfortable around them. Granny, however, had reveled in them.

Tori gave the sky one last uneasy glance and went back inside, closing and locking the door behind her.

Turning around, she came face-to-face with Devon, standing soaking wet in the kitchen.

His face looked ravaged, until he saw her. "Oh God," he whispered. "I searched for you and couldn't find you."

"I'm here," she said. "I just stepped outside to get some herbs for dinner."

He ran a hand over his face and shook off the water. "Do you have a towel?"

"Sure. Let me put this down." She placed the chives on the cutting board, then, stepping carefully to avoid the puddles on the floor, she headed back to the pool room. There, she pulled out a big fluffy towel from the large stash. Turning, she handed it over to him.

As he toweled off, she studied him. He looked much better. She walked around behind him to check his wound.

She stroked a finger across the freshly healed skin, amazed at the route the bullet had taken. It had caused so little damage when it could have easily been so much worse. He'd been lucky.

"How does it look?" he asked, twisting his head, as if trying to see.

"It's not bad. The pool did its job, and the wound's closed over. You'll have a small scar but a minor one."

"That's the least of my worries." He turned to face her, the towel around his neck. "I guess dry clothes are out of the question?"

She laughed. "I did try to get you out of those jeans before you hit the water, but you weren't interested in waiting."

"No, I was hurt, and I had such a powerful need to get into the water," he said quietly. "I had no idea this pool existed."

"Not many people do. It was Granny's, and now it belongs to me and my sisters."

"You're very lucky."

"We are. And it's a special pool," she admitted. "More powerful than the ones in the caves."

She walked over to another small closet and pulled out a blanket. "Strip down and wrap up in this. I'll get your clothes hanging up to dry. Hopefully they won't take too long. When you're done, come through to the kitchen. I've made a simple pasta meal for dinner."

"Thank you."

The sincerity in his voice had her heart warming.

She carried out his damaged shirt. The material was thin and light and would dry fast. She rinsed off the blood as best she could and then hung the shirt near the warm stove and left it to serve up the meal. Adding the cheese and chives, she finished off the food and served up two plates. Devon came into the kitchen and handed her his jeans. Tori hung them up next to his shirt.

"Sorry it's so meager," she said, indicating their plates. "I was actually surprised this much food was here."

"Doesn't Genesis come here a lot?"

"I don't know, but, when Granny was here, the kitchen was always fully stocked. Granny would never see anyone go without a meal."

He nodded and sat down awkwardly, trying to keep the blanket wrapped around him and, at the same time, bringing the chair close enough to the table to eat. Devon didn't waste any time digging in.

Tori smiled at his enthusiasm. She did appreciate a healthy appetite.

"Why didn't you stay in touch with your sister?" he asked between mouthfuls.

Her fork froze in midair; then she slowly popped the food in her mouth, as she contemplated what to tell him. She decided on the truth. "I was trying to put a large part of my life behind me, and she got caught in the backlash."

"That must have been tough on her."

"Looking back, I'm sure it was. At the time, she seemed invincible, and I was in too much pain to consider hers."

It was his turn to freeze. He stared at her, then slowly forked another bite into his mouth. She waited, and, when he didn't question her, she continued to eat, polishing off her portion. Retrieving the pot, she gave herself a little bit more and offered him the rest.

"Yes, please," he said, holding out his plate.

As she replaced the not quite empty pot on the stove, she gave his shirt a shake. It was drying well. She glanced out the window at the weird electrical storm. The storms on this planet had become odder in the last century. Scientists were all over it, but, of course, no one still had an answer. Perhaps it was because they were looking on a global scale.

Tori just wanted answers regarding her own small world.

AS HEROIC ACTIONS went, Devon pretty much sucked. He thought back over the last few hours. He had found her in the woods but then had managed to get hurt and needed her to save him. What the hell? He was a legal investigator, a problem solver. And this situation was fraught with puzzles.

He wanted Tori back in his arms and in his life and definitely in his bed. When he'd come out of the warm water, feeling calm and serene inside, he'd known exactly what he had to do. And the natural appetite drove him forward. To take her to bed. To make her his—again.

She'd always been his. Had never been anything other than his. They'd had stupid fights at a time when she'd been vulnerable. He couldn't even remember the details, except they had involved Grandfather and her spirit pet—which, at the time, he thought had been a joke. Nothing more than her imagination on overload.

Yet, after she'd left, Devon had heard enough about spirit pets to kick himself for laughing at her before. Not able to understand or to have their presence validated by anyone he knew at the time, ... well, it had swayed his judgment. Even Grandfather had said Tori was making it all up. Devon had been a fool for believing him.

He knew his grandfather had said something to her when she'd bolted. It wasn't just the spirit pet issue that had sent her on a yearlong run; something else had been involved. He needed to know what it was, but getting her to open up? ... Yeah, that wasn't so easy.

If he could get her into bed, he knew they could work things out. But she lived in her head so much that, the minute she got to worrying about things, she could blow something small into something much bigger. He was the one who had made the mistake of thinking small things didn't matter. Instead what he should have learned was that the small things needed to be nipped in the bud before they became something huge and horrific—if only in Tori's head.

Trying to take his mind off her, he studied the interior of the small cottage. It was cozy. Bright patterns covered the walls, and the floor was made of very old stone. There were a few modern amenities, but most were like the old stove—ancient. He could imagine her granny living out her days quite happily here. She would be safe in this place.

As the word popped into his head, he frowned. Why would he assume that Granny might not have been safe? The horrific woods outside should have kept almost anything at bay. Only the most determined predator would continue to work through the dense foliage. In a way, the cottage was ideally protected.

He glanced over at Tori, sitting quietly at his side, lost in thought. If she hadn't been here for over a year, and it was her childhood home, he imagined a wash of memories were running through her.

Tough times.

She'd walked away, and things had blown up behind her.

She had to feel guilty, and, even if she wasn't to blame, she had to feel a little bit of remorse for having left her eldest sister to deal with all this mess. "Did you have something to do with the woods outside?"

"Sorry?" She turned to look at him, puzzled.

At the confused look in her eyes, he almost didn't repeat

the question, but he figured that it was an elemental issue, and he'd really like to know. "Did you affect the woods outside?"

"Affect how?" she countered.

And he knew she had.

"Making them behave in such a crazy manner."

She shrugged. "Granny did most of that. They also protect me more than they would protect, say, … you."

"Interesting."

"The cottage is sacred ground." She laughed, although the sound was humorless, and he winced at the bitterness in her voice. "You do remember my granny was a stargazer, right? Something everyone laughed at my whole life."

"You really hated your childhood, didn't you?"

She stared at him in shock. "No, I didn't. Not at all. My granny was everything to us growing up, and she was mocked and shunned all the years I knew her."

"I didn't know her. I only arrived in town a few years ago. I never mocked her," he said quietly. "I know what the townsfolk said, but I've never had anything but the utmost respect for your granny."

Tori's shoulders sagged. "It's not you that I'm mad at. It's the world that treated her so unfairly. It's me—for walking away and leaving my eldest sister all alone to deal with everything. It's just … everything seems *off* right now."

"You should get in the pool and let it help you. You've had a couple tough days, and I am the cause of that. I'm sorry for the way I brought you back but not sorry for bringing you back. Those people needed you. … I need you."

He added the last part slightly under his breath, but she caught it.

And ignored it.

CHAPTER 15

TORI ROSE AND cleaned the dishes off the table. She tried to stuff his words down deep inside—where she could ignore them. Only she couldn't.

He was right though. The healing water would be lovely, the perfect answer for what ails her. She turned back to him. "I do need the pool. I'll show you to your room for the night, then I'll go soak."

He stood and looked outside. "So you don't want to try and walk out tonight back to our cars?"

She shook her head. "No, I really don't. I'll stay over-night and leave in the morning. You can leave if you want." She turned and walked toward the bedrooms. She stopped in Granny's room and laughed out loud. A newish double bed now filled the tiny room, Genesis's clothes tossed casually over the bedding. That was the biggest indication that things were good between Genesis and Connor so far. "Good for you, Genesis," she murmured, as she walked into Genesis's old room, with Granny's old big double bed and old hand-hewn posts.

As Tori stood inside the room, her heartstrings tugged at her. She'd spent many mornings sitting on Granny's bed, visiting. In her later years, Granny, although still spry, hadn't been so eager to leave the comfort of that bed.

When those happened more and more, the triplets knew

it wouldn't be long before they headed to the healing pools in the caves to stay for a night or two. Granny, even with her healing pool in her own cottage, had an affinity for the healing pools in the lower chain. It took years to be able to adjust to the waters and to the energy of those powerful pools.

The triplets would often sleep at one pool, knowing Granny would make the trek down to the lower ones, while her granddaughters slept. The pools had helped them heal much of their broken teenage hearts. Maybe that was why, despite their difficulties growing up, they had come out relatively unscathed.

Beyond being simply special, some healing pools helped with physical maladies. Others seemed to affect the mental state more, and still others, the emotional.

Granny said the pools on the lowest levels of the caves actually affected the energetic system.

Tori hadn't ever been that low, so she wasn't certain.

"Tori?"

She started, then glanced at Devon, standing awkwardly in the doorway of this bedroom. "Sorry, lost in thought." She waved a hand around the room and toward the bed. "This is Genesis's old room, and this was Granny's bed. You can sleep here tonight, if you are staying."

"I'd like to stay."

She heard the tiny catch in his voice and studied him carefully, wondering why. "The pool didn't kick you out, did it?"

He frowned. "What do you mean?"

"I mean, if the pool had done all it could for you, then it would have kicked you out of the water. That it didn't means you weren't quite done healing."

"I was in there for a long time and was worried about overstaying my welcome." He shrugged.

"Damn." She rubbed her temple. "It means you need to go back in."

"No, it's your turn."

Tempted, she thought about going in, while he waited, but then realized that wouldn't work. She wanted privacy to do her own thing in there. Including crying buckets full of tears, if they came. She wouldn't feel comfortable doing that, knowing he was waiting. With a decisive motion, she shook her head. "No. I'll go afterward." She waved to the pool room. "Go back in while I wash dishes. Maybe you won't need much more. Then straight to bed so that your body can rest and recuperate. This much healing is exhausting."

"And you?"

She smiled. "I'll be fine. Just rap on my door when you're on your way to bed."

Not giving him a chance to argue, she gently pushed him toward the pool, watching as he walked carefully, his blanket only reaching to midcalf, the muscles of his legs bunching with every step.

When he was inside the pool, she returned to the kitchen and made short work of the mess. Carrying a cup of tea for herself, she headed to her room to wait. She'd done that a lot growing up. If it wasn't an emotional healing, where one or the other sister needed privacy, then the pool would welcome two or three of them. But, when dealing with deeper issues, then they went in one at a time.

Her room hadn't changed since she'd been here last and was just as dusty. And neither had anyone slept in her bed from the looks of it. A poignant thought hit her, almost dropping her to her knees. Had Genesis come here to sit to not be so alone? Had it given her comfort to know it was her sister's space? Or had she lain here and cried because she was so alone?

Tori hoped not.

But she was starting to realize how bereft Genesis must have been as they all walked away from her. Especially after losing Granny.

And Connor.

A tough year for all of them. Maybe the hardest on her sister. Tori had made a conscious decision to go. Celeste probably had too.

Genesis had no choice. She had to stay. Powerless to do anything else when everyone had walked away from her.

Shit. Right now, Tori felt like the worst sister in the world.

And she wouldn't feel better anytime soon. Not until she could hug her sister and could apologize.

She sat on the side of the bed, wondering how to pass the time, when an odd sound caught her ear.

Tori rose and walked to the kitchen. She stared out into the dark sky, watching in surprise as landing lights heralded the arrival of a fancy hovercraft.

Tori felt a flash of panic. No one should have been able to find the cottage. No one should have been able to access the cottage.

No one except … her sisters.

When Connor stepped out from the pilot's side and when the passenger door opened, she caught her breath, … hoping.

It was.

Genesis.

Tori threw open the door and raced to her sister's side,

tears streaming down her cheeks.

And was instantly engulfed in the love that had always accepted Tori for who she was. Though she may have often been irritating, or a pain in the ass, Genesis had always been a loving sister.

DEVON SAT ON the edge of the pool. He'd only been in the water for a half hour when it gently rose and deposited him on the edge. He assumed that meant he was done. He was only slightly disappointed because the water was warm and deliciously cozy, but it was time to get back to Tori. He wished he had dry clothes to wear, but unfortunately it was back to the blanket for him.

Standing, he had just finished toweling off when he heard voices.

He straightened, then folded the blanket and wrapped it around his waist, before he strode out to the kitchen.

Through the doorway, he saw Tori and Genesis hugging and crying just outside the cottage. He smiled. Now that was a sight he felt happy about.

Until the glow of the hovercraft's landing lights was blocked by a body in the doorway.

Connor suddenly stood in front of him, wearing a huge grin. He motioned to Devon's state of dishabille, and his grin widened. "Did we disturb anything?"

"No," Devon said shortly. "Unfortunately."

At that, Connor broke out laughing. "I hear you there. Glad I'm past that point in my relationship."

"I'm not sure that I'll ever make it to your stage," Devon replied quietly. "Tori is not into forgiveness." Giving the sisters time and space, Devon walked over to the table and sat down. As he turned to face Connor, Devon noted the look on Connor's face.

"What the hell happened to your back? Is that a bullet wound?" Connor asked, his voice sharp.

Devon nodded, then motioned at his blanket-turned-kilt. "Yes, and the pool didn't leave me with much in the way of dry clothes either."

"I don't give a shit about your state of undress, but I do want to know everything there is to know about that damn wound."

Just then the two sisters walked in, still talking in high-pitched laughing tones. Connor reached out and tugged Genesis to his side. "Genesis, he was shot."

She stared at Devon. "Oh my Lord. Are you okay?" She turned to her sister. "Were you hurt?"

Before Tori had a chance to answer, Genesis had already turned back to Devon. "Turn around. Let me see."

Devon grinned wryly. "I'm fine, Genesis. It was just a close call."

She walked over to him, hands on her hips, and repeated, "Turn around."

"You might as well do it," Connor said, with a smirk. "She won't let you go until …"

Devon shook his head and stood, presenting his back.

He heard Genesis catch her breath. Then felt a gentle stroke across his back.

"Connor, this could have killed him."

"It was probably intended to." Connor paused. Then, in a harder tone, he said, "Now, start at the beginning and explain."

CHAPTER 16

THE EXPLANATIONS TOOK a long time. First, Tori had to explain about the bank robbery, hating Genesis's wide-eyed reaction when she realized how Tori's life had been in peril. Tori took a hold of Genesis's hands. "I'm fine. I just used my mind stuff on him."

Genesis grinned, then laughed. "You were always so damn good at that."

"She still is," Devon muttered.

Tori ignored him, but Connor smacked Devon across the shoulder. Tori rolled her eyes at the male camaraderie, but, after a nudge from Genesis, Tori continued on with the story. When she got to how Devon kidnapped her, Genesis smacked Devon on the opposite arm.

"Hey," he protested.

"You shouldn't have done that," Genesis cried out. "She could have been hurt."

Tori sat back and enjoyed watching Devon squirm. Genesis had always been good at calling bad behavior for what it was—unacceptable. Now that it was directed at Devon and not Tori—which it had been plenty of times during her growing-up years—it was fun to watch. Besides, Devon deserved it.

Until the tables turned and the rest of the story came out, with Devon sending her to the ground to protect her and taking a bullet in the process.

Then Genesis rose and hugged him.

Tori shook her head. *Devon always came out on top,* she thought sourly. Then she caught herself. She had no idea what the last year had been like for him, but he'd noticeably grown up. Matured. And she certainly had grown and changed.

"I'm fine," Devon said, when Genesis released him. "Honestly, I might have been shot when trying to keep up with Tori. The brush was closing around us so fast that I had to slow down to look. I could have been shot anytime. I honestly don't remember."

"I'm so sorry you went through this," Genesis said. "So much bad stuff has been going on that it's crazy."

"Your turn," Tori said. "What is all this bad stuff that's been going on?" And she sat back to listen. She heard about Connor being attacked, and Genesis bringing him right back here to the healing pools. Then about the Paranormal Center, Matt, the black rocks, and, yes, even the Portmans. Tori stared. "Good Lord. You went through all that on your own?"

Genesis smiled warmly. "No. I had Connor's help."

"And we both had Matt's help," Connor noted, with a grin.

"And Grandfather?" Devon asked in confusion. "If he was in the healing pool, why is he still …?" He stopped, lost for words.

"Still an asshole?" Connor filled in. "As much as Genesis can figure, when the healing pools were working on his physical body and brought him back to awareness, he crawled out as fast as he could—and that was before all the healing was done."

"Crap," Tori said. "That's no good. Maybe we should knock him out and bring him back to finish the job."

"If anything, it's made his opinion of the healing pools worse than ever. Instead of being a fan of commercializing the pools, he wants to destroy them."

"What?" Tori cried out in shock. "We can't have that."

"I know, but he's been heard muttering about it a few times." Connor turned to Devon. "What about you? Have you heard him talk about destroying the pools?"

"I haven't had to deal with him all that much lately," Devon said. "And I can't say that I heard him mention anything along those lines." He thought back over the last year. "He didn't talk to me much anyway, and, after that scenario with you two, he's even more reticent. It doesn't help that I'm also on the blacklist now too."

That brought up more cries of surprise and the need for more explanations.

Tori got up once to make tea for everyone, and, when that was gone, Genesis got up and made another round. The conversation continued until Tori realized that Devon looked peaked and seemed chilled. She excused herself to check on his clothes. Sure enough, they were almost dry. She bought them back for him. "Here. Get dressed."

He reached for them and excused himself. As soon as he was out of hearing range, Genesis leaned closer. "Tori, are you two okay?"

Tori shrugged, glancing at Connor.

The other man took the hint. "Don't mind me. I'll just go visit in the pool room for a bit."

And he walked out, leaving the two sisters alone.

"Genesis, I'm so happy for you," Tori cried out. "You deserve to be happy. I'm so sorry for walking away. Especially now that I hear how bad it was."

"It was bad at the beginning," Genesis admitted. "I was lonely. And missed Granny so much that I barely came here anymore." She looked around the cottage with a sad smile. "And I was so depressed, I neglected my duties."

Tori reached over and grabbed her hand. "You have no idea how sorry I am."

Genesis squeezed her hand back. "It's okay. You were doing what you needed to do, and I have Connor back in my life now."

"And I have Devon back in my life—but not the way you have Connor."

"Maybe not, but I think he wants to. He can't keep his eyes off you."

Tori shook her head. "I doubt that's true. I don't know what he wants, and I doubt he even knows. I know I'm not ready to have a relationship with him."

There was a small pause, then Genesis said, her voice rich with humor, "Sweetie, you already are."

DEVON GOT DRESSED quickly. He was almost sad that they wouldn't be staying here for the night, although it was late enough that they should be. It was a wonderful little place. And alone, he might have been able to cross the divide between him and Tori.

Finished, he cast a final look at Granny's bedroom to make sure he hadn't forgotten anything and caught sight of something under the bed. A roll of paper that had his name printed on the outside of it? No, surely not.

He pulled out the roll slowly. What the devil? He studied it without opening it. The paper looked old and fragile, and it was rolled up tightly so it could be easily stored. He had no idea what it was. Or why his name would be on it.

And he didn't know what to do with it. He didn't want the others to think he'd been poking his nose into stuff that didn't belong to him, but, now that he knew it was here, he really wanted to know what it was all about.

"It's a star chart," Connor said from the doorway. "Granny did them for a lot of people."

"So this is mine?"

"Not yours," he corrected, "but it might be *about* you though."

Devon nodded, and, with a flash of regret, he slowly replaced it. "She was really a stargazer? Wow."

"Oh yes," Connor said quietly, with a backward glance toward where the two women sat talking in soft tones. "And something the two sisters are sensitive about."

Devon collapsed onto the bed. "I had no idea."

"I know the feeling. However, I have since learned that all the star charts are real, that the stargazer dynasty is real, and that all three sisters have some of the same abilities as their granny."

"Really?" He'd been prepared to laugh at all the stargazer stuff. He was sure most of the people he knew felt the same. Especially Grandfather. He'd hated anything to do with the stargazer myths. "Grandfather really had us all believing what he wanted us to, didn't he?"

"He's been part of the lie for a long time. He benefited and continued to benefit, as long as the lie existed."

"And now that the sisters really own the land?"

"It's going through lawyers right now. Grandfather and his clan know the documents have surfaced but claim they are forgeries and how they have the legal ownership documents."

"Do they?"

Connor shook his head. "No. Basically everything here and in the pools, the forest, the town center, all belongs to the sisters."

"Jesus. That's a reason for a bullet right there."

"Two," Connor said. "That's why I wanted to talk to you. We have to consider the fact that Tori and Genesis are both in danger."

CHAPTER 17

TORI WAS TIRED and worn out. "Can I stay with you for a few days?"

Genesis smiled. "I'm actually living in the Paranormal Center with Connor. He works for Matt now. However, that means my apartment is empty and available."

"Nice. For you and for me." And it was. An empty apartment was a huge boon for her. And she was delighted her sister was moving up in the world. "So this is permanent with you and Connor?" She didn't know how to phrase it, to ask the personal details she had no right to know, but wanted to understand just what the relationship between them was.

"We're engaged."

Tori squealed and hugged her sister. "Oh my, that is wonderful news."

"It is. We were waiting for you and Celeste to return. I knew it would be soon. I wanted you both to be at my wedding."

"I'll be there," Tori said instantly. "Surely Celeste will come too."

"I haven't managed to track her down," Genesis said, "but there's time. All things happen when they're meant to happen."

"Oh Lord, that is such a Granny saying," Tori said, standing. "And speaking of that apartment, shall we go?"

"As soon as Connor is done filling Devon in about us." Genesis stood and smiled. "You know he is."

Tori shook her head. "He so is." She walked to the kitchen door and pulled it open. The wind had picked up. "We could also stay here overnight," Tori suggested.

"You do what you want to do. I love it here, but I'm heading home. We come to the cottage on our weekends a lot. In your case, maybe you should stay here and work a few things out."

"That's a good reason for leaving," Tori said instantly.

"No more running away, Tori." Genesis's tone was firm. "You tried that and look where it got you—right back here. You have bank robbers after you. Stay here and stay safe. Now that I know you're here and not lying in a ditch somewhere, I won't worry anymore. However, when you two didn't show up for dinner ..."

"Sorry. I had no way to contact you." She frowned. "That reminds me. Did you do something with the cottage alarm? It's different."

"I had to strengthen it after the attack," Genesis said. "Where's your phone?"

Tori shrugged. "Honestly I don't know. We used Devon's to contact you earlier."

Genesis sighed. "I just got a new one. You can have my old one." She walked out the door, Tori following, and over to the hovercraft and pulled out a large purse. She dug around inside for a bit, then pulled out a sleek pink phone, then reached in again and pulled out an older blue one. "This will work for you until you get a new one."

"But what about your number?"

"I had to get a new one when I started to live at the Center. High security and all that." She held up the pink phone and said, "Matt paid for the new one too."

"Nice. How come?"

"I'm helping out at the Center with the star charts. They are in the vault, and scientists are doing tests on them. He's also got the copies of all the land registry documents." Genesis hesitated, and her face closed down.

That was enough for a spiral of worry to fill Tori's belly. "What's the matter?" Tori asked.

"I didn't tell you about *all* the paperwork." She fidgeted with the purse, then pushed it onto the hovercraft seat and turned to Tori.

Tori held her breath and braced herself.

"There were adoption papers—for a fee. Granny bought us off Grandfather's sister when we were little. She had the DNA tests done to prove that we were Granny's blood kin. Then she had to buy us back."

"Jesus." Tori felt sick. "Is nothing what we thought?"

"No. Grandfather said his father had killed our mother and father years ago. Since his father is dead and can't be prosecuted, it's a closed case. We can't prove he had a hand in it, but, in my heart, I know he did."

Tori sat heavily on the side step of the hovercraft. "This is too much. I've hated Grandfather for a long time. I can't believe he actually had something to do with this. I understand about the property values and all the rest, but lives were at stake here."

"And many lives were lost." Genesis clasped Tori's shoulder. "I guess what I'm trying to say is that we can't trust him, even now. So, not only do you have to worry about bank robbers after you, you need to keep an eye out for Grandfather too."

"Great." Tori stared up at the dark sky. "Maybe it would

be best if I stayed here for the night. Set up a game plan."

"Honestly, I would. I'm sorry I don't have any more food and supplies for you."

"I'm fine. I don't need them," Tori said absently, her mind considering all the possibilities. She could go into the pool and heal. She could spend time alone to reminisce. "I think that's a good idea actually. Can I have the keys to the apartment? I'll have to return Vienna's car. That's the only thing."

"Don't worry about it. We can do that for you."

The sisters quickly exchanged keys, as the men came outside.

"Everyone ready?" Connor asked.

"Yes," Genesis answered, climbing into the hovercraft. "Let's go home."

Connor walked around the hovercraft, Devon at his side. Genesis waved at Tori. "Come by tomorrow."

"Will do." Tori backed up to the cottage door and watched as the hovercraft started up. The wind blew dirt and leaves all over. She quickly stepped inside and waited for the wind to calm down, then went to shut the cottage door.

And found Devon standing in front of her.

"Why didn't you leave?" she asked in surprise.

"Why didn't you?"

"I was going to enjoy some time alone," she said honestly. Until he winced, and she realized that she'd hurt his feelings. She shrugged apologetically. "This is home for me. I figured some time here to get reacquainted wouldn't be a bad thing."

"And I'm not letting you out of my sight while someone is hunting you down."

"I'm safe here," she said in surprise. "No one can get

through this door."

"That's not true. Genesis and Connor were already attacked here."

"And Genesis strengthened the protection energy afterward."

"That's nice." He stepped closer. "Until you know for sure that no one can come through here, I'll consider it still a possibility."

She shot him an odd look. "And if we are attacked? Then what will you do?" This was all energy-related, and he'd lost his abilities.

"Protect you. If I have to, I'll take a bullet for you."

Instantly she felt like shit. He'd already taken one bullet for her; she wouldn't dare let him take a second one. What if the next guy was a better shot?

She let him inside, closing the door securely behind him. "I don't need protecting, you know? But thank you for thinking of me." She smiled at him, probably the first real smile she'd given him since he'd walked back into her life. "It's nice knowing you were thinking of me."

He gave her a crooked smile in return and answered, "Always."

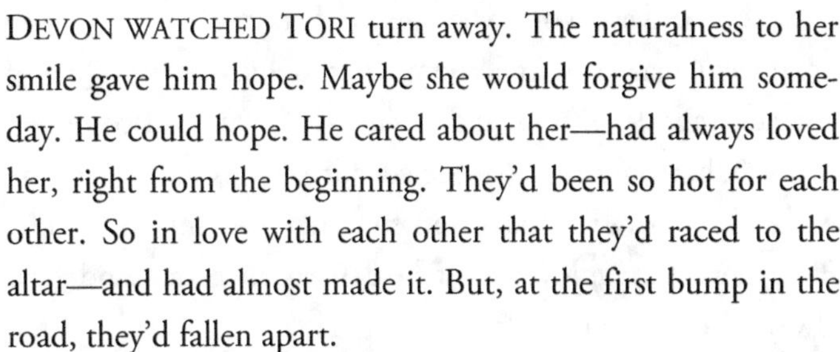

DEVON WATCHED TORI turn away. The naturalness to her smile gave him hope. Maybe she would forgive him someday. He could hope. He cared about her—had always loved her, right from the beginning. They'd been so hot for each other. So in love with each other that they'd raced to the altar—and had almost made it. But, at the first bump in the road, they'd fallen apart.

Then again, Devon didn't even know what the bump

was, before it had turned into a complete cliff.

Possibly because they'd had no foundation to work from. Yet, given the depth of emotions they felt for each other, they should have been able to work through this.

But they'd both failed that step.

He watched as she locked the front door. "Do you need to do any other kind of locks here?"

"I already have." She walked to the room behind the kitchen. "I'm going to the pool."

"Okay." He stood in the middle of the kitchen and watched as she left him standing here. After a moment, he headed to Granny's bedroom and the chart with his name on it. He unrolled the large sheet and studied the series of circles and lines. And the weird symbols on the circles. It certainly was a chart, but he didn't know what it was supposed to tell him or the stargazer reading it.

Could Tori read this? He looked in the direction of the pool. Instantly his mind was consumed with other thoughts. Was she in the water? Did she swim nude? Or did she have a suit? He really wanted to know. He rolled up the chart and returned it to its spot under the bed, then lay down on top of the coverlet. He stared up at the huge domed glass ceiling. He couldn't imagine the things Granny must have seen over the length of her lifetime.

He would ask Tori, when he got a chance.

Devon gazed at the room around him. It was full of character and love. As a single male who'd been raised by too many father figures, he'd missed out on this ambiance. He would have loved to have someone like Granny in his life. He'd not been unloved, but he'd been an extra. And he'd always felt like an outsider.

Devon's mother had died when his youngest brother had

been born.

Their dad had done his best, but he'd had to work to support them all, so he went away to find work and had left them in his brother's care. It was a situation that had worked for everyone but had left some things lacking in Devon's world. When he grew up, he went to college, then moved here to work for Grandfather, but he'd never been close to him.

Tori had been a perfect addition to his life. She gave him a sense of completeness.

Now if only she would see it Devon's way.

He closed his eyes, suddenly feeling weary, dropping atop the bed. The healing pool had left him tired the second time. It had felt wonderful.

The first thing he heard were whispers. Of man or of nature? Then the sound of brush moving around outside.

He sat up, his senses on full alert. What was he hearing? He closed his eyes and let his senses slide outward, suddenly delighted when he felt the first stirrings inside that he'd not felt in a long time. His senses were working—weak and stiff from lack of use—but they were there.

He spread them outward, searching, seeking the foreign energy outside. Only he couldn't find it. He frowned, forcing himself to relax further, letting his energy slide out farther. He felt it bump up against the protective energy of the cottage. He let it slip around the inside of the energy perimeter, wondering at the strength and power behind it. Was this Genesis's and Tori's energy? Surely not. It was old. Very old. Whispers of ancient knowledge and wisdom slid around the cottage and deep underneath.

Granny's energy, and that of the others who had gone before.

As he lay here, he felt the power of the cottage. The power under the cottage. The power within the cottage. This was a special place. A sacred place.

And he was an honored guest.

A heavy sigh of peace and contentment slid from his chest. He needed this, whatever *this* was. Tori had been blessed to have had Granny and this place in her life. They were both special. Tori might not have appreciated these things, but hopefully she'd learned now how special they were. Surely he would have appreciated these things a long time ago but wondered now if that were possible.

Connor had mentioned blocks put in place by Grandfather to limit Connor's abilities. Was Grandfather responsible for Devon's missing abilities too?

Devon couldn't imagine. His situation wasn't the same. He'd had his abilities, but they'd faded. He could still sense them there, but a cushion seemed to buffer him from them. Or his power link to them was so weak they couldn't charge.

Maybe the healing pool had helped resolve these issues. He'd certainly felt an improvement. But then, how much of that was from being close to the stronger energies of the cottage?

And, according to Connor, being close to Tori again also played Devon a helping hand. The sisters were special. Powerful. And Devon being separated from Tori this last year likely had something to do with his failing abilities.

Therefore, it made sense that the energies were stronger, when being close to her again.

He appreciated the insights that Connor had learned the hard way. Devon could hope that there'd be an easier pathway for him, but he suspected not. Tori was strong-willed.

And he wouldn't have it any other way.

He let his senses free, loving the freedom he hadn't had in over a year. After a moment's thought, he nudged the energy toward Tori in the pool. His energy knew where it was going and zipped over without any command from him. Like Connor had said, once matched, they were a pair.

Regardless whether or not the people in question acknowledged the match.

He sighed joyfully as he felt her energy stroke along his, just a gentle brush, a loving slide of two energies that knew each other well. In his mind's eye he saw the colors of her aura, the soft pinks and blues, blending with his darker greens and oranges.

He'd never understood the colors, but he knew they meant something.

Why hadn't he done this before, when he was with her? Maybe he could have soothed her when she was upset. He could have. He hadn't though. Why?

Because it wasn't part of their relationship.

Sex had been their relationship. And he was starting to realize the distance of this last year might have been a good thing. Painful but a huge learning curve for a better, brighter future.

Loving the closeness, he let his energy mingle with hers.

She wasn't exactly welcoming him, but neither was she chasing him away.

For the moment, that was enough.

CHAPTER 18

TORI STOOD, LETTING the healing waters sluice off her body, and dried off. The pool had brought tears to her eyes, as she released much of the pain and the grief of the last year. Now she was tired and peaceful. She'd sleep well tonight. The talk with Genesis had gone a long way to repairing Tori's sense of guilt over leaving.

It would be a while before Tori fully adjusted to being back, but she was glad to be home. To not be on the run. To be able to rest.

And, yes, to have Devon at her side. She'd felt his energy seeking hers.

And had allowed the connection. It was the first time he'd tried to do that, that she knew of. If he'd been of the same mind-set a year ago, they might have saved themselves a lot of heartache. Then again, maybe not.

Granny said things had to happen the way they did or else someone would miss out on valuable experiences needed for personal growth.

Tori was starting to understand.

Wrapped in a towel, she headed for her bedroom.

And stopped.

The air in the cottage had changed.

And not in a good way.

Her mind flashed with options. Instead of getting ready for bed, she quickly redressed. Hanging up her towel, her movements quiet and sure, she opened the door to the pool room and stepped into the large kitchen seating area. "Devon?"

"Over here," he said quietly, from the shadows on the side. She could barely see him, but she knew the cottage well. Making her way to him, she asked in a low voice, "What have you heard?"

"It's not so much heard as a sense of something wrong. The air is charged. Shadows are outside."

"*Hmm.* And yet the cottage should be protected."

"Should be?"

She shrugged. "I'm sure it's come under fire before and has ways to protect itself, but, as I don't know what they were, … I can't be too reliant on them." She stared out the window at the dark clouds billowing outside. "Look at all the energy out there—just outside the safety perimeter of the cottage."

"I know. Is there any way to leave this place without encountering whatever is out there?"

"There's supposed to be," she said in a low undertone. "I haven't used it before." She stared out the window. "I don't think this is an attack, more of a reaction to the changing energies of the forest. This is not good. Genesis hoped that, with the pools calming down, the woods would as well."

"Not to mention with you being back home again …"

She looked at him sideways. "Does that matter?"

He nodded. "You are part of the woods. Your energy helps stabilize the woods. When you were gone, they had a harder time. You know this."

She shrugged. "Yet I'm not very old, and they existed a long time before me."

"*Hmm.*"

Suspicious, she stared at him. "What?"

He shrugged. "Your energy while in Burnside, where I

found you, was less than your energy here. So it makes sense that, if you are doing better because you are closer to the forest, and then, as a forest creature come home, it makes sense that the forest will do better too."

She waved an arm at the strange lights outside. "Does this look like an improvement?"

"It looks almost … like a healing."

Startled, she stared out at the sky. What she'd originally taken for an ominous sign might just be something very different. "I wonder …"

"It doesn't feel negative," he murmured beside her. "It's powerful and unique, but it doesn't feel negative."

Moving quietly, she twisted to study his rapt expression. She didn't have the same kind of abilities her granny had, but even Tori could see that Devon was affected by what was going on outside. She thought about what he'd said. His phrasing. And she realized that meant … he had his abilities back. At least, some of them.

Had he realized?

She stepped back slightly to take a more encompassing look at Devon's whole body and saw the energy flying around his head. Not clear, not in color, but a distortion surrounded his edges. Fascinating. "What else can you sense?" she asked, keeping her voice low, calm.

"Energy fighting to reassert itself. It wants balance. It wants peace. What does it need to do to get it?"

"Something given. Something removed." Her voice had dropped to a trancelike state. She reached out her arms. "Something new." She opened the door and stepped out of the cottage.

"Whoa, what are you doing?" He raced behind her.

"It wants me," she said, her voice barely above a whisper. "I can help."

"No. No, you can't." He grabbed her arm. "You're scaring me. This isn't like you." He tried to tug her backward, but Tori bemusedly realized her body wasn't cooperating.

A part of her heard him, but she accepted the presence of something bigger than him here. Something was affecting her, but she didn't know what. She only knew one thing. "This is ancient energy. It needs feeding."

"No. No, energy doesn't work that way." He pulled on her arm again, trying to get her back inside the house.

Instead she stepped forward, then again.

"Tori, stop."

"Can't stop. It needs me."

"Whoa. No, it doesn't." He stepped in front of her. "No, it doesn't. Stop it. I don't know what 'this' is, but this isn't like you."

"No. It's what I'm supposed to be. I should be listening to the call of the energy all around me. This place is fantastic." She threw her arms open wide, almost knocking into him. "It's beautiful."

"Yes, it's beautiful, but you're scaring me. Come back inside, Tori," he pleaded. "Please."

"I can't. It needs me." And, under the influence of whatever strange magical energy surrounded them, Tori realized she really was caught by some pull which only she seemed to understand. She'd seen her granny do some weird things in her time, including standing out in the middle of a storm, as if she could absorb the power of the elements around her, but Tori had never seen anyone else do it.

And it had never been something she'd done herself. Until now. Her granny had reveled in it. Knew what it was and how to handle it. But she'd never shown the triplets what to do or how to deal with such a storm.

Tori doubted poor Devon had seen anything like this before either. And couldn't imagine that he would know how to deal with it, but she'd been wrong before.

God, she'd been wrong before.

So many damn times.

"It needs me," she cried and surged forward.

"No," he screamed. "I need you."

She stopped in her tracks, then slowly turned to face him. A light lit up deep inside. "Do you?"

"Yes," he screamed.

And the light around them disappeared in a flash, like a bolt of lightning to the ground, and he collapsed on the grass at her feet.

DEVON TRIED TO shift his position and couldn't. Something hurt. No, change that—everything hurt.

He lay quietly, trying to figure out what the hell happened. Had he been in an accident? He couldn't remember. In fact, he couldn't remember much. He blinked and squinted at his surroundings, realizing he was in Granny's bedroom. The faint light of dawn was coming in through the huge domed ceiling.

Then he remembered the energy. That special sense of being connected to the world. To the planet. Lord, he had no idea what had happened, but, if Tori had felt anything like it, and if that was any indication of her connection to the forest, he couldn't have imagined that she would have ever left.

He wouldn't have been able to. There'd been something in that energy. Something that had reached out and touched him. But had then grabbed on to her.

He shifted in the bed in an attempt to roll over and realized something was stopping him. He twisted around to see Tori sleeping beside him. Her face was drawn, as if she'd stayed up too late and had only recently gone under.

Slowly, so as not to wake her, he turned, so he could stare down at her. Lord, she was special. As he watched, he thought he caught movement out of the corner of his eye. He turned but couldn't see anything. There. No. He narrowed his gaze and watched, sure that something was moving in the room. Just as he relaxed, he saw it again.

A small odd … raccoon-type critter. Staring at him. He released his pent-up breath and whispered, "Hello."

The critter blinked at him. About eighteen inches tall and sitting on its haunches, the animal appeared more ghostly than real but not afraid.

Devon was afraid to blink in case it disappeared. But it slowly went down on all four paws and crept forward. Devon watched, wondering if this was a spirit pet.

"Jessie?" he whispered. The critter chattered, hopped up on the bed, and walked up to Tori's head, where he lay down in a ball and curled his tail around her neck.

Oh Lord.

Devon realized what a gift this was; spirit animals only showed themselves to those they trusted. Devon realized that, by saving Tori from whatever was after her, he'd been accepted by her spirit pet. Now if only that had happened a year ago.

Although, he thought, to be fair, lying beside her, he wouldn't have it any other way. Sure, he'd lost a year, but he'd also gained so much more that he wouldn't have if they'd done this in a different way. He stared down at Tori's beautiful features so close to his, lowered his head, and kissed her temple.

More a benediction than a kiss. More a promise rather than a caress.

He sighed happily and lay down completely, tugging her into his arms.

With the three of them close and connected under the dome, as the first rays of dawn appeared, Devon fell back asleep.

CHAPTER 19

TORI WOKE SLOWLY. Her body hummed with life. With spirit.

She lay quietly, loving the feel of morning. The sense of connectedness to the world at her feet, the sky overhead, the woods at her fingertips.

And yet … something in her world was so very different.

And so very right.

She was whole and … at peace.

Lying in Granny's bed made her smile. She loved her granny and wished she'd had a chance to tell her how special a person she'd been. How whole and caring a mother she'd been to the three of them. Granny had given selflessly, and Tori knew Granny had stayed on the planet longer than she should have to give her granddaughters the best start they could have. The pools had done that for Granny. And Granny had worked hard, keeping herself here longer than she needed to.

And it had cost her. In pain. Her old body had creaked and jolted with each step. She'd only been at peace when asleep and in her pools. She'd lived in this pool here, sometimes even drinking tea and napping in the water.

Tori hadn't understood. Her limited teenage mind-set had known but hadn't had the capacity of life experience to understand.

Now she did.

Her granny had been special.

And whatever she was, or had been, she'd gifted much of her skills to her granddaughters. They just had to train to use them and to learn how to expand them. Last night had been a big step in the right direction.

Tori still felt the effervescent experience breezing through her soul. Jessie lay curled up on her pillow, having joined them at some point in the wee hours. She reached up a hand to stroke his beautiful fur. Small enough to ride on her shoulder, he was half the size of Genesis's rare plumer, and Tori loved Jessie without end.

But Jessie wasn't the only male in the bed. Devon slept beside Tori. Heavy and large, the snores rolled out of his chest in continuous waves. She wondered briefly about getting out of bed and starting her day but didn't really feel like it.

Her body was in a state of total relaxation.

Devon's words circled her mind. He'd tried to stop her from walking into the energy storm last night.

She had no idea what was out there. Or why she'd been inclined to go.

But he'd been there for her.

She hadn't exactly been there for him.

When was it time to let the past go? When was it time to move forward? And in what direction? She wanted Devon in her life. She just wanted him on her terms.

How selfish.

And immature.

So much made more sense now. She'd been so upset after losing Granny, so hysterical that almost anything anyone did that wasn't fully supporting of where she was just pushed her in the wrong direction. As a result, she'd taken the wrong path, and the problems between her and Devon had blown up. Add Grandfather's jeers ringing in her ears, and she'd run not from Devon so much as from everything.

She owed him an apology.

She rolled over, Jessie slipping off the bed to head outside into the early morning sunshine, leaving her alone with her sleeping guardian.

She watched him sleep. So close to his face, she could see the stubble of his beard, the fatigue from the last few days. She hadn't considered the cost to him.

His eyes flew open, and she jerked back.

He reached out and snagged her close.

"Hey," he murmured in sleep-colored tones. "Didn't mean to scare you."

"It's okay. You just startled me." She rested against his chest, happier than she'd been in a long time.

"How are you feeling?"

Listening to the breath rumbling through his chest, she grinned and shifted away slightly, so she could look up at his face. "I'm fine. Better than fine actually."

Deep-blue eyes gazed intently into hers, searching.

She let him look. Could sense the gentle energy he sent out. "It's okay. I'm fine. I understand what happened last night and that you brought me back."

His gaze narrowed. "Glad you understand it. Lord knows I don't."

"No, but you knew enough to not let me go last night."

Leaning up on his elbow, he looked down at her, the look on his face making her heart lurch. Making her aware of the intimate setting they were in, the heavy emotions flying around them.

The intensity of the pain in his gaze.

"Let you go?" He shook his head slowly and whispered, "Never again."

She slid her hand behind his neck and gently pulled him down to her. "Good thing," she whispered. "I did a very foolish thing leaving you before."

His gaze widened. She placed a finger against his lips and whispered, "Later."

She reached up and kissed him.

The feel of his lips, the dry warmth of his touch, the sheer joy of being with him, … it was special. Her heart swelled. She withdrew slightly, but his head followed, staying close, almost touching, their breath mingling. His lips a heartbeat away. She relaxed onto her pillow, her gaze locked with his, asking and receiving the answer she needed. He followed her down to the warm sheets, his body resting beside her, his thigh thrown across her legs, pinning her down.

She was fine with that. This was exactly where she wanted to be. "I missed you," she whispered against his lips.

He paused, pulled back slightly, and looked down at her. "Not as much as I missed you," he whispered, his voice catching.

When he lowered his head this time, it was as if he intent on proving it to her. He didn't taste her lips; he ravished her mouth. He didn't just caress her body; he stoked a fire that had lain cold for a long year. A fire that eagerly jumped into flames at his sure touch.

She twisted under him, her body reveling in the nerve endings waking to his touch. Hell, they woke up, screaming for more. He quickly stripped the few clothes she wore and tossed them to the floor. His own boxers followed.

Not content to lie here passively, she slowly stroked and caressed his long, lean muscles along his spine to the round hard muscles of his buttocks, ready and waiting for her touch. God, she loved this. Sex had always been so good with him.

She took a deep breath, and the scents filled her nostrils. The sheer maleness of him. The shampoo he used on his hair. The aftershave triggering memories of days past. The sounds he made when she stroked him. The moan when she scraped her nails along his hipbone.

The way he would pause, then kiss her like there'd been no other women in his life. She hoped there hadn't been, but she had no plans to ask him. She didn't think she could take it if there had been another, but she had no right to expect such a thing.

Determined to throw off that depressing turn of thought, she slid her hand down between them and encircled him with her fingers. A shudder rippled through him, and she smiled against his lips.

"Witch," he muttered thickly. "Two can play that game."

And he slid down her body, his fingers racing ahead, remembering, exploring, blazing a trail for his lips to follow. And follow they did. Stoking the fire with each kiss, with each taste of his tongue, until she was crying out for him.

"No," he whispered. "I'm not ready."

"But I am," she said. "Come to me."

"Are you?" His fingers speared her damp curls, stroking just inside the plump folds. "Maybe you are." He reared up and spread her thighs. She lay open to his gaze, staring up at him fearlessly, until he lowered his head and kissed her on the nub at the center of her. His tongue laved the tiny nerve endings, which were screaming for more.

"Enough," she cried out and grabbed his hair, pulling him up to her. In one movement, he had his hands on her hips to hold her still, as he seated himself deep inside. They both stilled. She wiggled slightly, trying to adjust to the size of him. God, it had been a long year.

"Don't do that," he growled, resting on his elbows above her.

"Don't do what?" she asked and wiggled some more. "That or this?" And she clenched her inner muscles.

A hard shudder racked his body, and he started to move, driving his body forward and setting a pace that was brutal and yet at the same time not enough.

She met his every push with her hips raised, and still he rode her deeper and deeper. He shifted her leg to hook up over his hips and drove in again. This time she cried out and gasped in joy, as he went right to the heart of her. She was so damn close. He raced faster and faster, then reached down and stroked the nub hidden in her curls.

The climax ripped through her, her body arching as she rode through it, until he gave a shout, shuddered, and collapsed beside her.

***

WAS A HOMECOMING ever sweeter? With Tori trembling in his arms, Devon knew his own heart had swelled to its breaking point. He cuddled her close. He hadn't even considered that getting to this point was possible. The weird scenario last night had changed all that, and he couldn't be more grateful. She was special, and he'd needed her in his life for a long time. A year, to be exact. He closed his eyes, waiting for his own body to slow down. In reality, it just wanted to hit repeat and go again.

He hadn't known a time he wasn't interested in taking Tori to bed. She was the hottest, most caring lover he'd ever had. And he'd do anything he could to have her fully in this relationship, 100 percent. To know that she was committed. She'd blown his world apart when she'd left.

"Thoughts?" she murmured.

"I don't think I can stand it if you walk away again."

He felt her surprise, the jolt of rejection to the idea as her body jerked slightly. He crushed her closer, then released her. She had to want to be here. She had to want to stay, or it wouldn't work. And he was desperate to have it work.

So he let her go.

He rolled over onto his back, his arm still around her, and stared up at the dome ceiling. He swallowed and closed his eyes.

Silence.

And he knew it was over.

That this, his dream for the last year, was done and gone. He wanted to get up and walk out but didn't think his body would answer his commands.

He felt her shift on the bed, the mattress squeaking under their combined weight as she raised up to look down at him. He didn't dare look back.

"I didn't want to leave," she whispered. "I don't even remember what the argument was about."

He stiffened. Neither did he. He'd been angrier at her response than at whatever the stupid issue had been in the first place.

"But I wasn't running from you," she added.

His eyelids opened and narrowed. He opened his mouth to speak, but she laid a finger over his lips to stop him.

"I know I ran, but I wasn't running *from* you. I was running from the grief. The memories. The guilt. The pain. You and whatever argument I'd let boil into something too big to handle was a part of that. I needed to break away and to sort myself out. I needed to go away, and yet I couldn't leave you. So I let that argument become big enough to make the break happen."

He stared at her. What the hell? He tried to formulate his thoughts, to find an explanation, but there was no understanding this—or maybe it was women in general. He wanted to understand, if only to know how he'd recognize it, should it happen again.

"It wasn't you," she whispered painfully. "It was me."

And then she wouldn't say anything more. She curled up at his side and fell asleep.

Lucky her. He wasn't sure he would ever sleep again.

CHAPTER 20

I T WAS LATE morning by the time Tori walked out of her bedroom and into the kitchen. Her stomach was clawing at her from the inside. She needed food, and they needed to move.

She'd glanced at Devon, sleeping soundly beside her, and slipped out of bed as quietly as she could. She'd showered and dressed, pleasantly surprised to find her old clothes still here after all this time. And loving it, even if they were slightly big now. They were like pulling on a warm hug of memories.

Now in the kitchen, she needed to address another issue. Food. But the cupboards were more bare than full, and the cooler was empty. Too bad her sister hadn't brought something with her last night. Tori and Devon could use a good meal. Then again, they could get that as soon as they went back to town, either at the Center with Genesis or by shopping to stock up Genesis's small apartment.

Tori had no idea where Devon was living now. Especially if he'd walked away from Grandfather. She thought they all lived on the sprawling estate—land that, according to Genesis, she and her sisters apparently now owned. Tori grinned at the idea. She'd love to boot that grumpy old man out of the damn place. He'd been ruling this town since forever. Who the hell did he think he was?

According to Genesis, Grandfather had known all about the forged documents but had no intention of doing the right thing and handing them over. When Tori could, that would be one of the conversations she'd bring up with Matt. The Paranormal Council did have the money and the power to make sure Grandfather obeyed the laws, if they chose to do so.

Tori puttered around the kitchen, finding only leftovers or oatmeal for breakfast, and, as for the oatmeal, there was no milk. She did find granola bars. Warming up the last of the pasta, she arranged the little bit of food on a plate, added the two granola bars, and traipsed back to the bedroom with her meager offerings, only to find Devon was still asleep.

She placed the plate on the small bedside table and went to nudge him awake. He rolled over onto his belly and opened his eyes. "Hey."

"Hey." She sat down beside him, her gaze drawn to his back and the scar dancing across his spine. "There's almost no food here, but I brought the little I found. The teakettle is on, but no coffee is here."

"No coffee?" he murmured. "That's guaranteed to send me back to town."

"Granny wasn't a fan of coffee, so we never drank it growing up. We all developed a taste for it later in life, though tea is still our drink of choice."

He grimaced. "I prefer something stronger."

She laughed and stroked a finger along his back. "The scar is fading."

"The pool does great work."

"*Hmm ...*" she murmured absentmindedly. "It was a different experience for me this last time. I had a year's worth of healing to happen."

He reared up. "Did you need more time here? We can stay longer."

"No, I was there a long time." She shrugged. "The pool kicked me out this time. It doesn't usually do that though. We often just sat there and relaxed, as if it were more a regular swimming pool. So I'm not sure what's changed."

"Maybe the healing you needed to do wasn't in the pool, and it knew it at that point. Maybe it figured, if you left, you'd do what you needed to do. Then you could go back."

She laughed. "That's a whimsical point of view."

"Not sure about that. It was working on you a lot. There were weird lights and all kinds of sounds coming from the pool room. As I'd been unconscious most of the time it had worked on me, I didn't know if that was normal or not."

"Weird lights?"

"Yes." He shifted on the bed to lean up against the headboard. The sight of the sprawled male on her Granny's bed gave her a warm, cozy feeling inside. He was so damn masculine. So foreign to her. His body so strong and yet caring.

"There were colors and weird energy. Not big waves like the ones outside, but the same type of energy," he said, accepting the cup of tea she handed him. "And a little disconcerting, now that I realize it's the same energy from outside."

"The pool is ancient," she said, as she climbed up on the bed. She reached over for the plate of food and held it up for them to share.

They ate in silence. She knew something was changing, easing between them. But they'd have to leave soon.

That time sooner than she was ready for. An hour later, with the place locked up and settled for their absence, Tori turned with fond regret and led the way to the caves. Devon walked quietly at her side.

"I don't understand something," he said. "Last night. It was as if you wanted to go join the energy. What was that about?"

"I did. It felt great. It felt like home."

Silence.

She risked a glance at him, wondering where he was going with this. "Why?"

"Just wondering what you would have done. What would have happened if I hadn't stopped you?"

"I don't know. I'd seen Granny stand out in the middle of an electric storm before and assumed I would have stayed until I had that urge to join in. Maybe that's how she felt when she died." Tori felt more than saw his startled look and shrugged. "I can't say. Do any of us know what happens when we die?"

"No," he answered shortly. "And I hope to hell it's a long time before either of us finds out."

She laughed. "True, but it comes to us all at one time or another."

The entrance to the caves was up ahead. She slid into one of the hidden narrow entrances that had been Granny's special way inside and walked up the long incline.

She motioned toward the green luminescence that lit the tunnels and caves with a gentle glow. "This energy, this color, is normal. If I saw anything other than this, I'd be worried."

"Okay, that makes me feel better." He reached across and grabbed her hand. Instantly sparks flashed. There was no pain, but the surprise made him drop her hand and step back. "Please tell me that was supposed to happen too."

"Not as strong as that necessarily but shocks are definitely normal down here, particularly between two people with abilities." She studied his face for a long moment. "And your abilities are working again, aren't they?"

He nodded. "They appear to be, at least a little bit."

"Good." Satisfied, she turned back to the tunnel. "This goes on for miles down here. Keep alert. Maybe you'll sense something before we come to it."

"What do you expect to find?" he asked curiously.

"I'm *hoping* to find nothing but tunnels and healthy pools, but no doubt something is affecting the forest, and that could mean it originates here or in the other caves."

"I've never been down here, and I didn't know there were other caves," he said.

"Most people don't know about the others, but a large string of them are on this energy reserve, similar to all energy reserves. They are an enclosed system, and, if you damage one, you damage all. When the pools were damaged, the negative energy would move outward, even after the pools had healed, probably causing the same trouble. We also don't know if the same guy using those black rocks had something to do with the forests."

"And how would that have anything to do with the shooting yesterday?"

She shook her head. "Likely nothing. But I have to deal with one problem at a time."

He stayed quiet after that.

She led the way through the tunnels, watching as the various branches led off in different directions. In truth, she wanted to skip and dance for joy at being here again, but the reverence she felt toward the power of the caves kept her humble.

Granny had handled this energy like a pro. Then again, she'd had decades to work with it. Had aligned her life to be one with it and, in the end, had joined with it. Tori couldn't have been happier for Granny. It was what she'd wanted. And what Tori would love to see for everyone who had the abilities her granny had.

Tori continued down a path toward a junction. The tunnel that branched off to the left was dark. She started to walk past and stopped. No, it was too dark.

Following her instincts, she turned and headed inside the tunnel, Devon silently walking behind her.

DEVON COULDN'T BELIEVE the difference in his abilities down here. They were stronger and clearer, and the energy that surrounded the two of them was bright. Not peaceful but buzzing. He didn't have the same feeling, but he could see that, by staying down here and absorbing some of that for himself, it would have a similar effect. Maybe it would fade over time as he adapted to the energy, but he wasn't at all sure he would.

The dark tunnel did the same thing but differently. It pulled at him. Disturbed his energy. Gave him an uneasy feeling, as if he'd been rubbed the wrong way. Not bad but not … right.

Tori appeared to have no such qualms. Then again, this was her old stomping ground. And maybe this tunnel had always been dark and eerie.

He couldn't imagine what the triplets' childhood had been like if this had been their playground. What a way to explore the world and to learn about energy. The three sisters were all talented, and he could understand why.

It made Devon realize how different his life would have been, if his mother had lived. She'd been a healer. He could have learned so much from her.

The irony wasn't lost on him either—of a healer dying young. If he'd been a little older, a little stronger, then maybe he could have saved her.

At least he learned from her how to save his brothers the many times they'd gotten into trouble. Now he would like to give them both a good kick so they'd straighten out. But Devon had made plenty of mistakes of his own and had to let them do their thing, no matter how painful their actions and the resulting consequences might be.

And painful they had been.

The darkness deepened. Needing to, but not understanding why, he pulled his energy in closer, tighter against him. He noted Tori's energy snuggled up close to her body too. The light-purple color made him smile. On Glory, those with abilities couldn't affect the color of their energy. But Tori, and maybe Genesis too, were the exception to that rule. It seemed as if they had the ability to change the color of their energies somewhat. Tori had on deep-plum jeans, and her energy gave off a light-lavender tone. Earlier, when completely nude, she'd been glowing in gold. He understood looks and health affected them, but he was starting to wonder if maybe there was even more to it than that.

He'd never met Celeste, but he'd seen her around town a couple times before she'd taken off. She'd been very involved with animals and the Paranormal Council. Devon understood she and Matt had been an item, until that broke apart too. Seemed all three sisters were destined to go through heartbreak. Although now, Genesis was on the right track, and Devon could only hope that Tori's return would be the right thing for both of them. And that brought up the star chart he'd seen under Granny's bed. It had never seemed to be the right time to ask her about that, yet he really wanted to know …

Maybe now was a good time.

He opened his mouth, when she suddenly threw out her hand, stopping him in his tracks.

He tilted his head sideways, listening. Watching. He couldn't hear anything. He glanced over at her.

Her gaze was unfocused, intent on something that only she could see or hear.

He waited. When she didn't say anything, he asked in a low voice, "What are you doing?"

"Listening to trees."

He froze, looked around at the dark tunnel completely made of rock and dirt and entirely absent of any life form, and asked, "What trees?"

"Above. Ahead. Around."

He studied her energy; it was calm. Low. But high-res. She was connected to something. He could almost see it. Almost understand it but not quite. She was so intent, as if caught in some kind of web.

Something special was happening, a timeless interaction that he wasn't privy to, and one taking place in a language he doubted he could understand.

Then, as suddenly as she had stopped, she shifted, as if released from the web, and smiled up at him. "It's okay," she whispered. "I'm fine."

He nodded. "Glad to hear that. What just happened?" And why, after a year apart, was he seeing sides of her that he hadn't ever seen during their relationship?

"There's a disturbance in the woods up ahead," she said, her voice so serious that he turned to look in the direction she pointed out.

"But there aren't any woods out there."

"Up about a half mile, there are." She walked forward at a fast pace. "And we need to get there, fast."

CHAPTER 21

TORI COULDN'T EXPLAIN what she heard, but she knew the forest was in distress. She'd never heard this particular sound before. It struck her to the core. It had taken her a few moments to understand the sounds, and even now she wasn't sure, but urgency bit at her heels.

Again she wished Granny were here to help out, to translate what all this meant, as she had done when the triplets were growing up. She'd been a godsend then, helping her granddaughters understand the changes going on in their world, especially when their abilities first showed up, and how to learn just what they could do.

Too bad they hadn't paid much attention. Oh, they'd paid some, … but not as much as they'd needed to. But then, they'd never really believed in the day when Granny wouldn't be with them anymore.

Instead that time had come too fast. They hadn't had time to adjust to the major changes in their lives. Or the rippling ramifications as the energy around them disintegrated and reformed differently, with the loss of the main stabilizer of the forest. They hadn't thought about such things. Or about how the energy would change in their own personal lives.

Granny should have mentioned it. She should have warned them.

But Granny wouldn't have known what would happen when she was gone. But would Granny have known what would happen when she was gone, or thought they wouldn't have listened well enough, or even at all?

And Granny would have been right.

At the time before Granny's death, the three of them had been high on life. High on everything wonderful, believing that nothing would bring them down. That nothing would change. That their sunshine and roses would continue. Only now, Tori realized it was expected—that it should have been expected.

It was inevitable.

And none of them had seen it.

She hadn't until recently. After Tori had just recently talked with Genesis, bits and pieces fell into place. It would take time to reorder and to organize the rest of the pieces, but Tori knew they would fall into place eventually. They had to. Energy had been disturbed in a major way, and the fallout was still happening. Tori could only hope the three sisters survived this rocky road.

She knew Genesis was worried, and they needed to find Celeste and warn her. But, so far, they hadn't managed to locate her. Matt was working on it, but that wasn't their best option, as he was one of the main reasons Celeste had left.

Tori reached the end of the tunnel, her breath raspy after the race in the darkness. With Devon at her side, she slowed at the cave's entrance. Instead of bright sunshine outside, the sky was dark and cloudy. They were out of the protective energy of the cottage and the supercharged healing energy of the pools and now closer to the damaged forests.

"Why does it look like this?" he asked, stepping up beside her, his voice low and his hand on her shoulder, as though keeping her from running forward.

He didn't need to worry; she had no plans to go anywhere at the moment.

"I don't know," she whispered. "I've never seen it like this." No pretty lights flashing and dancing, like the night before. No sense of awe or joy in what she saw. There was shock. Fear. And a horrible sense of inevitability. "But I have to find out."

And she strode forward with a confidence that she didn't feel. The trees remained locked in front of her. They didn't move away, like normal. Instead they were still and dark, as if it was the middle of the night. Only it was a bright morning, and it should have been sunny and clear.

She made her way through the tree line and walked around the first of the trees. She had no idea why the place looked cold and stark, as if the forest here was already dead.

Devon picked his way through the brush to her side. "Why is it so silent?"

She shook her head. "It's the atmosphere." Glancing around, she gently probed at the trees to check their health, but they were closed up and quiet. Normally the branches swayed and rippled in the wind. But the air was still. Stagnant. Something had gone on here. Something bad.

They traveled deeper and deeper into the woods, seeing more and more of the same. Nothing moved. No birds sang. No wind rustled through the leaves. Even odder, the smell was rank, … similar to a skunk cabbage, but without the pretty flowers.

She wanted to see bright-green active life, but there was just the stark stillness of a dead world.

The only consolation was that she could see the trees were alive, if barely. They were frozen, almost to the point where death would soon follow.

Dried leaves crinkled underfoot, the lack of moisture a problem in itself. This area should have been feeding off the pool system, healing as it went around. The pools had been damaged, but, for some reason, they weren't flowing in this direction. She needed to find out why.

"I don't like anything about this place." Devon's voice sounded tight with anxiety.

"I love this place," Tori replied calmly, "but the water, the healing pool water, is no longer reaching this area. So either a knotted mess is somewhere—like what we found with your people caught on the other side of it—or something else is blocking the flow of the water."

"The knotted woods wouldn't stop the flow of water," he said.

"No, but that was an energy barrier more than a physical barrier—and that would stop the flow of water."

"Is that what you think happened?"

"No way to know until …" She stopped. And looked hard in front of her. "What on earth?"

A large warped barrier of wood and colors twisted in front of them. Energy? Wood? A combination of both? She had no idea. She looked across the wide divide and realized that it was man-made. "Who on earth did this?"

"Did someone? It looks more like an angry energy knot."

"No. Not quite." She planted her stance wider, her hands on her hips, and added, "Although you got something right. It is angry."

"Why?"

She looked at the amount of energy holding the barrier to the ground. Dark energy. It was locked inside some restricted area and couldn't move. Energy needed to be free.

It agitated and shifted and moved with the heat and the cold.

This construction kept it in place. Grounding it. But not the grounding that happened with natural energy, positive and negative grounding to neutral; this was grounding it to imprison it.

That was the first thing she had to do. Moving quietly to the left side, she reached out a hand and heard the crackle, as sparks flew from her palm.

"Easy. What are you doing?" Devon was at her side instantly. "This doesn't look like the last nasty mess you dealt with."

"It's not. But, in a way, it's not much different." At least, she hoped that was the case.

"What?"

And she realized she'd muttered that last bit out loud. "It'll be okay." She gave him a reassuring smile and took a deep breath, closed her eyelids, and carefully felt the energy. Granny had told them to use their other senses, to do more than just look at something, to hear deeper than with their ears.

Remembering those lessons well, Tori used her emotions to reach out first with her energy and to find the things that felt right or wrong as she came to them. She gave the quivering soft underbelly—deep inside the energy block— her attention.

It had heart, this energy. It had soul. It was alive. And quivering with need. The need to be free.

Soothing the energy with peace that she had dredged up from inside her, she sent waves and waves of blue and rose-colored energy through the morass in front of her. Waves rippled and danced, as they worked their way through the tiniest of crevasses to ease into the heart of the block. A block that didn't want to be a block. A block that had been twisted in on itself with negative energy, until it couldn't move past the space it lived in.

Granny's lesson had been clear—love was the answer to all things. It conquered fear. It released pain, and it healed the deepest of wounds.

She sent out wide waves of loving energy, warmth, caring, and soothing, and she covered the barrier in joy. In peace. At first, she was afraid it wouldn't work, but then she poured more and more energy over the massive barrier. It was so large that it was almost impossible to cover.

At that first fear of failure, she had to pull back. She had to remind herself that the universe had no shortage of energy. She had more than enough for her needs.

But it was hard to remember that when her foe seemed bigger.

She again closed her eyelids and sent out even more massive waves of energy, washing more and more and more over the place.

And still it wasn't enough.

Until Devon stepped up behind her and placed his hands on her shoulders. Adding his energy to hers. Adding his joy to hers. Adding his love to hers.

Laughing, she felt the power surge come up higher and higher, until she knew it would be enough. She sent out the same waves as before, letting them wash forward in ever-increasing pulses, until they washed over the barrier to float down the other side.

"Got it."

Now she let her energy slide inside the morass. It took a few moments to understand the locks and twists inside, but it wasn't long before she tapped into and unlocked the pattern to release the flow of energy. Instantly the hindered ball of energy swelled larger and larger, and, like any balloon with too much air inside, it burst—and threw out the massive amount of energy in a tidal wave of emotions.

She laughed as the wave hit her and washed over her. Through her. And through Devon.

"Glorious," he murmured in her ear. He squeezed her shoulder. "You did it."

"Yeah, this one." She reached up to squeeze his fingers. "With your help."

He slid his hands down her arms and tugged her against his chest. With his chin resting atop her head, he asked, "Do I want to know what that means?"

She shrugged but hugged his arm close to her chest. "I don't know honestly. But it seems the damage was too big for one blockage. There could be one at every entrance to the woods."

"Man-made?"

"Honestly I don't know."

"But maybe?"

"Maybe, but that doesn't mean it was intentional." She turned to look at the waves of energy flowing around them, the natural order slowly reasserting itself. "This will heal, but it will take a little while. After it's healed, it will help the rest of the forest heal as well. But, if the problem isn't resolved, I could come back here tomorrow and find that the blockage is back again, and all this was for naught."

"That would not be good."

"No."

"How do we stop this from happening again?"

"We need to check the other entrances. And we might need help."

"You mean …"

"My sister. Connor." She paused and said, "Matt and a

few others."

"Who are the others?"

"The others?" Well, now wasn't the time to bring up the issue, but it might as well be, given the circumstances. There would never be a better one. "The others are the various spirit pets. All of them are as affected as any of us by the problems in the energy field."

DEVON THOUGHT ABOUT the concept of spirit pets and tried to fit it into the animal he'd forgotten he'd seen in the night. He'd seen and done enough in these last few days to know much was possible. Knew his instincts were the big factor here. He needed to trust his instincts more. He wanted to learn more about these animals. The fact that their energy could be used to combat this stuff almost made sense—to a point.

"Would they consciously help?" he asked cautiously.

The sideways glance she slid his way made him jumpier.

"No, I don't think so. But they are instinctive creatures and do know when something is needed. Whether that is giving comfort or receiving it. Jessie often swims in the healing pools, mostly by instinct and for fun, but I don't know that, were he injured, he would know what to do."

"*Hmm.*" Walking through this minefield of a topic, he decided to not say anything else. Until a thought struck him. "Does Connor have a spirit pet?"

"He has reunited with his childhood dog," she said warmly. "According to Genesis, it was touch-and-go for a while, but they managed to make that connection happen." She laughed. "Like you, Connor never believed in spirit pets. Matt helped though."

"Matt?" Devon knew Matt but not personally. Devon, being on Grandfather's side of that fight for power in the Paranormal Center, had never been included in any social events with Matt or his friends. Devon wondered if maybe he would find a group of friends on this side now.

"Matt's pet is Darbo. To know Darbo is to love him." She laughed. "But most people wouldn't put the two of them together."

Being the Head of the Paranormal Council and supposedly a very powerful man in his own right, Devon could just imagine the type of pet—given a choice—that Matt would have. What Devon didn't know was whether these animals chose their humans or if the humans chose the animals.

He figured the conversation was worth continuing, until he stopped and looked around. "Where are we?"

"In the forest," she replied, but her puzzled humor had him confused.

"I thought you took care of the problem. Why are we going deeper into the forest?"

"I took care of one problem," she corrected. "There are several others."

"But you're tired. That took a lot out of you." He hated to see the fatigue in her eyes. She hadn't gotten much sleep last night, and he felt partly responsible. He wouldn't want last night to have been any different, but now, looking at her, … he realized he should have let her sleep. He continued. "And didn't you just say the others could help you?"

"Sure, but I have to know what we're up against first." And she turned and walked away from him.

His senses on high, he followed. She might have forgotten that the last time they were in this part of the woods, they'd been shot at, but he hadn't.

CHAPTER 22

IT REALLY WAS a new day. The two of them were together. Tori and Devon were in the woods. They had taken out another of the main problems here in the forest, and Devon was speaking about spirit pets. The conversation was loaded with pitfalls, and they were both tiptoeing through the minefield, but they were trying. She had to give them both credit for that. Maybe it was the passage of time and the span of distance; maybe it was just that they had bigger issues to worry about, but the issues they'd fought about before were not rearing their heads as issues now.

Then again, Devon hadn't been shot before. And she dared not forget he was still recovering.

"Why would they care to follow me here?" she asked him.

Devon didn't pretend to misunderstand. "I've been trying to come up with a good reason and can't. It's one thing to shoot you at the time because you stopped their robbery from happening, but it doesn't make any sense to track you down here. You can identify them, yes, but they were caught on the video feed anyway."

"Right. It makes no sense."

"Unfortunately we must consider other scenarios," he said, as they walked through the quiet underbrush. "They might just be pissed and figure that they need to eliminate you before you mess up another one of their plans. They might have heard about the problems here and that you and your sisters are going to be wealthy, and they figure they might be able to get a part of that."

"Ouch. I hadn't considered that."

"And we also have to contemplate that someone brought them here to get rid of you for a different reason." His voice slowed to a stop.

She looked over at him. "And that reason would be?"

"If you and your sisters aren't alive anymore, no one will be left to contest the land ownership issue."

She froze in place. "He wouldn't do that, would he?"

"I don't know. But I do know Grandfather's old and doesn't have too many more years to go. So who stands to inherit from him?"

"Crap. Nothing's worse than greedy and power-hungry relatives."

"Exactly." After a long moment, he stepped forward and pulled several branches out of the way from their path. "Maybe it's time we met with Matt."

"It's past time, according to Genesis. We need to meet up with all three of them and talk about this. And someone needs to warn Celeste."

"Do you know how to get a hold of her?"

Tori shook her head. "No. I went to hide away, and she went to find herself. If she couldn't do it, how could anyone else?" she added cryptically.

At Devon's questioning look, she shook her head and refused to elaborate. He had to understand energy to understand the mess Celeste was trying to sort out. And going to Matt for help almost felt like Tori was going against her baby sister at the moment too. "Let's walk to the forest corner closest to the parking lot and head over to the Center."

"What about the other corners? Do you need to fix those?" he asked her.

She nodded. "Yes, but I'm not sure how much I can do today." She pushed aside more brush, still worried at the lack of responsiveness. Normally walking for her was especially easy but not today. Was it her energy levels or the forest? Probably a combination of both.

The air lightened closer to the parking lot. It made her feel more positive about the problem. When they reached the closest corner, where she'd assumed there'd be problems, she found out they were wrong. "It's fine," she said in surprise. "Not glowing in health, but no energy mass is blocking it."

"Which isn't to say that there isn't a problem of some kind."

"No, there definitely is, but it's not as bad as the other one."

"Because you were already working on the area where the people were held?"

"Yes, to a certain extent." *But was it really?* "I honestly don't know," she said. "Maybe."

He laughed. "Let's do whatever we have to do. Then we can go home."

"Speaking of home, where is that for you?" she asked. The trees in front of her were dark and mainly healthy, low on energy from the ground up, but not necessarily so low as to be problematic. She gave them a wave of strong healthy energy anyway. At least enough to keep them happy for a little while. She walked the area, seeing little bits of congestion and problems in the flow, but, in a very big way, these plants were doing fine.

"Tori?"

She nodded. "I asked you a question. Where is your home?"

"For the moment, it's on Grandfather's estate. But I'll fix that as soon as I can."

"Interesting." Typical in a way. She tossed a last look at the forest, then turned in the direction of the parking lot. "Let's go. I've done what I can for now. Or at least," she amended, "until I see who else is available to help. I'd also like to catch up with Genesis a little more."

"You could call her."

She gave him a fat smile. "But I can't get a decent meal over the phone. Besides, I don't have a phone of my own either. Genesis gave me her old one for now."

He hooked her arm in his and led her toward his truck. "I can take care of that."

THEY DROVE INTO town and parked outside the coffee shop. When they walked in, Vienna raced to give Tori a big hug. "Oh my. Are you okay?"

Tori hugged Vienna back. "We're both fine."

"Ha." Vienna gave Devon a narrow-eyed look. "I'm not so sure about that."

Devon smiled thinly. "Tori is starving. Could we have a table? Me and her?" he added shortly.

"Sure." Vienna locked arms with Tori and led her to the corner table. "I always have room for Tori."

Tori giggled.

Devon ignored them both. He'd be shunned for a while, until he and Tori were obviously on the mend. Maybe then

Tori's friends would forgive him.

Until then …

He sat across from Tori at the restaurant and waited quietly for the women to finish chatting. He was starving too but had used up his good graces already. He stared out the window, his gaze absentmindedly watching as the cars drove by. Several long black models from the Paranormal Council drove by.

He studied the group of people sitting outside the restaurant. Small collections of chairs were set up for those looking to just sit and relax, unlike the more formal seating inside. Several people walked down the sideways, talking together. The passersby walked past two men standing off to the side—quiet, leaning against a tree, half hidden. Actually mostly hidden. They only were visible when they leaned out from their hiding spot.

Hiding spot?

He studied them again. Yes, hiding spot. They were waiting for someone. Watching for something.

He picked up his coffee and kept his eye on them, while Tori ordered and waited for their lunch to be delivered.

"What's caught your eye?" Tori asked, as she eyed him over the rim of her cup. "You keep looking across the road."

"And here I thought I was covering it up so well."

She laughed. "This is a small town. Everyone knows everything. If I didn't say something, one of the other people here probably would have."

He grinned, realizing she was teasing him. With a tiny nod of his head, he motioned to the men half hidden in the trees. "The two men keep popping out, as if looking for someone."

Her eyebrows shot up, and she turned to look. All she

could see were the trees. She kept one eye on the area and saw a man lean around the tree and look in their direction.

She gasped. "It's the man from the bank. The one who shot at us."

"Really? Are you sure?" He hadn't recognized them, but then he hadn't had a chance to see them clearly back in the woods. "He's too far away to see clearly."

"I can see enough."

"I believe you." He fiddled with the cutlery on the table, his gaze intent on the shadows. He tried to jack up his senses, but they barely spluttered to life. Not enough to be of use.

"Is it me they are keeping an eye on then?" Tori asked.

Devon nodded slowly, as the first man popped his head around the corner and stared in the direction of the restaurant. "Maybe."

"How do we find out?"

"We leave and see if they follow." He pulled out his phone and called Connor. After quickly explaining the problem, he ended the call and put away his phone. Vienna arrived just then with their meals. He waited for her to leave before leaning forward to say, "Connor is coming to the restaurant and will wait and see what they do. He'll track the men to see who they are following."

"That sounds like fun. I like the idea of catching these guys red-handed," she muttered. "They deserve to be shot for shooting you."

"They might have shot me, but I think they were shooting at *you*."

"Then they aren't after me to use for their own purposes. They'd be trying to shut me up." She picked up her sandwich and took a big bite.

"Especially if their goal is the property issue."

She chewed slowly.

He watched, but her first bite had soured to something nasty in her mouth. Then she'd spent her whole life without money, and, even now, to imagine someone trying to kill her just to take the little she did have just pissed him off.

"I can't stand the thought of them going after my sisters." She stared at him. "They could do what they would to me, but, if they tried to hurt my family, … oh, hell no." As he narrowed his gaze at her, she added, "I think we should confront them."

Devon slowly put down his forkful of food on his plate. "I don't think that's a good idea."

"Why not?" She took a bite and chewed slowly, as if working her way through the concept. "At least we would see what they have to say. Hear an explanation of why they shot at us. Between us, we could tell if they were lying."

"Maybe we could tell, and it wouldn't matter much, as they still wouldn't tell us the truth." He paused, looked at her intently, and asked, "Unless you have a way of making them tell us the truth."

She laughed. "No, I don't."

"Too bad," he muttered and took a bite of food. His phone rang. He fished it from his pocket. "Connor is in position."

Tori immediately looked out the window to find him. "I can't see him."

"Good. You aren't supposed to. Remember?"

They finished up their meal quickly. Devon paid the bill, and they walked out into the sunshine.

Devon was in between Tori and the men, a hand at the small of her back, urging her toward the truck.

"Don't push," she muttered.

Immediately he eased back. "Sorry, I didn't mean to."

"No. You're just trying to protect me." She reached for his hand at her waist and draped it over her shoulder, squeezing his hand. "And it's appreciated. But no more bullets for you either, please."

"Hey, that works for me."

At the truck, he opened the passenger door and waited until she got in. He closed the door and walked to the driver's side. He glanced around casually, then hopped inside.

"Did you see them?"

"Yes. They're both still there." He turned on the engine and drove past where the men had been standing, only he couldn't see them in the trees as they went past. "I can't see them now. They must have moved."

"Either deeper into the trees to stay out of sight or dashing for their own vehicle."

Because he wanted to give them lots of time to follow, if that was their plan, he drove slowly down Main Street, then took the turnoff to the Center. "I wonder if a meeting is going on at the Center," he said. "I saw three of their vehicles traveling in a convoy when we first arrived at the coffee shop."

"Maybe," Tori said, then shrugged. "I think lots goes on there."

"*Hmm.* I'm surprised that Genesis would be happy there, after being alone so much."

"I'm not sure that she is exactly, but I don't think that she's uncomfortable. Chances are, she's still adapting."

"That's all you guys have been doing for a long time."

"Yeah, it was definitely a tough year."

At the Center, he parked in one of the empty spots in the middle of the lot and walked around to help her out. They walked up to the front door. It was open, and music came from inside.

They stepped in and stood at the entrance, wondering what was going on.

"Maybe she's not here," Devon suggested. "Connor is out hunting down our bad guys, so maybe she went with him."

"Now that would make sense," Tori muttered. "So what are we doing here then?"

"Tori!"

A call from across the floor had Tori turning her head. "There's Matt."

Devon turned to study the man approaching quickly. He was long and lean and looked to be completely in charge. Devon shook his hand.

"Devon, nice to see you."

Matt engulfed Tori in a big hug. "You are looking stunning as always, Tori. I'm so glad to have you home."

Tori laughed quietly. "Maybe, but only because you're hoping Celeste is right behind me."

Matt winced. "Damn. Am I that obvious?"

"Yep." Tori linked arms with him. "So where is my other sister?"

"Probably hiding in her suite right at this moment. She did put in an appearance, but I thought I saw her making a rapid exit." He frowned. "Unless she snuck out with Connor. I told him that he couldn't go without her, but he wouldn't listen."

Tori laughed. "My sister doesn't like to be left out of anything."

"In fact, she also refuses to be left behind anymore."

Tori winced at the reference to everyone walking away on her sister. "Touché."

"Sorry. I had to say it once. Now we'll move on." He led the way past the people standing around and mingling, all holding brightly colored drinks in their hands. "Let's grab a few moments in my office."

Leading the way, he took the two of them down several hallways and into an office large enough for several people.

"Matt, life is treating you very well, I see." Tori wandered the room, looking at the evidence of his new position.

"Ha. It's the position, not the man."

She turned and smiled at him. "The man is the position."

He nodded once, as if giving her the point.

Devon watched the interplay with interest. He'd known some of Matt's history, but obviously Tori knew him much better than Devon had expected. He reached out as Tori walked past and dragged her down into the chair next to him.

She gave him a questioning look. He smiled blandly back.

Like hell he would explain.

Matt gave a bark of laughter. "Okay, down to business. Tori, what the hell have you gotten yourself into now?"

CHAPTER 23

TORI GASPED. "I didn't 'get' myself into anything. This isn't my fault."

Matt rolled his eyes, a grin flashing across his face. "Okay, so this isn't your fault. I still need to understand what the hell is going on."

"And I can't tell you, as I don't know." She glared at him.

"I'll do the explaining." Devon leaned forward and quickly outlined the events of the last couple days—all the way from the bank robbery through to what they found in the woods. Tori interrupted a couple times, but, within ten minutes, they managed to get it out.

"Well." Matt leaned back in surprise. "This is a mess. I knew about the people you saved, of course, but not from Grandfather. I didn't know the details, but it's hard to keep something like that quiet."

"And I had no knowledge of the event, until I was kidnapped. If you want to blame someone, blame Devon. He's the one who dragged me back." She turned to glare at Devon, but he leaned forward and planted a kiss on her lips, catching her by surprise.

"That's right. I did. And I would again," he said casually. "Those people needed saving."

"I know." She slumped back in her chair, watching as

Devon's long fingers gently stroked her slim ones. The man could turn her into jelly with just a look; add in a kiss, and she was a goner. With difficulty, she refocused on the men and realized they both were trying to hide their grins. "So what will we do about this?" she asked, determined to get things back on track.

Connor chose that moment to walk in. "Hey. I followed the guys. They were definitely keeping an eye on you. They came into this parking lot, then circled around and left again. This time, they went to Grandfather's. I stopped just outside the gate and watched as they were let in. Then I came back here."

"So it is Grandfather. Figures."

"It looks that way, yes, but we don't know for certain," Matt cautioned. "He's a different man since he ended up in the healing pools. Still a bastard but a different kind of one."

"Great. I'd rather the devil I knew."

"And that's a good point. We don't know anything about this mess, or what's going on here, so we can't assume he's done anything that he would normally do."

"But he does appear to be pulling the strings with the men."

"No," Connor said. "It could be any one of the people in that place. Several are relatives, many are in the will, and others are just plain loyal and would hate to see Grandfather's name dragged through the mud. They'd be happy to shoot you just on principle."

"Crap. So what's the answer?"

Tori was damn tired of the whole thing. Her instincts said to go and confront Grandfather. Maybe then he'd lay off, but, if Connor and Matt were right, then Grandfather might not even be the asshole behind all this.

She remembered something else that Devon had mentioned.

"We also need to consider that, if Grandfather's 'good name' was destroyed, and his business fell, who would step into his position of power?"

Matt slowly raised his head and stared at her. "Oh, very good thinking. Money and power are two of the biggest motivators. If we could figure out who would be in a position to take advantage of his trouble, then we'd have another angle to look at."

Tori nodded. "And considering that sex is the third biggest motivator, don't look only at the males in his world. Women are pretty cagey when it comes to landing on their feet."

The three men looked at her in confusion. She sighed. "Look at the women behind the men. Which one would benefit if her man were to rise to the top?"

Another long moment of silence passed, then comprehension hit.

Connor gave a bark of laughter. "I hadn't even considered that a woman could be behind this."

Tori rolled her eyes. "Of course not," she muttered.

"As much as I hope it isn't a woman, we will, indeed, check out all those who fit the parameters you described," Matt said, writing down notes. "It's a hell of a thing."

Devon nodded and added, "Also we need to consider that whoever is behind this is motivated by the land issue, and, therefore, not just Tori is in danger but also Genesis and Celeste."

Matt's pen stilled. "Anyone heard from her?"

"No. But just because we haven't found her doesn't mean the assholes haven't," Tori said.

Connor's jaw firmed. "I'll be sticking close to Genesis. We need to track down Celeste."

"As much as I'd like to help with that, I'd be more of hindrance than anything," Matt added quietly.

Tori nodded. "I hate to say it, but we'll never find her if you get involved in the search."

His face closed down, and he nodded. "I can put my men on the job and have them not approach her."

"That would help. As long as we know where she is, Genesis and I could go see her."

"With me," Devon said.

"Actually," Connor interrupted smoothly, "if you think you're going without either of us, Tori, then you'll have to think again."

"I wouldn't." She lied. No way would Celeste let either of the men approach her. The triplets had all been through too much lately for that to happen. Celeste knew the history of the men and her sisters. Celeste was gentle and innocent, but she wasn't stupid. "If you learn anything, let me know, Matt," she said. "However, the first problem is the men following us today."

"The bank robbers' names are Nate Parks, Tom Banks, and Paul Carney. All three are known to the police. There is a warrant out for their arrest. So far they've eluded capture." Matt read from the paper in front of him.

"You're serious? Eluded? They were right there in front of us." Connor raised both hands in frustration. "I suppose the police can't find them now? Right?"

Matt nodded. "Correct. But we know that Grandfather runs the police, and, therefore, we won't get any satisfaction in that quarter. However, now that we know these men are here, I've dispatched several men to go find them. We'll turn them over to the police in Burnside. They are wanted for armed robbery there. Remember?"

"Our system stinks," Tori snapped. "Grandfather shouldn't have that much power."

Devon had been mostly quiet but now stepped into the conversation. "I'm not sure he does."

They all looked at him.

"How do you figure?" Connor asked.

Devon stood and walked over to the window. "I don't know that I'm on the right track, but, over the last while, he's never been alone. Mason is always with him. Grandfather has henchmen keeping him safe."

"You think he's a puppet?" Matt asked in surprise. "I hadn't considered that."

"And I can't say for sure." Devon shrugged and turned to look at the others. "But, even if he is, how does that change anything? The town still looks to him to keep things running smoothly. They still fear him. He still has the illusion of power. But what if that healing pool did do something to him? What if it made him lose his edge?"

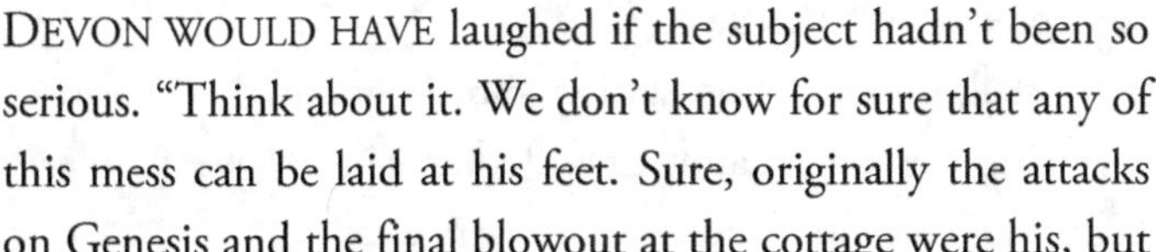

DEVON WOULD HAVE laughed if the subject hadn't been so serious. "Think about it. We don't know for sure that any of this mess can be laid at his feet. Sure, originally the attacks on Genesis and the final blowout at the cottage were his, but what about the ones after that?"

He turned to Tori, who stared at him as if he'd lost his mind. "Think about it, Tori. Have you ever *not* known a healing pool to do its job?"

"Sure, but according to Matt and Connor"—she nodded to the two people in question—"Grandfather refused to stay in the pool, once he reached consciousness, so the pool never actually finished the job."

"No, maybe it didn't, but the man is old. He could have a lot of health issues. Hell, he might need to live and to sleep in the pool for a week or more before the pool would be finished with him. He's got to have health issues, if he hasn't lived with the pools all his life. Everyone has something that can be improved. And if his unswerving *assholeness* was what the healing pool was working on, then who knows? Maybe a lot of progress was made in him."

"If what you're saying is true, who would you nominate as the most likely person to be the puppet master?" Matt asked.

Both Connor and Devon said, "Mason."

The two men looked at each other, nodded, and turned to face Matt. Connor said, "He's the head of security. The right-hand man."

"And he's married to Chelsea, Grandfather's favorite granddaughter."

Tori gasped out a breath. "I had no idea she got married." Tori shook her head. "I'm surprised that Grandfather would have let her. She'd always planned on marrying someone of her own station."

"Hell, Glory has no station above Grandfather. Short of marrying her own damn grandfather, she'd have to marry below her station, if she were to marry at all."

"True, but plenty of other top families are in other cities," Matt said. "She didn't have to marry the hired help."

Tori snorted. "That's true, but what you don't know is that Chelsea liked to play with the rough-and-ready bad boys. She was into the one-night pickups and would dump the poor suckers the morning after. And the wilder they were, the better."

"Maybe Mason is enough for her. He's the bad boy at Grandfather's."

"More than that, no one plays around on Mason. He would have dumped her, not the other way around."

"Okay, so we need to run a background check on Mason. See what we can find out about him."

Connor nodded. "I'll see to it."

"And I'll look into more details on Grandfather," Devon said. "My brother Karl is still very involved in the goings-on there."

"Do we really think that Grandfather might not be behind all this mess?" Tori asked, a note of incredulity in her voice.

"We don't know for sure at this point, but we need to keep our options open," Devon said.

She nodded.

Devon didn't trust Chelsea. He knew her too well. "And you and Genesis can put your heads together and figure out what's happening at the forest. We know something is interfering with the flow."

Disgruntled, she sat back but nodded.

He shrugged and flashed her a brief grin.

"I want to see the rocks," she said out of the blue. "Genesis mentioned one was here."

Matt nodded. "Get Genesis to take you down to the labs. And we have paperwork to do to get your membership set up in the Paranormal Center. Then we can have your history entered. Genesis is doing some work on the star charts that we have logged in here. In case you didn't know, we have several boxes of star charts from the cottage. And we've done a fair amount of copying of the original documents."

He looked up to stare at her. "I hope you're okay with all this. And that you understand what I'm talking about."

She nodded. "Somewhat. Genesis filled me in. I know original documents are in the cottage that can't leave. Ever. A lot of other things there can't be removed as well." She shrugged. "That was Granny all over. She was the last of her line, and some things were secret and special."

Matt nodded. "So I understand."

"I need to spend some time at the cottage and take a look at some of the documents." Tori gave a rather wan smile. "But it's hard. Everything there reminds me of better times. And Granny."

"It is hard," Connor said in empathy. "I know Genesis struggles with it every time we go to the cottage and the pools." He smiled at a memory and added, "There is one pool with a stone worn smooth by Granny that always brings tears to Genesis's eyes."

Devon heard the catch in Tori's breath. She'd struggled while in the cottage too. And he knew there would be many good days and many that would tug at her heartstrings, before she got over the loss. Being back was hard enough, but seeing your beloved grandmother in everything around you was that much harder.

"Then you should enjoy seeing the star charts preserved for everyone to see," Matt said. "And for our researchers to study."

She nodded. "I'm not sure how I feel about it yet. I know Genesis felt that something needed to be done, and this was the best option, or at least one worth pursuing. Personally I would prefer that they all stay safe at the cottage, and, until I see how they are treated here, I'm withholding my opinion and my consent on more being moved," she said coolly. "A decision made by Genesis will be honored for those you already have but not necessarily any others."

Matt grinned wryly. "Yes, you are definitely sisters."

She nodded. Then gave him a cheeky grin of her own. "And Celeste is just as bad."

He groaned. "I know."

Devon heard the undertones, but, outside of knowing that Matt and Celeste had been connected before she left, Devon didn't know anything more about that relationship.

Or when it had gone bad.

But it had gone bad, and he could only hope that Matt had a chance to repair the damage. But, from what Devon remembered about Celeste, she was the least forgiving triplet.

CHAPTER 24

GENESIS WALKED INTO the meeting just then. "Tori!"

Tori hopped up and hugged her sister. With a last glance at the men's smiling faces, she nudged her sister ahead of her and out of the room. "Girl time," she called back, laughing.

Genesis grinned. "It is so great to have you back."

"And I'm damned glad to be home," Tori said. "Matt said you could show me the rocks you found. I need to see if that has something to do with the problems in the forest."

Immediately Genesis turned and walked to the hallway on the left. "I'll be honest with you—they are downright freaky. But unless Portman Junior has been in the woods, no reason for those rocks to be there."

The elevator took the two of them down several floors. Tori studied the quiet glow on her sister's face for a long moment, loving this first chance to connect completely alone. "You're really happy, aren't you?"

Genesis smiled. "Oh, yes. Being together with Connor is heaven. I'm also, surprisingly enough, enjoying being here at the Center. It's as if I'd been alone so long in my life that now I can't get enough of people. We have a suite of our own here, but, if we want to, and we often do, we have dinner with Matt in the dining room. There is a big one for events and formal dinners and then a smaller, more casual one for just us. But it's nice because, if I want to be alone, I can be. If I want to have time for just the two of us, then I can as well."

"And the spirit pet thing?"

Genesis burst out laughing. "Once Connor managed to get over the issue, he's fine. Things became a lot clearer for him when Connor saw his own dog from years ago, now a spirit pet."

"Kona?"

"Yes," Genesis exclaimed. "And he's still around. Haven't you seen him?"

Tori frowned. "Not since I've been back. Which has been all of what, two days?"

"True. I know the spirit pets have been mostly invisible since Granny's death, but they are calming down now. So you should see them slip in and out more regularly soon."

Tori shook her head. "It's more a case of my burnt-out energy from when I was working on the forest. I've been shutting down my senses in the meantime deliberately, so that I can heal. Jessie's always with me, but I don't need to use energy to see."

"I wondered when I saw you. You are looking tired." Genesis studied her sister's face. "Are you sure you don't want to lie down?"

Tori shook her head. "Time for that later. Let's look at the rocks."

"Okay." The elevator stopped on the floor they wanted, and the door opened. Following Genesis, Tori walked into a pristine lab. Several technicians in white coats walked around, working on something.

"Those are our star charts, right?"

"Yes. I let Matt have the most recent ones. Can you believe that Grandfather was actually trying to steal the ones regarding his family? So no one would know what talents they had in his family line?"

"That's outrageous," Tori growled. "And so typical of him."

"And now, more and more townsfolk are asking if there is one on them."

"Of course there are. Granny did one on all the new births in town that she knew about." Tori frowned, thinking of how hard Granny worked. "Sometimes throwing more than one a day."

"And remember when we helped? Usually during springtime." Genesis laughed. "She called it calving season."

"Oh, she did." Tori grinned.

"I was never good at it though," Genesis said. "You were much better."

"No, yours were more accurate. My lines were never straight enough, and that left too many things open to interpretation." She looked at her sister. "And remember Celeste's? They were so damn perfect."

"And we hated that." Genesis's grin widened. "But she was the best of us all."

"Have you heard nothing from her in all this time?"

"Only once, and that just wasn't enough to say what needed to be said. She was hurting in such a big way."

"Matt?"

She nodded. "And Darbo."

"Darbo is adorable."

"You've seen him?"

Tori laughed, as she watched the techs analyze the writing on the star chart on the big screen wall. "He showed himself to me earlier. He gave me a big wink."

"Yeah, that's Darbo."

The two stood in silence for a long moment, enjoying the joy of just being together. "She has a point, you know. I don't think I could live with Jessie belonging to someone else."

"I know. But she's always had so many. She was like Granny in that way. She adopted the ones that had no one. Almost a babysitting service, until a new one was found."

"Like Darbo. Only she didn't want to lose him."

"And I'm not sure that Matt expected to end up with him either."

"No, but when the spirit moves, the spirit moves."

"Exactly. And, from Darbo's point of view, he would have both of them now."

"Only Celeste left."

"And they all lost out," Genesis said sadly.

"And so did you," Tori added quietly. "I'm so sorry for leaving. I know it must have been very difficult for you."

"It was. But, as Granny always said, things have to happen …"

"… in their own time and in their own way," Tori jumped in and finished for her. "So true." She walked into the room where the star chart shone on the wall. "Is that a holographic image?"

"Yes, we were trying to protect them. This way, they can study the charts and not damage them."

"Sounds like a great idea." Tori nodded appreciatively. "I have to admit I was worried when I heard what you'd done."

"And I was worried too, but I had a lot of decisions to make and no time or help to make them."

Feeling the intensity coming from her sister, Tori turned

to face her. "I know you did the best you could. But I am glad that the original land ownership documents stayed in the cottage."

"Me too. It felt wrong for them to leave. As if they couldn't be taken out."

"I'm not sure they can be," Tori said. "I do remember Granny saying something about the fact that the things that are there, need to stay there."

"I remember that. I wondered about the wisdom of removing the star charts, but they were all ones that we were around all the time. Some we had helped her with. Some we'd done on our own. I figured, if any of them could leave, it would be those. And they were all done in the last couple years. Matt has mentioned several times about getting more, but I think, with the older ones, the ones that Granny had done a long time ago, we'll just use the holographic machines to take images and leave them all there."

"That would be my suggestion as well." Tori liked that. Keep Granny's originals in the cottage, their home. Some of them were well over one hundred years old and the specialists should have the images to work from. "Have they asked you for any help in deciphering the charts?"

"Yes, I work down here two days a week." She pointed to the computers on the sideboard. "We're rendering digital images and then entering all the analyses. It's quite a job per star chart. I hadn't realized just how much information each one held." She sighed. "Or how long it would take to input the data."

Tori nodded. "I can see you doing that." She paused. "Actually is it possible to help you do that?"

Genesis looked at her in delight. "I'm sure it's possible."

"I don't suppose it's a paid position, is it?" Tori asked

hopefully. "I'm broke. If it weren't for your little apartment, I'd have nowhere to stay."

"I won't be keeping the apartment anymore, so you can have it, if you want. We can transfer the lease over."

Tori pondered the idea. "Maybe. I'll stay there for a few days or weeks and see how that goes."

"And what about you and Devon?"

Tori winced. "I'm not sure. Things are unbelievably good compared to where they have been, but, of course, that was so bad that anything is an improvement."

But she felt the intensity of her sister's gaze and the knowing look in her eyes. Heat flushed up her neck. "Yes, we're that close again." At her sister's big grin, Tori rolled her eyes. "But it's not perfect."

"Of course not. It takes time to sort through all the problems and to find a meeting ground. Then it takes more time to make it flow."

"Well, you're glowing, so I presume you and Connor have resolved your differences."

"Yes, but it's a work in progress," Genesis said. "It wasn't easy, but the danger did make us work out our differences."

"Well, I certainly have the danger factor. I hate knowing Devon got hurt."

"This has to stop. We must get to the bottom of this, before anyone else does get hurt."

"Ideas? All we do is talk. I need action. Something to do that actually moves this process along."

"You need rest," Genesis exclaimed. "You haven't had any time for anything. You've been on the run so much."

"And sleep last night was weird. There was another electrical storm at the cottage. Apparently I was more interested in joining with it than anything else."

Genesis turned to stare at her sister. "Electrical storm? Join?"

"It was the strongest one I've seen yet," Tori admitted. "Incredibly strong."

"I always hated those …"

"*Hmm*, and I always loved them."

"They must be stronger because of the forest imbalance."

"Maybe. Where is the black rock?"

Genesis pointed out the glass cupboard on the far side of the room. "It's over there." Motioning Tori to follow, she walked over and unlocked the outside cabinet. Inside sat a large glass box, churning with dark energy.

"Wow," Tori said softly. "So much … power is in there."

"I know. And it needs to heal, but I'm not sure how to help it."

"It almost hurts to look at it." But she didn't turn away her gaze. She couldn't. It needed her, but she had no idea how to help it. Genesis was chattering away, but Tori was barely listening. "I was thinking that it needed a positive source of energy to heal, but I can't just open up the glass and let it loose."

"No, it will steal the energy from everything around it. And, in most cases, just perpetuate the problem."

"Unless we can find something or someone strong enough in positive energy to feed it back to health," Tori suggested.

"Exactly. And a person strong enough to stand back at a distance and to move the energy in the right direction." Then Genesis groaned. "Actually the energy wouldn't need to move at all. The pull these rocks exert is damn powerful. They will take what they need from the closest thing. So having that special person who can direct the energy is more important."

"How many rocks like this are there?"

"There were dozens, but most … healed themselves using Portman Junior's body. This is the one I recovered from the pools."

Tori stared in fascination at the swirling mass, as it darted around the corners of the box, searching even now for a way out. She shivered, sensing the force inside, that need to be whole again. "It's pretty scary."

"*Mmm.* And that's why it's here, until we can find a solution."

"I'm not sure I can help it, and yet I should be able to. I'm the forest worker. The one with the affinity for all things in the woods, but this?" She'd never seen anything like it. And couldn't imagine such a thing were possible. "Portman Junior must have been incredibly powerful to do this to the rock."

"Very, and, of course, with that power came abuse, and he caused all kinds of mayhem."

"And I'm feeling that now."

"What do you want to do from here?" Genesis asked in concern. "Go to the forest and look at the knots happening or head to the apartment and settle in? You do look tired."

"I am tired," she said, "but I'm not sure what to do. I want a game plan before I rest. I can't just let this go."

"Understood. That storm would have had a negative effect on your system. It might have tired you right out."

"Actually it had the opposite effect," Tori admitted. "I was buzzed for a while, then completely wiped out." She flushed, remembering. "Okay, so maybe not completely wiped out."

Genesis laughed. "Why you don't go to the apartment and lie down. It would be a good way to recharge, while the men do their thing."

She nodded. "I was trying to leave them alone for a bit. Discussions are heavy."

"About?"

"I don't know exactly, but Devon is unemployed now."

"Ah, Matt is building a team." The sisters looked at each other knowingly. "Let's leave them to it."

***

DEVON WATCHED THE sisters leave with misgivings. He knew they wouldn't take off and do anything on their own, but he didn't like being separated from Tori.

"They'll be fine. Besides, I want to talk to you for a few minutes."

Devon switched his attention to Matt. "What about?"

"You're unemployed now, correct?"

"Yes." He glanced at Connor in time to see a quickly concealed grin. "Why?"

Matt looked at Connor, then back at Devon. "I need a hand here. I've hired Connor to be my right-hand man, and I'm looking for someone to head up the investigative security team."

Devon's eyebrows shot up. "Why me?"

Matt grinned. "Well, I could say to keep it in the family, but I also need your particular set of paranormal abilities. You're a problem solver. Your mind works differently than mine or Connor's. And that's a good thing. You'll come at the problems in a unique way. I need that."

"Interesting." And it was. It was also problematic. "You know how Grandfather will react, right?"

"Outraged. Pissed. And feeling like I'm stealing all his men, yes." Matt eyed him carefully. "How do you feel about working for the enemy?"

"You're hardly that." He was still reeling from the *keeping it in the family* comment. "Besides, there aren't too many good options. I was considering setting up my own company. But this might be a good alternative."

"Think about it. You don't have to answer right now. And, with everything going on, maybe take a little longer. It could get nasty, and Grandfather might do more than sling some verbal mud. Unlike Connor here, you are blood family."

"Not really, not enough to count. At least in his eyes. Chelsea is his favorite, but, being female, she's not even close to what Grandfather wants. He always wanted sons and grandsons to take over his empire."

"He had sons, but he never gave them enough control or status to keep them in the business. And neither was he ready to hand over control. Now that he might be, they are all old and aren't interested anymore. The younger generation isn't trained and ready to step in. You have to groom your successors, and Grandfather failed to take that step."

"True. Both his sons are out now anyway. Whether by choice or by disagreement, they are no longer a major part of the company."

"I didn't know that." Matt frowned, making notes on a large pad in front of him. "They appear to still be figure-heads."

"Yes, they are, but both ganged up on him a few weeks ago, looking to step up and to move him out. He retained control. And he's pissed."

The three men sat in silence.

Connor added, "That would be an interesting move on their part. Mason will be more subtle. And the two brothers just gave him the opening he needed. They are out, but he's moving up. More discreetly."

"And Chelsea is always right there," Devon said. "Tori was right."

Matt nodded. "They are the ones we need to look at first. And we can't forget Grandfather's sons. If they took out the triplets, that's a guaranteed reinstatement into Grandfather's good graces."

"True."

Devon stood. "I'll start there. And I don't need to think about it. Thanks, I accept the job offer—starting when the women are safe. Until then, I'm not leaving Tori's side." He nodded to the other two and walked out.

CHAPTER 25

ORI UNLOCKED THE door to the small apartment. She understood that much of the furniture had been destroyed during the prior break-ins, and Genesis wouldn't replace it, as the lease was up soon. Now Tori had to decide if she wanted to keep it in the next ten days, and she didn't know whether that would be enough time. She stepped in and turned around. Damn, it was small. Even at the worst of the places she'd stayed at, she'd had enough room to turn around in. She walked through to the small bedroom and the tiny bathroom.

As she walked back out, Devon just walked in with her one bag. She needed to return to the cottage and pack up some of her old things. It would be a while before she could afford new clothes. But then again, no reason for new. She had lots she'd left behind.

Nothing like getting shot at to put things into perspective.

"I'll go grab the groceries." Devon exited the apartment.

She picked up her bag and took it into the small bedroom. The closet had a set of shelves and a small hanging rack. Plenty of space for what she needed. She quickly unpacked. Returning to the kitchen, she found Devon unloading the bags of food onto the counter.

"Looks like you're feeding an army here," he said.

"No, I'm just hungry. And more so since being at the cottage."

"Because of the healing pools or the electrical storm?"

"No idea." And she didn't care. She unwrapped the makings for sandwiches and quickly put together several.

"We could go out to eat, you know?" he said in a conversational tone, watching her.

"Not required. I'm low on funds, and you're low on employment." She didn't add that she had no job at all, so her money was now gone. She would have to talk with Genesis as to whether there was more money available from Granny's estate. "I already owe you for the groceries."

"No, you do not." He sat down and grabbed a sandwich off the cutting board. "I'm eating too." He took a big bite. "And besides, I got offered a new job today."

She froze, then looked over at him. "By whom?"

"Matt."

She relaxed. "Good. I was afraid someone from Grandfather's clan had approached you."

"Well, I was approached in the market, while you were getting the apples. But I turned Mason down. Gently, of course."

She swallowed hard. "And you didn't say anything?"

"I was thinking about it, but I wasn't sure what to say. Besides, I need to stay on good terms with them. Especially if we want information."

"Did he know about Matt?"

"I'm sure he knew that we'd been at the Center."

She nodded. She stared down at the sandwich, now tasting sour in her mouth.

"It's a great sandwich," he said. "Thanks."

She nodded. "It's the least I could do."

He shot her a curious look. "What's the matter? You're not eating."

"Yeah, I am. Just pacing myself." She picked up the sandwich again, determined to throw off the pain and the heavy reminders. She'd been the idiot who'd kept walking away. She could have turned around and come back at any time. Only, in her case, she didn't have a reverse gear. If it weren't for Devon forcing her to come back, she'd still be out there, trying to forage a living without him. "Thank you."

He paused, the sandwich halfway to his mouth. "For what?"

"For bringing me back." Then she took a big bite and refused to say anything else.

After cleaning up the rest of her meal, she turned to Devon. "If you don't mind, I need to go to lie down now. I'll see you in the morning."

He snorted. "Yes, you will, but you'll also see me now. No way I'm leaving you alone."

"There's no room for you here," she said on a laugh, her insides warming at the thought. "Remember? This is a one-person apartment. There is no room."

"Then you should have thought of that before we came here. We could have asked to stay at the Center."

She shrugged. "If the offer had been forthcoming, I might have taken them up on it. Instead I'd already mentioned the apartment, so …"

"Right." His phone rang. He glanced at the number on the screen. "It's Mason."

DEVON ROSE AND walked to the doorway and opened it,

stepping out to stand on the tiny landing at the top of the stairs. "Hey, what's up?"

"Grandfather wants to talk to you."

"About what?" His mind twisted on the possibilities. Go or stay? And why now?

"He didn't say." Muffled voices were in the background. "Be here in ten." And he hung up.

Damn. Devon didn't like the sound of that. He quickly dialed another number he figured he'd be using a lot in the future. "Matt, I've just been ordered to Grandfather's side. Not sure what's up. I don't want to take Tori, and I can't leave her alone."

"I'm fine," Tori protested behind him. "It's not that bad."

He shot her a warning look, as he listened to Matt arrange for security while he was gone. "Thanks. I'll check in when I'm done." He ended the call, realizing that, although Tori was ready for bed, it wasn't that late yet. "I'll be back within the hour."

A car pulled up outside the building and turned into the parking lot. Connor got out. He loped up the stairs. "Matt tagged me. I was still in town. Genesis is safe at the Center, so I'll visit with Tori while you're gone."

"Ha. I'm going to bed. You can sit here alone." Tori snapped before turning and walking back inside.

"Sorry. She doesn't like the idea of a babysitter."

Connor shrugged. "Too bad. Besides, I'm used to this. She's so much like her sister."

"Good to know." Devon grinned. "I'll be back as soon as I figure out what's going on." He was halfway down the stairs when he heard Connor call down, "Watch your back, Devon. Remember that you've already been shot once."

"Speaking of which, did Matt pick up those men yet?"

"No sign of them. We're thinking they might have left town."

Devon frowned. "Not good. Who knows when they'll show up again? Or where."

The truck was dark and quiet. He unlocked the driver's door and hopped in. Turning on the engine, he pulled the vehicle out of the parking lot.

Just as he hit the main road and turned toward the large sprawling estate that Grandfather had claimed as his, he thought he heard a sound behind him.

He slowed and looked in the rearview mirror. Nothing. Puzzled, he kept going at full speed, yet felt he was no longer alone.

CHAPTER 26

T ORI CURLED INTO as small a ball as she could behind the rear window. She would never have made it, if not for Connor stopping to talk to Devon. Of course Devon listened to Connor but had ignored her concerns. Well, no way in hell she would let him go on his own. Grandfather would chew him up and spit him out as roadkill.

She'd been there already.

The property was also huge, and, for all they knew, the men who shot Devon were there. She knew the place, as she'd been living there for a few weeks just before the wedding, thinking that it would be her new home. The start of a wonderful life. Well, she'd quickly learned that was all bullshit. Grandfather was one scary dude.

And Devon had been shot once. No more.

Jessie chattered quietly in her ear. She smiled. She wouldn't have made it without his help. Like all spirit pets, he could appear and disappear at will. However, unlike other spirit pets, if Tori was hanging onto Jessie, then Tori could disappear too. Invisible, she'd raced out of the apartment and down the stairs ahead of Devon. Thus, when he had un-locked the driver's side door, she'd slipped into the bed of the truck. Nice timing because otherwise she'd be sitting in the parking lot, looking for a way to steal Connor's car to follow Devon.

She worked off her instincts. While she had had no plan when she'd bolted one year ago, her instincts told her to run, and she'd spent those last twelve months following those same damn instincts. Here she was doing it again.

The truck slowed. She narrowed her gaze, knowing that she might need to be invisible again if anyone were watching the gate. She didn't know when security left for the night and when the gate was locked. Those who came and went had a security pass, but she doubted that Devon was on the acceptable guest list any longer. Especially after he had been tracked to the Paranormal Center.

They would know Matt would be involved, and that would change everything.

She hated the thought of Grandfather pulling something nasty on Devon. She didn't trust that old bastard one bit.

The truck turned into the big estate and drove up through the long driveway without stopping, so she presumed the gate had been left open for him. Even more suspicious. She didn't doubt that it would lock and close behind him.

So maybe it was Grandfather's vehicle, after all. She shrugged. So what? She and Devon could get off the property and call for a pickup. Connor might not be talking to her for a while after pulling her Houdini act, but Genesis would understand.

And Tori would leave it to Genesis to fix the situation with Connor.

The truck rolled to a stop. Devon shifted into Park and turned off the engine. The lights in front shut off. Tori took a quick peek at their surroundings. A long parking lot ran beside the building, but he'd chosen to park in a way that would make leaving easier.

Smart boy.

He opened the door and said, "Good evening, Mason. What's up?"

If he'd move just a little bit, then Tori could squeeze out without being seen, but, no, he was leaning on the window and talking. "Why the cryptic order?"

"I said, he wanted to see you."

At the low menace in the voice, Tori had Jessie turn them invisible again, and then she sat up and stared outside. They couldn't see her, but she was damned if she wouldn't see what they were up against. Mason stood on the front porch, but all the lights inside appeared to be off. Normally the front porch was lit up like a Christmas tree. But tonight, only one light was on. And that made her more suspicious.

"And I'm here, but the lights aren't on. Has he gone to bed so early?"

"He's not been feeling the best. But, no, he's awake. Come in. He's waiting for you."

Devon stepped out of the vehicle and closed the door, the latch only partially catching. On purpose? Did he know she was there? No, he would never have driven out here if he had.

She waited and watched as Devon walked up on the porch and followed Mason inside.

She didn't trust the dark dangerous-looking man one bit.

Scrambling into the front seat and holding on to Jessie, she opened the truck door just enough to slide out.

She stood in silence. Not a breeze or a birdcall or the sound of a dog barking—there was nothing. A little too close to the absolute silence of the damaged woods. She studied the vast building, her gaze carrying on to the other houses on the property. She thought one was Devon's to use—or at least, part of one. Suites were available for family and staff, if they needed it. A good idea until you were no longer part of the family.

She crept up onto the porch and further back along the deck. Inside the house, darkness stared back. Nothing was moving. If Grandfather was still up, where was he? Somewhere deep in the bowels then.

A step crackled on the gravel nearby. She froze. And turned slowly. Crap. Guards must be nearby.

Even though she was invisible, Tori quickly stepped into the flowering bushes that bordered the long deck. Holding her breath, she let her energy blend with the brush around her. Soon, even if they were looking directly at her, they'd have a hard time seeing her in the greenery. Her affinity for the woods helped her a lot. She hadn't done much more than play with the skill over the years, but she and Jessie had done the hide-and-go-seek thing a lot when he'd been younger. He'd been much better at it than she was.

She felt his paw slip into hers, as she crouched in the shrubs. The guards were talking between themselves and not paying any attention to their surroundings. Lazy and not doing their job. A moment later, the two guards walked away from the porch and disappeared into the darkness.

She shrugged. That worked for her.

She stepped out and walked back onto the porch, heading in the direction Devon had gone. Suddenly a hair-raising feeling of warning filled her belly. Something was odd. … Something was wrong up ahead, but she didn't know what. She flattened against the cedar siding and poked her head around the corner.

And gasped in shock.

The men from the bank. Crap. They were just sitting there, relaxing with a beer. Not a care in the world.

She ducked back around the corner, pulled out her phone, and sent a quick text to Matt. She didn't know that he could get the men here—it was private property, and, with Grandfather controlling the police, it wouldn't be easy. But at least she had proof they were here. Only … she didn't.

She turned on the camera on her phone and turned off the flash. Would she get anything worth seeing this way? She didn't dare let them know she was here, and the flash would be a dead giveaway.

She was trying to be quiet, but her raspy breathing was impossible to hide, even to her own ears.

Maybe she should retreat and go around the back.

Suddenly the door opened, and a woman walked out of the house. Chelsea. Tori clutched Jessie's hand and held her breath, pressing her body as tightly as she could to the house.

Chelsea was busy talking on the phone. "No problems. We've got this taken care of." She laughed, but the sound was coarse and hard. "No, he's done. We'll move on to the sisters soon enough."

Still talking and walking, Chelsea carried on into the night, heading away from the main house. Tori watched the woman walk confidently in the dark toward the largest of the secondary houses on the property.

Then again, why wouldn't she? She was used to shadows.

And she'd probably married a predator.

DEVON FOLLOWED MASON inside, his senses on high alert.

He sent out a probe, looking for anything wrong, his mind pulling together the bits and pieces of information he could find and then trying to formulate an image. Something here needed to make sense. And so far it wasn't quite there. He understood that Jessie, Tori's spirit pet, had been in the truck—if not on the drive to Grandfather's, then recently, and Devon was picking up on Jessie's latent energy, but that information was lacking a lot of detail.

He had no idea when the energy had been there or how much of it. And was it Jessie's energy alone or mixed with Tori's energy as well? This was the first time he'd actually been able to direct his energy since the cottage. Power rippled underneath the surface. Power he hoped to be able to tap. One day. It was there but not accessible. Yet.

Devon pushed aside his frustration and focused on what he had at his disposal, collecting other bits and pieces of information. He noticed that Mason appeared at ease, but he was a man of power himself. Carefully contained, like a panther on a leash, but there, always ready to pounce. Why hadn't Devon noticed it before?

"Where is Grandfather?" he asked again, his mind busy cataloging the information. No one home. Dark. No lights on inside. No lights on outside. There would normally be a well-lit exterior. No one was around, including the house-keeping staff. The halls were unusually silent. Grandfather preferred light classical music to play throughout the house, and usually people bustled around, working, no matter what the hour.

Although Devon was reminded of a few times in the past when silence had reigned. An ugly silence. This wasn't the same.

Mason continued to lead him into the bowels of the

house. He'd never been back here before.

Out past the long glass doors, he thought he saw shadows outside. He stretched out his energy, trying to pick up identities. Did he know that person? Or were they strangers?

His energy hooked onto the signature of one of the men who'd chased and shot them. He almost stumbled.

"Problems?" Mason asked smoothly in front of him.

"No." He walked over to study the night outside the glass doors. Through the slightly opaque glass, he could see several men sitting outside on the patio chairs.

"This way," Mason snapped.

"Why? Where is Grandfather?"

Just then, one of the other long-term henchmen walked over and spoke quietly to Mason. Devon tilted his head slightly, trying to hear what was said, but without any luck. Damn it. He approached, a smile on his face. The two men separated quickly. "Hey, Gordon."

Gordon nodded stiffly in response, turned, and left.

"It appears you took too long. Grandfather has retired for the night." Mason waved his arm back toward the entrance of the house. "You'll need to come back tomorrow."

With that, he turned, motioning Devon to move on. With a last glance out the window, where the men sat smoking, Devon turned and followed Mason back to the entrance. What just happened?

Back outside, with the door firmly shut behind him, Mason waved him off to the vehicle. "I'll call you tomorrow. I'm sure Grandfather will want to see you sometime."

Devon nodded and, without any further excuse to stay around, he slowly walked toward his truck. "Oh, by the way, Mason ..."

He turned to look at Grandfather's right-hand man. "The police are looking for three men who were involved in a shooting yesterday. Keep an eye out in case they come around." He opened the truck door, pausing to look back at the silent man. "After all, we want everyone here to be safe."

With that, he got into his truck and started the engine. The area in front of him flooded with brightness, as all the porch lights lit up simultaneously. And yet Mason somehow still managed to remain in the shadows.

CHAPTER 27

TORI SIGHED WITH relief, as she scrambled into the passenger side of the truck just in front of Devon, sitting down. "Damn, that was close," she whispered to herself.

Devon drove slowly down the long driveway. Inside, Tori was shaking. The three men from the bank robbery were there. No sign of Matt yet, and, for some reason, Devon's trip was over very quickly. If she hadn't gotten nervous and decided not to follow Devon around the house, she might have found herself on the road walking back to town. And that was a damn long walk.

They approached the security gate, and the bar slowly rose. The powerful truck lurched forward.

Grumpy, she slumped down in her seat. How would she get out of trouble now?

The truck drove down to the highway, the narrow road weaving around the trees. At the highway, they turned right and headed into town.

She shot a look backward. No sign of anyone. She let go of Jessie so Devon could see her.

"Feel free to start the explanation anytime," Devon said abruptly.

Uh-oh. She stared at him in the darkness. He reached across the seat and held out his hand.

Shit.

Slowly she placed her hand in his. He squeezed her hand—hard. Then released it, putting his back on the steering wheel. At the same time, she realized he was staring into the rearview mirror. She twisted around. Lights were coming up behind them. Fast.

"Are we being followed?"

"It looks like it."

She pulled out her phone, quickly texted her sister, then told Devon, "I contacted Matt earlier. Let him know the men who shot you were there."

He glanced at her sharply. "You saw them?" he snapped. "Were you seen?"

"No, I wasn't seen." Disgruntled, she turned to look out the window and the mirror at her side. The lights were high up on the tail vehicle, so a truck. And it was approaching very quickly.

Devon handled his truck deftly. As he should; he used to race the damn things as a hobby, if she recalled correctly. One of those things he couldn't afford to do once he got older, but apparently the skills he'd learned had stayed with him. He sped up, and the truck following appeared to have trouble keeping up.

She checked their speed. Oh, crap. At this speed, there'd be no way to survive an accident.

A straight stretch was coming up. She sucked in her breath as Devon gunned the accelerator, and the vehicle shot forward. Within seconds, there was no sign of their pursuers.

She turned around and sank back into her seat. Closing her eyes, she focused on calming her breathing. The truck still shot forward at a crazy speed, but not as bad as earlier, and he was gradually slowing the vehicle.

"Now ... about that explanation ..."

Damn. "No explanation required," she muttered. "You were shot once. I wasn't going to leave you to face the same assholes alone. I decided to be your backup."

She felt more than saw his incredulous look. "You were going to be my backup?"

"Sure," she said. "I've got lots of experience hiding. Remember?"

His glare shone like black granite in the gloomy light of the truck. "I didn't need backup. You were supposed to be home, where you would be safe."

The truck turned the corner at Main Street when they were approached by four large vehicles in the opposite direction. Driving the first one was Connor. Tori gave him a cheerful wave.

If he saw her, he gave no sign. Just then, a text came in from her sister. "They are heading to Grandfather's to pick up the men."

"Damn it. I should be there," Devon said.

She winced at his tone. "Then pull over and change vehicles. I'll drive home."

"Like hell you will. I know I can't trust you to stay behind."

"That's not fair. In this case, several reinforcements are going. Earlier, it was just you." She waved once more at Connor. This time, he glared at her and pulled ahead. "*Oops.* He's not happy with me either."

"Did you expect him to be?" Devon snorted. "You can't treat people like fools and expect them to like it."

"I didn't mean to." She stared straight ahead, refusing to budge on the issue. "I did what I had to do."

And she refused to say any more.

SHE DID WHAT she *had to do*? Really? That was supposed to be a good enough answer for him? Devon's irritation warred with his amazement at the fact that Tori could go invisible—and how cool was that? He'd only realized it when he'd seen the shimmer of energy on the porch and Jessie at her side. His heart had frozen in fear. He'd left the door open long enough for her to get inside and then headed straight out. His throat had been locked down, and his jaw would be sore all day tomorrow from clenching. And now that she was safe, and he could finally relax, that was all she had to say?

He pulled up to the Center and parked. The night was black, and so was his mood. He never said a word as he walked toward the building. When they were almost to the entrance, the front door burst open, and Genesis came running out. Tori opened her arms and hugged her sister.

"Inside," he said, motioning them both indoors, where they could at least believe that they might be safe. He no longer believed it at all, but this gave the appearance of it.

Extra staff bustled about in the big common room. Devon nodded to several of them and headed to Matt's office. The sisters chattered at top speed behind him. It appeared they were heading for a good herbal tisane. He grimaced. Hell, he was hoping Matt kept a bottle of something much better in the office.

And he did.

Thank God.

After some rummaging, Devon struck pay dirt. He opened the bottle and poured himself a stiff drink. He lifted it to his lips, heard the door open behind him, and, ignoring whomever had entered, tossed back the contents. The firewater hit his throat and made him suck in his breath. But it felt wonderful sliding down into the raw fear in his gut.

"Better?"

Matt.

Devon turned around. "I owe you a bottle. Sorry for not asking, but I really needed this."

Matt laughed. "I do understand. I have to tell you. Connor has been in here a time or two himself."

"I can imagine," Devon said, with feeling. He refilled his glass. "May I pour you one?"

"Sure."

Together, the two men sat in the office and shared a drink.

After several moments, Devon finally felt calm enough to speak. "Honestly, I had no idea she was in my truck. I never saw her. I can't imagine how she got in, and neither did I see her get out. But she was there. I only saw her at the end, when I caught sight of Jessie."

"Jessie?" Matt said sharply. "You saw him?"

"I saw him the first time after the weird electric storm, where Tori almost sacrificed herself to the elements, then again tonight." He leaned back and swirled the golden liquid in his glass. "On the way there, I thought I recognized something, energy of some kind. But I couldn't tell how old or how much there was. I just had this horrible feeling that someone was in the back of the truck."

"And you were right."

"Ha." Devon took a healthy slug. "I realized the men who shot at her were outside on the patio, when Gordon spoke to Mason, and suddenly Grandfather wasn't available to speak to me anymore. He'd retired for the night."

"And you couldn't hear what they said?"

"No, and I tried. Now that I know that Tori texted you and that you sent out a team, I have to wonder ..." He eyed Matt carefully, seeing the older man staring back at him, strong and steady. "... if you don't have a mole in the

Center."

Matt's eyebrows shot up. He sat back, a thoughtful expression on his face. "Interesting."

"I thought so. The timing works." He shrugged. "Then again, there could have been any number of reasons for Gordon to talk to Mason, but it wasn't a casual conversation. It was sharp and urgent."

"They probably got a tip that we were heading up there. Which means that my men will find nothing."

"Probably. The robbers weren't hiding anywhere. They were sitting on the back deck, smoking. They weren't afraid at all."

"Why would they be? They have the protection of the most powerful man in the area."

"Exactly."

Matt's phone went off. He answered it and listened quietly. "Devon thinks that we have a mole and that they were tipped off the minute we made a move toward them."

"Damn," Devon muttered under his breath. Sounded like the men were gone or had at least moved farther out of sight. Maybe Tori had the right of it, after all. If she'd stayed, she could have seen where the men went. Damn.

Matt put away his phone. "As we suspected, the men are gone."

Devon nodded. "Of course they are."

"But Connor managed to plant a listening device outside, close to where they were sitting."

"Highly illegal," Devon said, with a narrowed glance at Matt.

"Not when we know they are harboring fugitives. Tori actually took pictures of the men sitting on the deck on Grandfather's property, which completely changes things."

That it did.

CHAPTER 28

TORI COLLAPSED IN her chair. "Connor doesn't understand."

Genesis explained, "He'll need a while. They seem to think that they should supposedly look after us. It's a male thing."

"Really? I'm not supposed to do something to look after Devon? When there's something I'm uniquely in a position to do?" She shook her head. "Ha."

Genesis grinned. "I know. It's silly. But ... we love them, so we do what we have to do."

"I know." She leaned her head back. Now that the excitement was over, she was tired. Somehow she had to make her way back to the apartment. But what about Devon? He had no place to stay. The apartment was seriously small. It might do for a single person but not for two.

"Do you want to stay here tonight?" Genesis asked.

"Is that an option?" Tori asked hopefully.

Genesis bounded to her feet. "I'll get it organized. Tons of rooms are here. They keep a lot of the visiting dignitaries housed upstairs during the many meetings. I stayed in a couple rooms when I was first here too."

"A couple rooms?" Tori couldn't imagine. "Why more than one?"

"The first one felt like it had been searched, so I moved

to another one. Connor was supposed to find me, only he never did. Figured I was trying to avoid him and trying to put some distance between us.”

“Really?” Tori shook her head, laughing. “Men.”

They walked upstairs and past the curved staircase on the left. There, Genesis called someone over and asked him to prepare a room for Tori for the night. “We’ll figure out what to do tomorrow. The apartment really is cozy, but it’s too small.” Casting a sideways glance at Tori, she added, “The bed is damn small.”

“As if you and Connor ever slept.” Tori glanced in the direction of Matt’s office. “Do we wait and see if they come out of the office anytime soon or do we knock? Alternatively I could just go to bed. With the adrenaline wearing off, I’m tired.”

“Come on upstairs, and I’ll grab you something to sleep in. I have a spare toothbrush too. You’ll be fine for the night. We’ll grab your bag tomorrow.”

“I can hardly just move in. This is the Paranormal Center. I’m not even sure I’m a member.”

“You’re my sister. And you’re a member. I put in your paperwork when I did mine. I knew you’d be home soon.”

Tori stared at Genesis. “You were always scary that way.” She linked arms with her sister, so damn glad to be able to. And that brought up memories of their other sister. “Any idea when Celeste is coming back?

“Soon,” Genesis said, “but she’s not coming back easily or happily. She’s got a lot of hurt still to deal with.”

“That’ll happen faster here, won’t it?”

Genesis shook her head. “Matt’s here. The animals are here. Granny is no longer here.”

“Right. That’s understandable. Still, it will be nice to

have everyone back together again."

Genesis squeezed Tori's arm. "Yes, it will. I'm so happy you are back now." She looked around carefully. "Any sign of Devon seeing your spirit pet?"

"I think so. He says he's seen … something."

"Well, that's something, at least." Genesis thought about it. "He's never had a pet either, has he?"

"No, I don't believe so. It'll be hard to hook him up with one."

"Oh, I'm not sure about that. Quite a few disconnected ones are around. They'd love to be adopted."

"Is that possible?" Tori loved the idea of Devon having a spirit pet of his own. "*Nah*, it won't happen. He has to believe in them first."

"Give him time."

Tori glanced at Genesis, skeptical.

"You never know." Genesis led the way upstairs and down the hallway. "Let's get you to your room."

"NICE TO HEAR what they think of you, isn't it?" Devon muttered from the shadows by the stairs. The women had walked so damn slow, so intent on their conversation, that the two men hadn't been seen. "I have seen her spirit pet. Now that I have, it's much easier to believe in him."

"Except it's the other way around," Matt said comfortably. "The spirit pet has to know that you are safe for them to show themselves to you. Then, when they trust you, they will let you see them. It's not so much your choice as it's their choice. Yes, you have to be open to the possibility, but it's ultimately up to them."

Devon glanced over at him. "Really?"

"Really." Matt grinned. "Right, Darbo?"

And the tiniest squeak came from the far side of Matt's head.

DEVON TWISTED SLIGHTLY, so he could see what was making the noise. If it wasn't for the grin on Matt's face, Devon might have thought he had imagined the whole thing. With his grin still reaching from ear to ear, Matt turned slightly.

"Oh Lord," Devon murmured in shocked delight. Taking a deep breath, he said, "Hi."

The tiniest creature he'd ever expected to see—a lemur?—sat on Matt's shoulder, one long arm hooked over Matt's ear. His huge eyes stared up at Devon.

"Devon, this is Darbo. Darbo, this is Devon."

After a moment of shocked surprise, then a tiny squeak came again, and Darbo tucked up against Matt's neck. That was when Devon noticed the long tail that wrapped around Matt's neck, presumably to help him keep his place. "Hi, Darbo."

Darbo stared at him with his big eyes, then made some kind of guttural grunt that had Devon glancing at Matt for translation.

Matt said, "He says hi."

"Interesting pet."

Matt shrugged. "Humans are chosen as much as we choose. We have the right to say yes or no, but ..." He shrugged. "I couldn't imagine saying no."

Neither could Devon. "And those of us without a spirit pet, how do we find one?"

Darbo squeaked in a high-pitched but rolling tone.

Devon watched him closely, but he barely moved his lips. *Amazing.* "Do you communicate with him?"

"Of course, but it's not like you and me, and it goes way beyond having a real pet in your life."

Devon glanced over at him. "Really?"

"Absolutely. They are on the same wavelength or something. We can speak without words. He says something, and I more or less interpret the responses."

That made sense and also spoke of a connection that Devon hadn't yet experienced. He wondered what that would be like.

And suddenly, sharply, he had felt he'd missed out. "Any way to get one now?" he asked.

"The person to talk to would have been Granny. She was the guardian to the many lost or displaced spirit animals."

"And yet she's gone."

"Maybe Genesis or Tori would know," Matt suggested.

"Maybe …" But he wouldn't be asking Tori. Not after the earlier troubles they'd had over her spirit pet. Now that he could see them, he remembered how angry she'd been and justifiably so. They were a special part of the paranormal world, and he'd been out of that scene so much.

Why was that?

He'd had abilities—not tons—but Grandfather only ever considered him of minor-league ability. Mason, on the other hand, was a heavy hitter, but Devon didn't know in what area. His power was low-lying, always there, but more a growling-in-the-background kind of power. "Are snakes ever a spirit pet?"

"Yes, it's possible." Matt considered the idea. "Although I don't think that would be a common animal." His gaze sharpened. "Why?"

"It's what I think of when I see Mason."

"That does seem appropriate." Matt's brows furrowed slightly. "As for getting a spirit pet, just send out a mental call and see if any animal is interested."

"Just send out a call?" At Matt's nod, Devon had to wonder if it were that easy.

And did he want a spirit pet, or was it just a new thing he wondered about having missed out on? His childhood hadn't been harsh by any means, but, when compared to Tori's, it had been dull. Boring. She'd had the advantage of Granny. Sleepovers in the caves, spirit pets, electrical storms, healing pools. Devon's life of school and after-school activities seemed dull.

She wouldn't agree. She'd been hearing too much from the townsfolk about how odd Granny was. How they avoided her—unless they wanted something from her of course.

He'd seen the fickle nature of people enough to know the love/hate relationship between the aging stargazer and the people around her.

Granny had been a blessing to the triplets though. Devon couldn't imagine what their life would have been like without their grandmother rescuing them. He didn't understand all the details in that regard but realized they were probably still figuring out a lot of it. And the secretive nature of the issue kept everyone from discussing it clearly.

At least with him.

CHAPTER 29

T HE ROOM WAS beautiful. "Wow, this is a guest suite? Who are the lucky guests who've stayed here?" Tori stood in the center of the room, slowly turning around, trying to take it all in. "I know we weren't exactly poor, but we never saw anything like this before."

"As I said earlier, it's taken me a bit to get used to being around such opulence." Genesis laughed. "Matt talks about redecorating, but it's not exactly a priority or in the budget."

"What? He doesn't like gold brocade on the walls, huge sconces in the crown moldings, and—what are those? Velvet curtains?"

"And let's not forget the carpet."

"At least it's a nice carpet. With wood flooring being so common, carpets do give it that royal touch." She crossed over to the couch and sat. "This is really wonderful. Thank you so much."

"Thank Matt. He's the one who said to give you a room here. I would have done so, but it's not my place."

"And speaking of your place, where are you living?" Tori asked.

"Come on. I'll show you." She relocked the door behind them and led the way down the hall, where she pushed open large double doors into an identical hallway. Only she stopped at the first door on the right and, using an energy key, she unlocked the door and led Tori into a massive apartment.

"Oh my." Tori stood in awe. "This is all yours?"

"For the moment, but the arrangement is a little loose. There's no lease for it. I don't pay rent. Connor doesn't pay rent. He is working for the Center though, so this is one of the perks."

"Nice perk."

"Yeah, it is." Genesis quickly crossed the room to close a window, whose curtains were billowing wildly in the wind. "I had no idea it was so stormy out."

"Yes. I think they are getting worse. I don't remember storms like that from before." Tori yawned. "If you don't mind showing me back to my room. I think I need sleep first and foremost."

"You're right—the storms nowadays are different. And nobody seems to know why." Genesis stared at the window for a moment. "Yes, it's not far, but I'll show you the way back. I'm sure Matt is done talking with Connor and Devon by now."

"Maybe, but I'll be asleep before I hear any update."

"You do look tired."

"Ever since that lighting storm actually."

"Did you protect yourself going in?" At Tori's blank look, Genesis reminded her of Granny's lesson. "It's important to keep your energy neutral when going up against powerhouse energy. Otherwise yours will brush up against it and get burnt, and you'll feel something afterward for a long time."

That was one lesson Tori had definitely forgotten. "Then I'd say that's what I did." Damn. "But I had Jessie with me. He's been recharging me for the last year. Without him, I wouldn't have survived. I didn't have the same affinity for the other woods that I do here. I'm sure I would have grown to adjust to those forests eventually, but I never really stayed in any one place long enough to get that level of awareness."

"No, this is your home. These are your woods."

Tori nodded and followed her eldest sister back down the hallway. "I know, but the effects should pass quickly, won't they?"

"They will, but be patient. You brushed up against the storm. Recovery could take a while."

In her room and finally alone, Tori headed for a shower. When she walked back into the bedroom, wearing a robe she found hanging on the back of the door, she found Devon standing in the middle of the room.

He looked at her in surprise. "Oh, I'm sorry. This is the room Connor showed me."

"And the room Genesis showed me." Tori frowned. Was it her loving sister's shenanigans, or did they only have the one room to spare? Tori decided she could put money on the former.

"Although this is probably a good idea," Devon added. "After all the mess we've been through, I don't think you should be alone."

She snorted. "That's the line you're using? The damsel in distress one? You're the one who got shot."

He clasped his hand to his chest. "You're right. Please stay and protect me all night," he said, a woeful look in his eyes.

She rolled her eyes. "As if that'll help."

"Whatever works. We could also just be happy to be together, to be safe."

That was worth thinking about. She nodded. "There is that."

"The being together or the being safe part?" he asked hopefully.

She shot him a look. "It was going to be both, but now I'm rethinking the choices."

He laughed and stripped off his jacket. "The bed is huge. And I promise to not touch, unless you want me to."

"Right." She rolled her eyes and walked to the window. As if. She couldn't keep her hands off him now. And to think the fact that they had been put in the room together didn't even seem pushy on her sister's part, clearly Genesis knew and understood more than Tori knew.

She heard Devon approach from behind. Warm hands rested on her hips. His gentle warm breath caressed the back of her neck. "I'll ask for my own room, if you'd prefer."

His tone of voice was so serious, so calm, she felt better. He wouldn't be embarrassed to get his own room. Or to have everyone else know.

She might, if she had to do the same thing. Still, it didn't solve the basic underlying problem—what did she want? They'd opened up that relationship once again. She loved him. Always had. But that didn't mean she wanted to go there again.

"Would it help if I said I loved you?" he murmured, his warm breath stroking her neck, while his hands slid up and down her arms. "I'm sorry for the events that made you run from me. I'm even sorrier that you felt you couldn't come home anytime this last year. All this time I've been waiting for you, not knowing how much time to give you or if I should be chasing you down."

She bowed her head. She couldn't let him keep thinking

he'd been the reason. Slowly she turned to look up into his loving gaze, the emotions firing up something deep inside. Tonight wasn't about sex. It wasn't about embarrassment. It was about commitment.

Something they hadn't discussed. Maybe now, she realized, they didn't need to. They'd made their commitments a long time ago. She'd gotten angry and walked. But her anger had been at life as much as anything.

"It wasn't you. It wasn't even us. I'm sorry I was so stubborn that I couldn't see to make my way home again. I would have. And sooner." As she looked back mentally on her circuitous route, she realized she would have come back around again. She would have deluded herself that it was to check in on her sisters, but he'd been tugging at her heart for a long time.

Why? She'd been so stupid. "I'm so sorry for putting us through this. I couldn't deal with everything. When Connor and Genesis looked to be blowing up, and Celeste and Matt disintegrated, I thought relationships were all garbage. So, as soon as we had our issues, I let it affirm my suspicions about my life and how it was all falling apart, and I had nothing of value left."

He winced.

She reached up and stroked a finger across his mouth. "I'm sorry."

He kissed her finger. And cuddled her close. "It doesn't matter anymore. Maybe your granny was right—everything had to happen for a reason."

She frowned from within the circle of his arms. "Granny said you were my partner. But, at that point in time, she'd said the same thing about my sisters' partners as well." She looked up at him. "And I thought she'd been wrong then too."

"I saw a chart with my name on it at the cottage," he confessed. "I didn't understand what it all meant though."

"I'll go over it with you," she said absentmindedly. "A lot of stuff is in there. Granny was a wizard at reading the stars."

"But, for a time, you thought she was a failure."

She nodded. "And I'm the one who was wrong."

"You just needed to learn and to experience a little more of real life."

"Maybe." She rubbed her forehead along his jawline. "It's nice to be home."

He slid his arms around her back and held her close. "I'm happy to be here too." He then nudged her chin higher. Her eyes fell closed, and she waited. For his kiss.

His acceptance.

His benediction.

After what felt like an eternity, his lips gently stroked across hers, his tongue soothing, tasting.

Her lips parted, her tongue reaching out to wrestle with his. Only the teasing was gentle torture. And she wanted so much more. She slid her hands up his chest, his neck, to clasp them together behind his head. Her fingers slid into his curls, and she tugged him down to her. Their lips crushed together, their bodies locked from chest to hips.

And still, it wasn't close enough.

Desperately they kept their lips together, as they stripped the clothes from each other. When they were finally undressed, both of them fell into bed, laughing.

Cool sheets met heated skin, … and neither noticed, as lips melded with lips. She moaned at the feel of him under her hands, as she stroked and caressed. She wanted more.

Needed everything he had to give.

And now.

But he was taking his time.

She pushed up on his shoulders, until he rolled over. She rolled with him and sat up.

Immediately he grinned, his hands sliding up her belly to cup her plump breasts. She moaned, then sighed. "That feels so damn good."

"It is good. It's great. You're great." One hand slid down to her belly and played with the curls below. She sucked in her breath and threw her head back. She loved being with him. Loved everything about him. She slowly rocked back and forth, her body teasing his by stroking up and down on his shaft. His hips lifted in response, his fingers grasping her thighs to speed up her pace. She shifted and rose, then with one hand guided him to her.

And came down on top of him, seating him deep inside.

"So good," he murmured.

At the squeeze of his fingers, she started to ride, her thighs rising and falling in a rhythm as old as time. The pace was slow and steady, but his fingers were getting firmer and stiffer on her flesh, his head twisting on the pillow.

She tossed her head backward.

And picked up the pace.

He grabbed her hips and pulled her down hard, his hips grinding upward inside her. Then he arched beneath her and groaned. His seed spurted deep inside.

And sent her over the edge.

With the explosion still rocking her, she collapsed on top of him.

She barely noticed when he shifted their positions and tugged her up against his side, pulling a sheet over both of them.

And she slept.

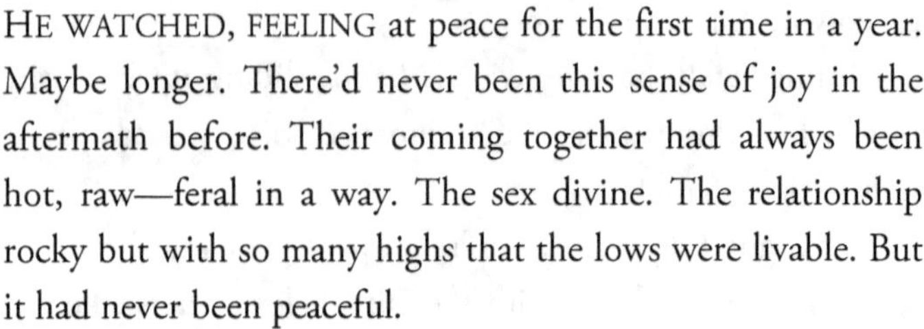

HE WATCHED, FEELING at peace for the first time in a year. Maybe longer. There'd never been this sense of joy in the aftermath before. Their coming together had always been hot, raw—feral in a way. The sex divine. The relationship rocky but with so many highs that the lows were livable. But it had never been peaceful.

Now he understood what it meant.

And he thought he could get used to this. It was so much easier to look at life from this new position.

Now the challenge would be to keep it. His thoughts hardened. Those bastards who shot him needed to be picked up, and they needed to solve this forest problem. He wouldn't want Tori caught up in another electrical storm, based on what he had seen. She'd been a little too willing to walk away from everything they had.

That whole event had freaked him out.

As he lay here, Tori shifted restlessly in his arms. He gently stroked her back. From the corner of his eye, he watched as something moved. No longer disturbed by the odd movement, he watched as Jessie curled around Tori's neck and shoulder, one eye on Devon.

"Hey, buddy. It's all right."

Jessie appeared to study him for a moment, then closed his eyes and slept.

Nice for him.

Sleep was the furthest thing from Devon's mind. Staring at Jessie, he considered Matt's words. Could Devon get a spirit pet? Did he even want one? Yes, he really didn't have to think about that. To have an animal that connected on an energy level, that was his pet alone—and where that thought came from, he had no idea, but considering how he'd grown up with two brothers …

But wanting it didn't make it so.

And although Genesis and Tori had energy affinities, that didn't mean they could help him.

He didn't really know what kind of animal he hoped he could have, just one that would want to be with him.

"You're thinking too loud," Tori said drowsily.

"Ha, you should be sleeping."

"I would be, but you were making too much mental noise." She yawned. "What are you worrying over?"

"Well, not worrying exactly." And he wasn't sure he wanted to share. The spirit pet issue was still touchy, and he didn't want to set off fireworks. Jessie took that opportunity to roll up like a cat with his belly topmost, looking like a beautiful furry ball.

He chuckled. "Jessie is quite the character."

"Yes, he is," she murmured, half asleep. She opened her eyes. "You really can see him now?"

He nodded. "It started after the night of the energy storm."

"Good. That's the way it should be. We grew up with dozens of spirit pets hanging around."

"Dozens?" He couldn't imagine.

"From Granny. And Celeste has an affinity for animals, both spirit and flesh. Both were always in and out of the house, as she found homes for them."

"She can help spirit pets find homes?" Okay, now he really wanted to find Celeste.

"Sure. Granny did all the time too. Or helped them to

cross over."

"*Hmm.*" He wanted to ask but figured it was a silly request.

"Of course it's not like adopting a flesh-and-blood pet. That affinity from animal to soul is everything."

"I can imagine."

"Maybe by the time she gets home, you'll know if that's something you'd like to do. You just have to put out the mental call, energy-wise, and see if someone, some animal, answers." She yawned and rolled over. "You could also ask Jessie. They are all connected."

And she closed her eyes, snuggling in deeper.

Devon stared at her for a moment, before his gaze switched to Jessie. "You?" he asked in a low voice. Jessie raised his head and stared at him. There was almost a question in his question. He studied the spirit pet and sensed a weird tingling in the ethers. He had the strangest feeling that Jessie was asking him something.

Just in case, Devon said, "Yes, please."

CHAPTER 30

"PLANS?" TORI SIPPED her coffee, loving the morning thus far, sitting at the center of a large table, having just finished breakfast. In fact, she was feeling pretty-damn satisfied with life in general this morning.

Hell, maybe she'd get back on track with her world. In some ways, her yearlong hiatus had sent her back a few steps, even while it had moved her life forward.

"The forest," Genesis said. "That needs to be our priority at this point."

"The three men who shot Devon need to be picked up."

"We must find them first," Matt said smoothly. "Connor, you're on that."

Connor grinned. "With pleasure."

His feral smile had Tori's eyes widening.

Devon's smirk was fun to see. "And me?" He looked over at the women. "I'll be with you two."

Tori rolled her eyes. "Of course you will."

"He's right. You two don't go anywhere alone," Matt said. "Got it?"

"Got it," the sisters said in unison.

"I need to go to the lab and check on how the work is progressing, before I can go anywhere. Then I was hoping to go back to the cottage." Genesis looked at her sister. "If that works?"

Tori nodded happily. It didn't matter what the suggestion was—all was good with her today.

As they headed toward the first room in the lab, someone raced past, shoving them in the process. Tori called out, "Hey! Watch out."

He didn't acknowledge the two women, nor did he slow down. He quickly disappeared from sight.

Genesis had her phone out and was talking to someone.

Tori wasn't paying much attention to the conversation. Her gaze was locked on the direction the man had disappeared. It had looked like an escape. "Genesis, where does that lead?"

Instantly a loud noise crashed overhead, as a siren began to wail.

"Damn, I knew it." Tori took off after the man.

"Knew what?" Genesis cried from behind her.

"He didn't belong here."

She raced down the hallway and into a maze of doors and more doors. She spun around in frustration. "Where does any of this go, Genesis? Is there an exit here?"

"I have no idea," Genesis cried out, panting with exertion at Tori's side. "I haven't been down here much."

The alarm kept blaring in her ears. She clapped her hands to the sides of her head. "That needs to stop."

As if obeying her command, the alarm stopped. And a heavy silence ensued.

Genesis's phone went off. Followed by Tori's.

Tori answered.

Devon snapped, "Where are you?"

"We're in some hallway off the labs. A man went running past us. Then the alarm sounded."

"Stay where you are." And he hung up.

"I hate it when he does that," Tori snapped, putting away her phone.

"Did you get that same 'stay where you are' order?" Genesis asked, her voice tinged with humor.

"I sure did."

Genesis shook her head. "Not sure what they expect us to do but stand here, looking like idiots, while they all run around trying to solve this problem."

Tori motioned to the long hallway behind them and the double doors that opened to let in the three men. "And there they are to rescue the damsels in distress."

Genesis sighed. "I really don't like that role."

Tori glanced at her, caught her sister's eye, realized that they were thinking the same thing. With their abilities, they wouldn't ever be in that role. And they broke out laughing.

They were still giggling when the men reached their sides.

"What's so funny?" Matt shook his head. "Never mind. Where did the man go?"

Tori shrugged. "I tracked him to here, and I don't know why, but I can't see much energy here."

"That's purposeful. After those rocks came in, we had to try and keep the energy fields down here neutralized."

"Not such a great idea now," Connor said, glaring down the hallway. "Do we have any idea what he wanted?"

One of the doctors came through the double doors and raced toward them. "He took the box with the black rock."

Genesis groaned. "No. Not that. It'll create chaos wherever it ends up, if they take it out of the box. Worse, the person who takes it out will die. Bet no one warned him of that." She studied Matt's face. "Time to beef up the security around here."

The doctor interjected, "It was the new technician we hired." He held out a tablet that displayed the image of a man. "This is him. He came highly recommended." He gestured frantically. "Now I might have to consider that he was too highly recommended."

"And who did the recommending?"

"The Portmans. Portman Senior runs the Paranormal Center in Big Glory."

"As it was Portman Junior who created the damn black rocks, I wouldn't think that was a recommendation at all." Tori narrowed her gaze.

The doctor looked down his nose at Tori. "That's why we were happy to bring him on board. He'd seen the rocks before because of Portman Junior. He had experience with them."

"And yet apparently what he really wanted was the rock. What are the chances he had plans for it that didn't include research?" Matt turned to make his way back up the corridor. "Connor …"

"Coming." Before he turned to follow, Connor shot a hard look at Genesis. "This has nothing to do with you. We'll handle it."

And he raced after his boss.

Genesis snorted. "Like hell."

"Thank you," Tori replied. "I'm glad to see you aren't taking those kinds of orders lying down."

"You might want to consider it, Tori," Devon said calmly. "Connor has a good reason for warning her."

Tori shot Devon a look. "I'm fully aware that he might." She paused, then gently asked him, "Shouldn't you be helping them?"

She caught the quiver of Genesis's energy as she waited

for the answer. Her sister wanted to go after the rock.

"I'll be staying with you two," he answered, his voice clear and knowing, his gaze shifting from one to the other. "So no trying to get away from me."

Tori gave him a wide-eyed, innocent look. "Never." And she turned away, rolling her eyes at her sister, with a big grin on her face.

DEVON DIDN'T TRUST them. "You know trying to ditch me would be the worst thing you could do right now, correct?" he asked in a silky voice.

She pivoted and said, "I wouldn't try. Even though I could do it without putting in that much effort." She turned sharply to walk away from him, her back rigid.

Good, she could be pissed off all she wanted. As long as she stayed safe. And playing games was no way to do that.

Genesis reached out a gentle hand. "We won't. Honestly."

He studied her face, then nodded. "Good." They turned to walk after Tori, who hadn't slowed at all. "Where to now?"

"The caves and the woods. We need to find out what's happening there. Matt will work on the missing rock, and Connor is supposed to be tracking down the men who shot at you. So what we can do is start looking closely at the woods. See why the energy system there is off."

He nodded. "I'll drive."

CHAPTER 31

THE WOODS SMELLED … dead. The undergrowth had rotted down to a mulching moistness that Tori couldn't remember ever seeing before. On the positive side, it wasn't everywhere. It wasn't even in a large area, but it was definitely at this one place, leading to the corner of the forest they hadn't checked out yet. And she didn't like this preamble.

There was no energy feel to it. No life to it. Just a dead and dying, *having given up hope for anything better* feel to it.

And that disturbed her more than she could imagine.

"Why?" she whispered. "I've never seen anything like this. This was my favorite area to play. What happened to it?" At a loss and hating the sadness and grief inside her at the sight, she wandered the path, wondering if she could even bear to move farther inside.

"I don't know why this one is the worst so far, but it's been low energy for a long time. A year, in fact," Genesis said delicately.

Tori turned to look at her. "What?" She shook her head. "Why a year?" Then she realized. "Granny?"

Genesis nodded. "Partly." She walked forward, the dry leaves crunching underfoot. "Her death was a huge climatic shock to all the systems. And, when we didn't step in to heal them, well …" She waved a hand. "This is the result."

Tori frowned. She had the strongest feeling that something more went with her sister's story that Genesis was reluctant to bring up. "Is it really just our lack of effort? Or is there something else going on?"

The barest of winces whispered across her sister's face.

"Tell me."

Genesis hesitated. "How were your energy levels when you were traveling?" she asked.

"Sometimes good, sometimes bad," Tori said. "It depended on where and how far away from the forest we were."

"Right. That makes sense." Genesis glanced at Devon, then back at Tori. "And, of course, you had Jessie."

Tori nodded. "Jessie was huge at keeping me charged. I don't know how he got the energy sometimes. When it was really bad, we were bedridden, but, since I had a living to make, I couldn't give in to that often. So I had to pull more energy than I've ever pulled before just to stay alive." She studied the woods around her. "The other woods didn't seem to have the same affinity for recharging or not the same affinity for recharging me."

"Exactly." Genesis's voice was so low Tori almost didn't hear her.

She studied her sister. "What am I not understanding?"

Genesis shifted uneasily.

"Gen? Talk to me. You know something, or suspect something, that I don't understand." She was aware of Devon, ever silent at their side. He was studying the bushes around them but hadn't added to the conversation yet.

"I think you weren't charging from the other forests, as they weren't your forest. Jessie could because, as a spirit animal, he could pull from anywhere, but not enough for you too. So when you were low and needed the energy to stay alive, you pulled from ..." She broke off.

Tori frowned at her sister, not sure where she was going with this. "From?"

"From here."

Tori stared at her sister in disbelief. "Genesis, no way I could pull from here. I was miles away."

Genesis just waited.

"I was like … thousands of miles away."

Genesis stared at her mutely.

Tori looked around at the dead forest. "How is that possible?"

"This is your forest."

"But I wasn't here." No, it couldn't be. She couldn't be responsible for this mess. "No. I have pulled from this woods for years, and there was never any of this kind of damage."

"But you never needed so much, never gave in return, and never took at a time when Granny's energy wasn't there to balance things out. Since her death …" Genesis sighed. "Since her death, everything is different, and we are now responsible for everything we see here." She waved her arms around. "Including the damage."

Tori walked around the forest, her mind consumed, as she cast her thoughts back to the last year. The times she really needed the energy to survive. How she'd specifically thought about the woods here at this corner because they were her favorite. How she'd smile all the time, knowing that this place was here and was special and how connected it had helped her feel to her own family and home.

She'd really pulled the energy as she'd needed to.

And because she hadn't been here to see the damage and to break down the blockages in the flow, the flow had slowed to a trickle, until they'd eventually stopped altogether.

Before, she presumed Granny's energy had kept that

flow moving, as it was supposed to. All the things that Granny had done to keep everything perfect … had stopped when she'd stopped too.

For all Tori's running away a year ago, thinking she'd been so good at it … She collapsed onto a rock. "Oh my God. I didn't know." What had she done? "I'm so sorry," she whispered. "I would have come back if I'd known."

"I know you didn't do it on purpose. And it wasn't just you …" Genesis sat down beside her. "We were all guilty. After everyone left, I couldn't go to the cottage for a long time. I did the minimal amount of work I had to do here to make sure all was well—and, when I say minimal, I mean just that. It was six months before I could come to the pools and not cry. I was lost and felt forsaken at the very center of me. I had to get over it, deal with it all. That's when I found out that the one group had been trying to commercialize our pools, and then the black rock mess started. None of this could have happened a year ago when Granny was alive."

"No." Tori shook her head. "It's our fault. She kept this place in perfect running order."

"And, in truth, we didn't know we would have to. Granny didn't assign us death duties or anything."

"No, she shouldn't have to." Tori raised her face to the sky, feeling a heart-crushing pain like she hadn't felt before. "We've failed her. And Mother Nature. No wonder the electrical storm wanted me." She stared at Devon. "Maybe it needs me."

"Yes, it needed you," Genesis confirmed. "And, if we can't fix this place back up, it'll probably require one of us for that too."

"What do you mean, require one of you for what?" Devon asked, his voice hard.

Genesis answered Devon's question. "As an entirely different power source. Another thing Granny managed on her own."

"Sounds like Granny should have done more training with you three," Devon stated, "if she expected you to handle everything she had taken care of. After all, she'd been dealing with this for what? Forty, fifty years?"

"Over one hundred," Tori said quietly. "Our mother was supposed to be the next one and to train us, but she died before she could."

"Murdered by Grandfather's father apparently," Genesis added sadly. "And the whole system went off-kilter."

"Or rebalanced, as there would only be one stargazer in each generation and always a female."

"But this time three of us were born."

"Maybe that was nature trying to spread the duties," Tori said, her joke lacking humor. "And it is, for all three of us. Celeste was the guardian of the animals." Tori stood still and looked around at the underbrush, missing the sound of scurrying underfoot and the birds flying outward through the branches and leaves. "No more animals are here, are there?" She turned to face her sister.

Genesis slowly shook her head. "Not now. Not since the death of Granny, and they are all gone. In fact, I doubt the woods could sustain animals any longer."

Tori closed her eyes and cried out softly, "What have we done?"

DEVON DIDN'T KNOW that his input would be welcome, but he wanted to try and help. Anything other than have one of the triplets be a required sacrifice. A discussion he planned to take up with Matt and Connor at his first opportunity.

"You might want to consider that it's not your fault. That Granny's death caused an energy vortex that required an adjustment. Since you didn't know at that time, we are now at a recovery-and-repair stage. You now know more is required of the three of you. That all of it works together and that we need Celeste home to do her part. But this is fixable. If Granny alone could run all this, then you three together can run all this."

"The damage is extensive," Tori said. "We might not be able to fix this." She picked up a dead leaf and crumpled the golden paper-thin leaf into powder. "No water has been here in how long?"

"The healing pools were a big problem, but they're running again," Genesis said. "But I'm not sure the pools can reach this area."

"Right. That brings us back to the woods and their blockages. If we can keep the water flowing and healing the woods, in theory, the animals will return. Over time."

"If we can track down Celeste, then that time frame will shorten considerably."

Tori nodded. "I'd place my money on Matt finding her."

"True enough. But that doesn't mean she'll be willing to come home."

"Why not?" Devon asked. "If she knows she's needed?"

"She's got a heart as rich as gold," Tori said, "but, when her relationship with Matt blew up, I've never seen her so devastated."

"She could have healed in the meantime though," he argued. "You did. Genesis did."

The two women looked at each other, then back at him.

"True, but that doesn't mean the same magic will work for her. She gives so much that, when someone takes advantage of her good nature, it's a betrayal she finds hard to forgive."

Devon opened his mouth to say that she'd get over it, but he didn't think the women would appreciate the comment. And, true enough, he didn't know the details and shouldn't give an opinion, as he didn't know Celeste. But he did know Matt, and that man was determined to find her and to fix whatever had gone wrong.

He'd put his money on Matt any day.

CHAPTER 32

TORI SAT IN meditation in the middle of the dying forest. She was clearing the debris of the energy field, as her granny had taught her a long time ago. If the forest were healthy, then she could do this from her bedroom at home—wherever home ended up being. However, with this level of damage, it would take more work, more energy, and, therefore, she couldn't be pulling energy and not returning energy.

So she was here. Devon sat with her, and Genesis was at the creek. She was doing something similar.

The woods were the current problem. Somehow the roots were blocked from the water. Like a thirsty man without a mouth, they couldn't access it because of the barrier. And it wasn't just in this section of the woods. The barriers were everywhere. Miles of forest to fix.

The knotty mess she'd unlocked when she'd first arrived had stayed open and, given the right tools, that corner of the forest should be working on healing itself. It would still need more help, but she had to focus on the areas that were worse off. Eventually all the energy would rise up, but the fastest way was to strengthen the weakest link, so they could all help each other.

Another big knot of energy appeared to be somewhere below her, and she didn't understand that. No caves were down there—at least, not ones she knew of. But something had to be there. And, in that case, she needed to find it. "Devon, I have to see if caves are underneath us. I can feel the blockage, but I can't see it to unlock the mess. It's somewhere below."

"Many caves are down there," Genesis said. "I can help you look."

Devon was on his feet, ready to go. "What about the road access? We could drive to the other side and come in from there."

"Let's try that."

The truck was only a ten-minute walk away, and, by the time they made it in and were driving away from the damage, they felt better. Until a large black SUV pulled up behind them. Tori glanced over at Devon. His face had gone hard, his gaze on the rearview mirror.

His fingers clenched the steering wheel. Tori turned to look at Genesis and found her texting Matt.

The black SUV pulled up closer.

Tori sighed. "Here we go again."

"Yep, hang on." Devon gunned the truck, and it ripped forward. Smaller, lighter, and more powerful, it could easily stay in front of the SUV.

"I can't see the driver," she said. "Genesis, can you?"

She shook her head. "No, but I've sent a picture of the license plate to Matt."

Tori nodded. "Good thinking."

Devon lurched the truck to the side and pulled off the side of the road, taking cover behind the brush.

She let out a shocked gasp as she realized he'd brought the vehicle to a stop. "What are you doing? It's not safe to stop, is it?"

Barely before she had finished speaking, she heard the sounds of the vehicle approaching. And they all watched as it steamed past.

Once the SUV had rounded a bend and disappeared from view, Devon spoke up. "Now we have to make a decision. Do we follow it or go to the caves?" He glanced from one to the other.

Both women immediately said, "Caves."

"Matt can track the truck," Genesis added.

Devon nodded. "Good. Give Matt our plan, and I'll get us to the caves." He pulled out onto the road, made a couple sharp turns, and took them down a back road.

A few minutes later, he pulled into a deserted area and parked in the trees. He pointed up ahead. "The parking lot is right over there."

"Smart thinking." Tori and Genesis hopped from the vehicle, when Genesis's phone beeped. "That's Connor. He's picking me up at the parking lot. Are you okay to go alone?"

"Of course," Tori exclaimed. "I'd feel better if you did go back with him." She grinned. "Now that we lost those guys, we'll be fine."

They walked to the small parking lot, approaching the area slowly, in case the wrong people were waiting for them. Several parking lots were around, but this one was empty. They remained at the tree line, staying out of the open, until a similar SUV to the one they'd seen earlier pulled into the lot.

"Any chance we were wrong about the earlier vehicle?" Tori asked.

"Absolutely," Devon said, "but we'll be cautious about everybody right now."

After a quick hug, Genesis left with Connor, leaving the

other two alone. Tori turned back to Devon. "Ready?"

He nodded, and they headed toward the cave entrance. The healing pools here weren't as strong as some of the others, but they were more accessible for many people. Even so, few used them. The path was empty, and not much traffic had been through here in a long time.

"I haven't used this entrance in a long time," Tori said.

"I've been here a couple times," Devon said, "but not in the last few months." He paused and added, "It doesn't look much different."

"That's too bad." She moved ahead, her stride purposeful. "I was hoping the poor condition was a recent change."

"No, it's been looking dead for months."

Grimly she carried on, filled with worry.

"Is it because of the healing energy of the cottage that the area surrounding your home is so vibrant and healthy?" Devon asked.

"Yes, exactly," she said. "And there is an extremely strong healing pool keeping the area alive. The problem is here, the energy block, combined with the weaker pools, has completely ravaged this area. Whoever did this took advantage of the vulnerable spots."

She felt his hard gaze.

"Do you really think someone did this on purpose?" he asked.

"The three of us had a part in creating the damage, and we didn't even know about it. What are the chances that other people could be negatively affecting the energy level? I'd say there's a pretty-damn good chance, especially with those black rocks."

"A horrible thought."

"Yes, but we can't take anything for granted at this

point." The lighting in the cave was darker than she expected. Gloomy. She stayed to the right and walked past the pools. The water moved with a slow, sluggish energy, as if going to sleep or just waking up. She hoped for the latter. That would match up to what Genesis had said. It took time for energy to filter, and it took a lot of time and effort to get things moving, but that process normally sped up over time.

The pools, if they were healing, should be in much better shape soon. They'd be fine to sit in now and to have a refreshing swim, but they wouldn't afford much healing to people.

"Do you think Mason could have anything to do with this black rock mess?" she asked out of the blue.

"I don't know why he would, but considering that we've had no problems here for years and years, to now think that the Portmans and Grandfather *and* someone else are all causing trouble is a bit much."

Something along that same train of thought caught her attention. "It has to do with Granny too."

"In what way?"

"It's all gone bad in the last year. When Granny died, the gentle hand-holding on the energy field she'd kept on everything—our townsfolk included—has all disintegrated."

"That makes a sad kind of sense." He stopped at her side to look back the way they'd come. "Isn't it a bit much for one woman to have handled?"

"Yes, except she would have cared for each individual area slowly over time. My mother really should have been in the sequence of caregivers, but, when that couldn't happen, Granny had to pick up so much more responsibility." Tori frowned and paced a few steps. "Something else to think about is that, as the Portmans' pool commercialization was in progress, and Grandfather had been involved in Granny's mess, what was Mason doing? How much was he involved in this mess? With the black rock being stolen?" She snorted. "We don't know whether Mason is in this up to his eyeballs or hasn't had anything to do with it at all."

"It would be nice to think that way, but the bottom line is, I never saw Grandfather here, and I did see the men who shot us."

"Right. I forgot about them," she said. How could she have? "Any word on them from Matt?"

"Not yet."

"Damn."

They walked farther into the tunnel. Tingles raced over her skin, and she stopped in her tracks. "The energy mass is coming from over there."

"Are you sure?"

She hurried forward. "As sure as I can be."

"Now let's hope it's a quick answer to the problem."

She didn't bother answering. Since when had anything been easy?

DEVON WATCHED THE endless dark walls march by. He'd been in a lot of dark places that he didn't like and a lot of dark places he did like. The jury was still out on this one. There was an air of waiting, of wanting. Not a desperate energy yet, but that sense of knowing something was wrong and needing it to stop.

He hoped Tori was the one to do that.

With a quick glance at his watch, he realized how late it was. Maybe they should have gone back with Genesis and Connor, but they really needed to get a break in this problem. His stomach growled, and he thought that perhaps they should have brought something to eat with them. That could have stopped some of this sense of wanting to leave and go back to the Center. Food kept you focused and on track.

He was looking forward to working with Matt. Devon wasn't so sure about being the head of security though. Was that the type of work he wanted to do now? It made him think of Mason and all that bullshit. Who wanted to be included in that garbage? No one.

Then again, the Paranormal Center wasn't Grandfather's empire. Devon respected Matt. Saw the vision he was working toward. Devon wouldn't mind being a part of that.

A suite for him and Tori might also be part of the deal. Considering that Connor and Genesis had a similar package, it wasn't out of line. And that would be nice for everyone. Genesis's apartment definitely wasn't big enough for him and Tori, and Devon was essentially homeless.

It was all about choices.

Odd sounds dragged him out of his contemplation. Animals? Running water?

He tugged Tori to a stop and motioned with his head in that direction. She nodded. "I hear it too. I need to see what's going on."

"I'll lead." He stepped in front of her and sent out an energy probe. The air was filled with a luminescent light, but it was actually harder to see, as the depth perception was off.

He rounded a corner and came to a stop. *Voices were ahead.*

Chittering sounds came from behind him. He spun around to find both Jessie and Tori staring at him, bland looks on their faces. He glanced down at Jessie. "I gather he wants to go and take a look?"

Surprise lit Tori's features. "Yes, he does."

"Fine. We'll wait here."

She smiled at him. "It's lovely to see the interaction between you two."

He grinned. "Now to get my own."

Her eyebrows shot up. "Are you sure you want one?"

"Maybe." He shrugged. "You all have a special bond that I don't have. I'm out of the loop on this one." Something caught his ear, and he turned back to the noises coming from up ahead. He frowned. "Did I just hear Mason?"

"No, really? I hope not." Tori leaned forward, tilting her head toward the sound. "I can't tell."

Then came a sound they had no trouble hearing.

Shots rang out. Three of them.

CHAPTER 33

T ORI CLUTCHED DEVON'S arm, her heart stalling at the sound. "Please tell me that wasn't gunfire."

"It was." He tugged her close. "What we don't know is what their intended target is."

Another shot rang out. Cold and short. She winced. A second one came on its heels, followed by a third.

"Six shots? I don't like the sound of that."

"Nor do I."

And that was no good. Okay, so she might not have a good connection with the men who'd come after her—or with those in Grandfather's pocket either—but she certainly didn't want anyone dead.

The gunshots also meant that someone was playing for keeps.

She wasn't any good at healing people, but maybe she could help anyone who was hurt.

"Shit. I hate it when things go south," Devon whispered.

She did too. They'd gone more in that direction than any other in the last year. Was it possible that Granny's energy had also kept the townsfolk on the straight and narrow too? Because damn, ... since she'd been gone, the shit had gotten real.

Silence reigned for several long moments.

Devon tugged Tori behind him and slowly peered

around the corner. If they'd been just a couple minutes faster, they would have walked into the middle of the mess. He could only guess at what had gone on here, but those last three shots sounded like insurance, to make sure the intended targets didn't get back up again.

And he knew three men who had become a liability. But for whom?

Devon crept forward. Tori jerked his arm back, hard. "Stop. You can't go out there. They'll see you."

"I think they're gone," he whispered.

"Thinking is not the same thing as knowing." She squeezed his hand. "Wait for Jessie."

"How long will he be?"

"He's returning now."

Devon waited a few minutes, then felt something brush against his legs. "Is that him?"

"Yes, he's still invisible though," she said in a low dark voice. "It's bad. He says dead men are there."

"Yeah, I figured. What about the others, like the man with the gun?" he asked urgently.

"They are gone."

"They? How many?"

"He doesn't know. He saw one for sure."

"I'll take a look." Before she could grab him, he slid around the corner and crept forward.

Following on Devon's heels, Tori sent out as much of her energy as she could afford, searching for the other energies. And found them. But they weren't vital and powerful. In fact, as she moved closer to the men on the ground, their energy was snugged up tight against their bodies and fading quickly. They were already dead, their bodies cooling, the energy disappearing as their body temperature dropped.

She shook her head in denial. This wasn't supposed to happen in her hometown. It shouldn't ever happen, but she certainly hadn't expected to see a dead man, let alone three of them, murdered in her lifetime.

She stood at the foot of the first man. He was the man she'd forced to open the door of the bank to let her go. She glanced over at the other two, knowing they'd be his cohorts. And they were. "Three dead men who were wanted by the police."

"Meaning three men who had become a liability."

"And the last time they were seen was at Grandfather's place."

"Right."

"So did he do this?" Tori bit her bottom lip.

"Grandfather himself? No. He doesn't get his hands dirty. On his orders? Very likely. By Mason? Most likely." Devon moved over to the farthest male and crouched to examine the bullet hole. "I've already contacted Matt. He'll need to get a crew down here."

"Now that's too bad," said a man behind Tori in a hard, deep voice.

She stiffened.

"Both of you stand up, please," Mason ordered.

Devon shot a look over at Tori, his gaze warning her. She stood up slowly and turned to see Mason and Grandfather, standing there watching them.

Grandfather's face was a mix of emotions, from anger to sorrow.

She knew instinctively that the pool had had some effect on him. Not completely but enough that he was, indeed, struggling with his personality and his life choices.

Mason, on the other hand, appeared to be enjoying himself. Then again, the high-res gun in his hand gave him a confidence she'd love to experience.

Still, she had other weapons. In her mind, she mentally said, *Put down the gun. Put down the gun.*

It didn't waver.

She tried harder. *Put down the gun, and walk away. Turn around, walk away.*

Mason just grinned at her. "Don't bother. Your tricks don't work on me."

That had never happened before. There had been times when she'd had to work harder to overcome someone's resistance, but never where they'd known what she was doing and had been immune.

She didn't like it.

She still had Jessie though.

"Oh, and if you're looking for your pet, don't bother—within seconds, he should be history too."

"What?" she gasped. "What are you talking about?"

Jessie, she cried out in her mind. *Where are you?*

She heard a loud squeak of pain and fear, then nothing.

Her heart pounding in her chest, she took a step toward Mason. "What did you do?"

"Oh, I didn't do anything. But predators have predator spirit pets too."

Mason's smile made her blood run in icy rivers through her veins. "You have no reason to hurt him," she cried out.

Mason shrugged. "He's a pest, running around and sticking his nose in places it's not wanted. Who needs that?"

She didn't know what to say. She was desperate to save Jessie, but she also needed to save Devon and herself.

Mason waved the gun between Devon and Tori. "Devon, walk closer please."

She heard his approach, as he complied with the order. He was probably trying to give her time to do her thing, she thought hysterically, only she couldn't. Why wasn't Mason susceptible to her talents?

"You heard me say that I've already called Matt," Devon said.

"Doesn't matter. I have to get rid of him soon anyway."

Tori moaned. Why the hell was this happening? "Grandfather, why are you doing this?" she asked.

The old man opened his mouth to answer, when Mason brushed aside her question. "It doesn't matter to you. You're dead regardless. As if anyone would let your stupid paperwork stand in the way of a fortune." He snickered. "And I'm not fool enough to let that slide through my fingers."

She glared at him. "I asked Grandfather, not you. What's the matter, is he a puppet now, and you're the puppet master?"

"You could say that." Mason didn't appear too bothered either way. "Then again, the land should belong to me. And, with the forest about to completely die off, huge potential is there for development."

"You're crazy," she cried out. "You can't develop the forest. It won't stand for it."

"It might not if we were to do things your way, but we aren't." He grinned. "Too damn bad those assholes couldn't even shoot you properly. I figured they'd love a chance to hunt you down and to get their own payback after you turned them into fools. They didn't even want money for the job."

"Too bad they were so incompetent then," Devon snapped. "Seeing as how they failed completely."

"Well, they won't fail again," Mason said comfortably, a sneer on his face.

Grandfather just looked confused. And that bothered Tori more than anything. Mason appeared to have no conscience, but where did Grandfather stand on that? She'd heard nothing nice about him or from him, but the pool seemed to have had some effect on him.

Grandfather, she whispered, *speak up. Don't let him control you.*

Tori saw no answering spark in his eyes and no connection of energy. She could usually see if she was getting through to someone. With him? … Nothing.

She glanced over at Mason, grinning like a crazy man. Shit. He knew what she was trying to do.

He raised the gun.

She caught back her breath, her instincts telling her to bolt out of here as fast as she could.

Devon gripped her arm. "You're going to shoot us? You think that's the answer?"

"Sure, why not? It's an easy solution. Gregor," he called out. "Come over here."

A large gorilla-looking spirit animal walked toward him, a limp Jessie in his arms.

She cried out, barely able to see the energy of Jessie's body. He wasn't dead, but he was in really poor shape.

Mason growled. He waved the gun at them again. "Turn around."

"Why?" she cried out. "Is it easier to shoot us in the back?"

Devon's grip on her arm tightened. She glanced over at Mason and realized he wasn't quite in control. In fact, a cry came from Grandfather. He crumpled to his knees, his hands on his head.

Mason turned to look at him. "If I didn't still need you, I'd put a bullet in your head," he said, his voice filled with disgust.

Grandfather stilled and quieted.

As Tori watched him, she couldn't tell what was going on—as if being given a command that she couldn't see and hadn't sent. His face was twisted, and he appeared to be in pain. She didn't understand. "What's going on?" she snapped. "What's wrong with Grandfather?"

"Oh, nothing. He's just having a fit," Mason said non-chalantly. "As usual."

So much disgust filled his voice that she stared at him. "You really are the puppet master, aren't you?"

"Of course. I should thank your sister too. She made this possible. In fact, she's directly responsible for your plight. Too bad you won't get a chance to thank her yourself."

He lifted the gun and pointed it at her. "And, by the way, I have no problem pulling the trigger and shooting you in the front or the back." He pulled the trigger.

And all hell broke loose.

❧

DEVON PUSHED TORI to the ground, his own instincts sending him down on top of her. The sounds of a horrible fight to the death made him cringe, and he heard Tori cry out beneath him.

He'd set something in motion and had no idea where it would stop. Hell, the way things sounded, he couldn't even be sure that it would stop.

But he sure hoped so and damn soon. The sounds of an animal fight and the screams of pain and terror would haunt him forever. But, when it became obvious that Tori couldn't do her usual mind trick, he had to come up with something to save them.

Taking a chance, he raised his head, realized the chaos was still going on around them, and hopped to his feet. Helping Tori up, they took off into the shadows.

Then the cries stopped.

And silence reigned.

With Tori's hand in his, Devon kept running as far and as fast as they could go.

CHAPTER 34

TORI RACED BEHIND Devon, her breath catching in her chest, as they bolted into the dark passage. "What the hell just happened?"

Devon shook his head, but he didn't take the time to answer. He kept dragging her ever onward.

After several long moments and no sign that they were being followed, she pulled her hand back and slowed to a stop. "Devon, answer me," she said, gasping for breath.

Hands on his hips, he turned to face her, his breath ragged. "I didn't know if it would work."

"If what would work?" she asked in exasperation. "I couldn't see much, but something was attacking the damn gorilla."

He nodded. "I called out for anyone to help save Jessie."

She stared at him. "And it worked?" How incredible was that? And yet why not? She had no idea how Devon had managed to do that, but she was grateful. "Jessie is alive, you know. The gorilla thing didn't kill him."

"I know." He stared down at the ground, his breathing easier. "He's with us."

She studied him carefully, then glanced at their surroundings. Jessie was indeed with them, and he sat on the back of a very large black cat. Jessie was injured and appeared to be struggling to hold on. Tori held out her arms, and

Jessie awkwardly jumped into them. She cuddled him close, watching as the cat slowly circled the two adults, his glowing eyes studying Tori and Jessie before he walked over to Devon.

"Amazing," she said quietly. "I've never seen a large cat spirit animal."

"Is it … friendly?" he asked quietly. "I know I called it, but …"

"It's alone. Untethered, or unmatched, so to speak," she said. "Or it wouldn't have answered your call."

"Meaning?"

The cat stared at him, his huge green eyes glowing in the darkness.

"He really is beautiful, isn't he?" Devon whispered, his gaze on the powerful animal.

"He is." She didn't say anything else, wondering if he had any idea what was happening, or rather, what could happen. She glanced back the way they'd come. It seemed no one had pursued them, and she was damn glad of that. It wasn't over, but hopefully Matt and his men could get here and could capture Mason. Of Grandfather's fate, she had no idea.

A heavy rumble caught her attention, and she pivoted, startled, Jessie cuddled protectively in her arms, to find the huge black cat weaving around Devon's legs, almost knocking him over in the process. The rumble?

The huge feline was purring.

She watched in shock as Devon reached out a tentative hand and connected with the spirit animal. She caught her breath. Such an amazing amount of power was hidden in that animal. If Devon could connect, and it appeared they were, it would be an amazing spirit pet.

If he wanted it. The cat was alone and open to the idea, but this wasn't a cute and cuddly cat. It was a massive feral animal.

In front of her, the cat fell to his side and exposed his belly for Devon's touch. And, with a big grin, she watched Devon and the cat reach out feelers, both of them slowly accepting the other.

She never thought she'd see the day.

Tears collected in the corner of her eyes.

It was so special, so intimate, seeing this bond being offered and accepted.

Jessie gave a low chitter in her arms. "It's okay, Jessie. I'm fine. Better than you are."

The sound out of his mouth was closer to a warble than anything else. She smiled, her heart full of love, as she watched her protector and lover find an equally strong spirit partner.

For they weren't pet and owner, like Tori and Jessie. These two had come together in mutual agreement. They were bonding in respect and admiration. Love would be a heartbeat behind.

"Tori?"

A quiet voice called from the shadows behind her. The cat surged to his feet, his teeth bared and a low howl in the back of his throat. Devon reached down a hand. The cat sat and glared at the shadows. Matt walked out slowly, his wary eye on the cat. A group of men walked out behind him.

"When you choose a pet, Devon, you choose a pet."

"Apparently," Devon said quietly. "His name is Storm."

"And is he aggressive?" Matt asked.

"Not if you aren't, I don't think."

Matt nodded. "Let's see how this works." He reached up

a hand. "Darbo, your turn."

Tori watched closely, as Darbo made a tiny singsong sound that had everyone stopping to listen. She glanced over at Devon, seeing the surprise and concern, as he glanced down at the big cat. He was new to the world of spirit pets, but, as long as one was calm and nonaggressive, then everyone would get along. The only exceptions were the spirit pets, like that gorilla, whose violent and aggressive natures made them instant matches with humans who had the same nature. There was an old Glory saying that water always settled at its own level.

It was true of people too.

The cat roared, but it was a playful sound, not an angry one. Jessie piped up in a weird chatty tone, and Darbo spoke again. They had a short conversation only the animals could truly understand. Tori gathered bits and pieces of it but not the entire thing. Storm padded over softly, until his nose was shoved up against Darbo's chubby belly.

A collective gasp escaped from all the humans.

Then Darbo reached out his long arms and wrapped them around Storm's neck. Darbo chattered away softly, while Jessie interjected at various points.

Then, like the sharp edge of a knife, the conversation ended. Darbo appeared to fall asleep, and Jessie curled up in Tori's arms and closed his eyes. Storm walked back around Devon, coming to sit down by his leg. He slanted a glittery look up at Devon, a rumble deep in his throat, as if saying, "Okay, we're done."

Tori laughed. "Glad they worked that out."

Matt grinned. "Now maybe we can get down to business."

"Right, speaking of which, we need to fill you in," Devon said and proceeded to do just that.

"I think while we were dealing with the hierarchy stuff, the bad guys got away," Tori murmured.

Matt shook his head. "I have a team on the other side."

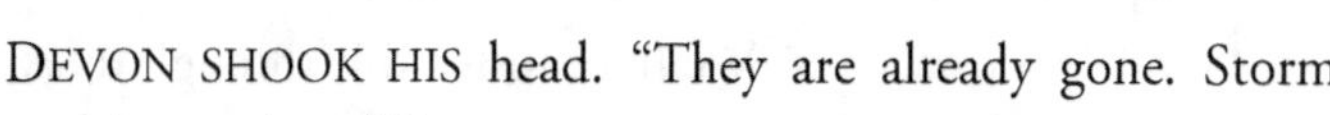

DEVON SHOOK HIS head. "They are already gone. Storm saw them take off."

Matt looked at him. "Damn."

He sent the men forward to look. "This place is a maze."

"If they go home …" Tori suggested.

Matt shook his head. "Grandfather will, but Mason will go underground. Still, once he lawyers up, there won't be any touching him. You didn't see him shoot anyone, did you?"

Both Devon and Tori shook their heads.

"And he didn't admit to killing the men, did he? He might have threatened you both, but he'll wiggle out of that. He never fired the gun in your vicinity either, did he?"

"Hell. No, he didn't. And neither did anyone else see him. Just Grandfather, who appeared to be under the influence of something wrong, and us. So no one to confirm our story."

"Exactly. I need the gun. I need Mason. Preferably both standing over the bodies with the smoke still floating up from the weapon."

"That's not fair," Tori cried out.

Devon understood how she felt. Unless one of them had actually gotten shot and someone caught the shooter, they would have a hell of a time stopping the asshole.

"Too bad you didn't think to ask him about the black rock," Matt said.

"No guarantees he would have admitted anything about it. And I'm not sure that he didn't have some kind of mind control over Grandfather happening too," Tori said, her tone defeated. "He was also immune to my power of suggestion."

"Now that's an interesting twist." Matt motioned at the direction his men took off. "Are you coming?"

Devon nodded. "Yes. We have to see this through. Next time it could be our bodies on the ground you are collecting."

"It almost was us this time," Tori said, her voice pained. She fell into step behind Matt.

Devon and Storm brought up the rear. He glanced down at the large animal walking at his side. Who'd have thought he'd end up with something so … perfect?

He grinned. Not him.

The cave where the bodies lay was awash with bright lights. Matt's crew was busy wrapping them up to take to the surface. Other men were working the scene. Devon studied the workers. He didn't recognize them, but they appeared to be officials of some kind. He thought the police were in Grandfather's pocket, but, from the looks of it, Matt really was making changes.

And that made Devon all the more eager to join the company. This planet, this city, these people, all needed change. Needed to see their leaders in the right light. It would be something to be a part of. Something he would be proud to help make happen.

Accepting Matt's offer was the best decision Devon had made in a very long time.

CHAPTER 35

TORI STOOD OFF to the side and watched the men work. Her mind was caught on the puzzling problem of Mason's mental shifts and his apparent control of Grandfather.

How had he been immune to her suggestions?

And how could she get around it, if she had to go up against him again? She'd been vulnerable this last time. She couldn't afford to fall into that same situation again. Not now. Not when they were so close to having the type of life she'd been waiting for and had wanted to have since forever.

The last thing she wanted to do was lose it all now. And for what? Land they couldn't keep and secrets they'd been keeping too long.

She leaned against the far wall, watching the men work. The sight of death bothered her but more because of the senselessness of it.

A whisper behind her had her turning to look out at the forest. An entrance was behind her. That was how the men had been brought in before being shot. She couldn't imagine all three standing, waiting for the bullet with their name on it.

Maybe Mason had the same ability that she had.

That would explain much.

The whisper came again. Not human and not animal. It

was the forest again. Calling her. She cast a glance over at the others, but Devon and Matt were deep in a discussion over something. She walked toward the entrance, where the forest waited for her.

She'd never been afraid of the forces of nature. She had too much of her granny's blood to let that be a part of her existence, but she knew that not everything in the forest was sunlight and roses.

At the entrance, she stopped and studied the deadness. A darkness was here that hadn't been here before. They needed to find that blockage to let the forest heal.

She studied the ground, spotting a dark river she hadn't noticed before. But then, this area was all new to her. Her gaze tracked the low-lying energy. It was sluggish. Dark.

And incredibly unhappy.

Good, this was it. This was the strongest lead yet to the blockage. This energy should flow smooth and powerful; instead, it wallowed in place.

An entrance to the cave system was just a little farther down. She followed the dark river right to it. She studied the entrance, then realized that, given the circumstances, she shouldn't go alone. She turned back to find Devon, but he was already here, standing with his hands on his hips and glaring at her. Storm gave her a matching glare from his side. She raised both hands in mock surrender. "I was just coming back to get you."

He stared at her, silent.

She walked up to him. "I think I found the entrance to where the problem is."

"Good. Let's go." He motioned with his hand. "Lead the way."

With a quick grin, she turned and raced back to the entrance. "With any luck, we can disarm this and get back in time for dinner."

"I don't doubt it, knowing you."

She walked down the entrance incline. "This one looks to go deeper than the others."

"Probably just a steeper entrance."

She shrugged. The caves seemed to all have little cubbyhole entrances from the forest side that all connected to the major spaces below. It was the nature of the land.

The descent was steep. She walked carefully, still carrying Jessie in her arms. When she finally got to the bottom, she watched the dark energy wallowing at her feet. Confident that they were in the right place, she walked forward quickly. This should be easy enough.

Behind her, Devon called out, "Wait."

She froze, then slowly looked back. "What's the matter?"

"Storm."

She studied the big cat. The ridge of hair along his back stood up. His top lip curled in a silent snarl. "Well, he doesn't like something here."

"Probably the energy." Devon stood at her side. "Why don't we have a light again?"

"I've never really needed one before. Usually I work in the woods, and it's either sunlight or moonlight helping me out." She studied the darkness. "And there's normally the energy glow in here. This is blacker than I'm used to for a cave."

"Goes along with the dark river."

She opened her senses and used it to lighten the air around her. "I can see better now with my energy brighter."

"Good. Can you see where the problem is?"

A long cave stood in front of them. She walked down

the tunnel. The air became damp, full of the earthy smell of roots and moisture.

At the end of the straight section, she caught the ripple of water. She ran toward it. "It's another healing pool," she cried out.

"How can it be? It's black."

She pointed to the center of the water. The black rock, no longer in its protective box, sat atop the water in the center of the pool. The box it had been in sat on the edge of the water.

"Is that the one from the Center?" he asked in shock. "Why here? And why aren't we affected?"

She studied his energy. And her own.

And knew. She said simply, "Because of Storm. He's protecting us."

DEVON STARED AT her, then turned to look down at Storm. "You're right. I didn't even think of that. My senses are open, and my energy is out wide, but I'm already so used to his presence that his energy has already blended with mine, and I didn't recognize what he was doing."

"It's amazing. I knew he was powerful but had no idea what he could do."

"Do you think their abilities develop and grow?" Devon asked. He studied the huge cat. Power emanated from his shoulders, and he wore it as his birthright.

"It's possible. The thing is, how do we get the rock out of there? And seal it up again? Also, this was recently stolen, so someone came here and put it in the pool deliberately. But it hasn't had enough time to cause this level of devastation. What did that earlier?"

He pointed to the blurry shapes in the water beside the bigger rock. "It's not the only rock. What are the chances that the previous rocks weren't strong enough to bring about the devastation that the person doing this needed?"

"Maybe, but why the pools and the rocks anyway? It makes no sense."

"It will. We just don't know how it all fits. Let Matt bring the scientists down here. They can retrieve the rock." He turned back to the way they came.

And came face-to-face with Mason.

"Hell, not you again," Devon growled, his hands immediately forming fists. "What are you doing here anyway? And what possible reason could you have for this damn rock bullshit?"

"It's none of your business, but I'm trying to collect the rocks, thank you," Mason snapped. "Some asshole has been stealing the collection from the estate. We've been trying to retrieve them."

"What?" Tori asked. "You have more of these?"

"Had. They've gone missing." Mason waved a gun at them. "Portman left us a few examples of what he could do."

Damn. Devon was getting tired of always being the one without any firepower.

"Besides, you should be able to retrieve the rocks, can't you, stargazer girl?" Mason asked in mocking tones. "Your stupid sister apparently saved the day the last time."

"That's not quite the way I heard it," Tori said, her voice tight. Devon glanced at Tori. Her face was pinched, and he knew she was actively looking for some sort of solution.

"Sure you did. She's got the affinity for water. You're the one with the affinity for land. So the rocks are there on the ground, at the end of the water. Pick them up, wrap them up

safe, and bring to me."

TORI TURNED TO look at the rocks. They were above the water, and she could in theory bring them over, but the cost to her personally would be huge. She remembered Genesis having wrapped them up and that not being enough. Her spirit pet had managed to wrap them up enough to carry out. The box was there. She could put it in the box and then collect it for Mason, as ordered. But what would he do with it then?

The last thing Tori wanted to do was give him another weapon he could wield on his own.

"Get it now." Mason's voice was deadly low. "I can just shoot your lover if you'd prefer, and don't think your spirit pet will save the day this time."

"No, I'm going." Storm's energy was dedicated to protecting them from the ripple of black energy. He couldn't fight another battle and win. The closer she got to the energy, the more it would try to claim her energy as it tried to rebalance. Hence the forest struggling down here. Not only was the water now poisoned and no longer able to feed the forest, as it needed to be fed, but the rocks were stripping the positive energy from the forest. She had to give the rock what it needed, or else it would take more from everyone around.

And somehow she had to lock it up. And, on top of that, she had more than one rock to deal with.

Damn. Her mind spinning on possibilities, she waded into the pool, feeling it clutch her legs, her skin. Making her hot, odd. The closer to the rock she got, the more she felt it latch onto her energy and draw her closer. Like a fly to a spider, she was caught.

Because it needed positive energy, large energy.

Instead of giving in to the fear and the panic her body was shouting through her nerve endings, she filled herself with love and sent lightning bolts of bright healing energy toward it. Surrounding it, suffocating it in positive energy—the kind it needed.

Instantly the negative energy of the cave lessened. She felt the forest sigh in relief above her. It needed this. She had to free it. But how?

Then she realized she didn't need to do anything. The rock was land. It was the forest. It was her affinity. In fact, it was a part of her. She was okay to send her energy into the rocks because she was one with all things. She could give the rock everything she had; the world around her would just give her more energy.

She stretched out her arms and tilted her head toward the ceiling above her. She cried out to the forest to come and to feed from the healing waters. That she was removing the poison so that they might live again.

The air crackled around them.

Sparks flew.

In the background, she heard the men.

"What is she doing?" Mason cried out. "I just want her to bring me the box with the rocks safely inside."

"And that's what she's doing," Devon replied. "But you can't ask an energy worker to do anything the way you want. They have to do things the right way."

Tori laughed, her arms wide and her heart open. "Take what you need. Return to the space you were in before being damaged. Rejoice in being whole," she cried out. And she pushed out the energy in her system and poured it in the rocks. She surrounded it. Swamped it with love, damn-near suffocating it with the joy of being itself and one with the others. She closed her eyelids but felt the energy change. The temperature eased up, and the darkness dissipated.

Unusual sensations washed over her. She loved it. She turned in a wide circle and saw the men standing there, staring at her. With a big smile on her face, she reached down and picked up the rocks, placed them in the box, and brought them over to Mason. She handed it to him and said, "Here. They are yours."

He stumbled backward, his gun hand waving wildly around. "Stop. Don't come any closer."

"Why?" she asked. "You asked for the rocks. I brought you the rocks."

"Tori," Devon spoke up behind her, his voice gentle. "You're not all there."

She stopped and turned to look at him. He motioned at her body. She looked down to see a seething mass of energy whipping in and out of where her body had been. Her form was still there, but it was full to bursting with the energy that raced through her system.

"Oh, that." She turned toward Mason and the rocks, now on the ground. She lifted the lid to show him the rocks were neutralized. "Isn't that what you wanted?"

"No." He shook his head and backed away, his voice trembling with fear. "No, that's not what I wanted at all," he yelled, lifting his gun and pointing it at her.

And he fired the weapon once, then twice. Instinctively she reached out her hand to stop him and watched as his body jerked once, then twice in response.

And collapsed.

Devon raced over to Mason. As she watched, Devon

checked the man over before slowly standing and studying her. "He's dead."

"How is that possible?" she asked, confusion coloring her voice. A feeling of horror filled her. She hadn't killed him, had she?

"He's been shot." He stared at her, his gaze narrowed, like when he was in deep thought. "I think when he shot you, the bullets hit your energy, and either they were deflected or bounced off you and flew directly back at him."

She shook her head. "No, that's not possible."

"It wasn't possible before. But now …" He motioned to the wild energy around her and said, "I think it is."

Mute, she could only stare at him, her eyes huge. Then she gazed down at her body, glowing bright and strong in the dark. And gasped. "It's the energy field."

And, with her words, it was as if another surge swept over her. It appeared to power up her energy field again. Spreading her edges out farther, connecting her even more deeply to the world around her. Just like the electrical storm. Only different. But bigger. So much bigger. And growing.

Devon could imagine her being one with her woods. One with the trees. One with the earth.

She was one with Mother Nature.

She gasped. "Devon, I'm so lost … and found …"

"I'm here, Tori. I'm here. Stay with me, please."

Her head flung back, as the energy between them swelled. "It's so much. I feel so connected."

"Stay with me, Tori. You belong here with me." He couldn't believe what he saw. She was glowing, a huge ball of blue energy, the edges so thin and sprawled out that she looked to be one with the forest. "Tori, please …" he cried out. "Stay with me. You are connected to me. I love you."

She threw her head back again, as energy billowed around her, through her.

"Please," he cried louder, desperate to get through to her. "You are one with the forest, but you are also one with me. It's not time for you to leave. You are not your granny."

"No," she whispered, "I'm not. She was so much better than I am."

And her energy slowly pulsed in front of him.

"And that is how it should be. You have your lifetime to grow, to learn. To hone your talent, so you can be just like her."

Then a weird stillness came over her body, a shimmering, as if she were considering his words, and he had to wonder if he'd gotten through to her. If she'd heard him—really heard him. She was so special and so very hard on herself.

And he loved her for it.

Hell, he just loved her—any way he could get her. And he realized he might need to tell her again.

"I do, you know," he said in a slow loving tone. "I love you just the way you are. You don't have to be anything other than you. It's the way you are supposed to be—perfect right now."

He reached out to touch the glowing energy and noted no shock, no spark, no pain—just … joy. Joy of having her there. Joy in feeling her in his heart. Joy of having survived a horrific event—to be together.

Overwhelmed by emotions, he closed his eyelids and waited. Something touched his fingers. He opened his eyes to see Tori, the bright glow around her fading, as he watched the woman he loved appear before him.

Her eyelids closed. Her fingers in his.

He squeezed her hand.

She opened those beautiful eyes and smiled at him. "Hey."

He tugged her into his arms and held her close, running his hands up and down her back, so damn grateful to have her in his arms once again. "Thank God," he murmured against her hair. "Thank you for coming back to me."

"I was never gone," she whispered. "I was always here. For you. For everyone."

"As long as you're here for me, I can deal with the rest," he whispered. She'd never be easy. She would always feel pulled to do more. To be more. Good for her. He'd be there for her, no matter what she chose to do.

If she'd let him.

"I will."

He realized that he'd spoken out loud, and she'd answered. "Good," he replied, his smile warm and tender. "Then the rest is up to us." And he pulled back to look down at her, her gaze so full of love, his heart couldn't contain its boundaries. It overflowed with emotions.

She slid her hands up to either side of his face and tugged him down to her.

And kissed him.

Her energy flowing to his and his flowing to hers.

Connected in all ways—once again.

This concludes Book 2 of Glory: *Tori*.

Read the first chapter of Glory: *Celeste*, Book 3

Glory: Celeste (Book #3)
Chapter 1

CELESTE CHANDLER COULDN'T go much farther. Her leg throbbed with pain. She should have returned before now, not waiting until the last minute. She closed her eyes and breathed through the discomfort. Then she took a deep breath and started again.

Finally Granny's cabin was just ahead of her. Celeste cautiously glanced around. Good, she was still alone. Her nerves tingling, her body tense with excitement, she stared at a wall of greenery, blocking her view. She was almost home, for the first time in over a year. And she had to admit that her heart ached with yearning to reconnect. She was the youngest of three triplets—by mere minutes—and she'd missed her sisters terribly.

So much had happened, and she didn't really understand all the changes. But she was home now, and, after she healed, then eventually she'd contact them all and catch up. Finally.

It was as if the bomb blast from Granny's death had destroyed the core of their lives and had blown the family apart. Genesis had stayed home to hold down the fort, which was always her thing, being a homebody and the responsible eldest sister. Tori, the middle child, had run as far and as fast as she could. Celeste? Well, she was like neither of them, but she'd gone into hiding close by to find herself. Close enough to keep track of the goings-on, but far enough away that no one could find her. Not that anyone was looking.

Except Genesis. And, damn, Celeste felt bad about that. Living several towns away, she'd been close enough to hear a lot of what had gone on but not enough to know all the details.

Her coworker, an avid gossip, who drove from town to town making deliveries, had shared that Genesis had been involved in a major kerfuffle, but she had a new partner, and they were living full-time in the Paranormal Center.

That had caused Celeste a ton of sleepless nights. It shouldn't matter, as she'd been the one to walk away from Matt, the new head of the Center. ... However, no way would Celeste ever be okay with him being in a serious, committed relationship with her sister.

It had been weeks before she had found out that Genesis's partner was not Matt, Celeste's former fiancé.

After she could breathe again, she'd mentally beaten herself up for being such a fool.

Celeste leaned against a thick tree, catching her breath. Just a few more feet. Then she'd be safe. And home. Once she'd heard her other sister, Tori, had returned home recently, Celeste knew she was the last one to return to the fold. Granny had always said that she was the slowest of the bunch, and that was fine, as Celeste did things in her own time and rarely made mistakes.

Boy, had she been wrong. Devastated at the loss of the woman who'd raised them, destroyed by what she could only imagine as being a complete betrayal by her lover and the man she thought was hers forever, Celeste couldn't cope and had walked away. One year ago.

Leaving Genesis to mop up the mess behind Celeste.

She owed her sister a lot. Just the thought of seeing her again made her arms ache for a hug. Genesis and Tori were special. They'd been the idols Celeste had looked up to. The models she'd always tried to copy.

And look at what she'd done.

Smurg, her owl spirit pet, flew down to land on a sweeping branch beside her. The look in his eye was one she'd seen many times before.

"I know. It's a big step. And, once again, I can't force myself to take it."

Smurg tilted his big feathered head and stared at her with those wonderful owlish eyes, silently encouraging her to take this step.

And she was rather desperate to do so. Her leg, injured only a week ago, hadn't improved. And now it was at the point that she was afraid she'd left it all too long. She needed Granny's healing pool. But it was on the other side of the energy barricade.

And, the minute she crossed it, she would trigger an alarm that would tell her sisters that Celeste was here.

Was she ready for that?

Did she really have a choice?

Her leg throbbed and pounded the longer she stood here. She looked back the way she'd come. That was the biggest issue. She wouldn't likely make the trip back with her leg like it was. And was she truly alone? The entire way in, she couldn't shake the sensation of being followed. Tracked. An abrupt flash of fear spurred her into motion.

"Okay," she whispered to Smurg. "I'm going."

A small paw slipped into hers. She looked down at Minkel, the spirit meerkat, who walked ever at her side. Her spirit pets were the only reason she'd survived being alone as long as she had. And technically the pets meant Celeste was never truly alone.

Granny had had many in her care. Some had left with Granny upon her death. Many others had left with Celeste, and some had found new homes. It had hurt to lose some of them. But she'd come to understand that these were needed changes. Granny would be proud of Celeste. Granny had often told Celeste how possessive she was and how she must learn to share.

Sharing was one thing, but what about when sharing didn't work, and you lost a special pet? How did one lose a special someone when you were bonded by love?

Silky the lemur whispered reassuringly in her ear. Celeste tilted her head into his warm belly. He stayed snugged up in the crook of her neck.

"I know. I know," she said. "You guys just don't understand how hard this is."

But that wasn't true. They did understand. They'd been here at the cabin before too. They had loved Granny as much as Celeste had. They'd been lost in the spirit world, as they'd never connected to their human soul mates or lost them before their time had come. Granny had been the one to rescue them.

But Celeste had an affinity for the spirit animals, and they'd bonded to her in a big way. But some were hers in ways she hadn't realized, until she lost a few and had seen the bond had only gone one way.

Silky murmured encouragement.

And Celeste knew she'd procrastinated enough.

Hopefully her sisters would give Celeste time to heal, to adapt to being here, before they crashed into the silence her world had become.

She bowed her head and raised her arms. In a gentle series of flowing movements, she opened the energy barrier and stepped through the oversized foliage to the protected space around the small cottage.

It looked just the same, as though it had been frozen in time. As soon as her gaze landed on it, her tears started to flow. Would she ever adjust to Granny no longer being here? She'd been the stability, the rock, the driving force behind the three sisters. So much of their history had been mired in mystery, but Granny had forged a strong path for them. And, when she'd died, it was as if everything died with her.

How sad was that?

But first things first. Celeste shuddered as the pain in her leg deepened. As if it knew they were somewhere it could get help—but maybe didn't want that help.

She hated her wild imagination. How could her leg scream at her to leave this place? To go away before it was too late? Too late for what?

At the cottage door, it took another moment to open the locks. She frowned at the double-energy alarm system in place.

Trouble had been here.

And recent trouble.

She stepped over the threshold and carefully relocked the door. Dropping her bag on the table, she hunched over, her pain so severe that she could only focus on the healing pool. It called to her, yet her leg injury screamed at her forward progress. As if it didn't want her to move forward. She didn't bother looking around. She'd known that the cabin was empty of people as soon as she'd entered the protected space.

Good. She stripped, dropping one item at a time, as she crossed the room to the closed door on the far side. She pushed it open and cried out in joy.

Inside, in the deep recesses of her mind, she'd been afraid that the healing pool wouldn't be here. That something really bad had happened to damage the pool.

Instead, the waves of glittering blue water surged toward her. Reaching for her. She kicked off her shoes and slowly, painfully removed her pants, crying out as her sore leg was free at last. Her socks and panties hit the ground afterward. It was all she could do to sit on the edge of the pool and swing her leg over the side, when the water surged up her calves and up to her thighs. By the time it hit her hips, she was lifted above the glistening waves for a tiny second, then slowly lowered into the bubbling pool below.

She cried out once, before her head was completely submerged, and then she sank to the bottom of the pool. Relief and joy washed through her.

Her last rational thought, as Silky detached from her ear to float at her side, and Minkel perched on the edge above, was, why had she taken so long to come?

MATT HANDED THE sheaf of papers to Connor. "Check out the disturbance at Grandfather's place. Take Devon with you. The investigation is going well over there, but something is still not as stable as it should be. And we need it to be."

As Connor reached out to grab the papers, Matt froze, his senses firing up inside. His hand still holding the papers, he slowly sank into his desk chair. "Jesus. Finally."

Connor frowned. "Matt? What's up?"

Matt released his pent-up breath and murmured, "Your soon-to-be sister-in-law just arrived."

The office door burst open, and Genesis raced in, Tori one step behind her.

"Matt," they both cried out.

He held up his hand. "I know. I can feel her too."

The two sisters hugged each other.

Genesis frowned. "She's hurt. She's triggered the healing pool."

"It's the first place any of us would go. Just think of the emotional trauma we all felt after Granny's death. Celeste is confronting that for the first time," Tori said softly, her hand gently stroking Genesis's back.

"True." Genesis stared out the window at the darkening sky for a moment, before she whispered, "Yet it seems that it could be."

Another odd eruption of noise came on a different level, as their spirit animals conversed.

Matt stared as Darbo spoke with several other spirit animals crowding into the space. They could connect to Celeste's animals in a way that no one else could. And, in this case, since Darbo had been hers at one time, he had a deeper bond than most.

"She's hurt," Matt said, standing abruptly. "Darbo said her leg is bad. Can barely walk, Minkel says."

"Then it's a good thing she's in the pool," Connor said, wrapping an arm around Genesis. "Let's keep calm, everyone. We knew this time would come. We all want this. It's a good thing. I know she's hurt, but we can't go rushing up there and scaring her off. She's come back on her own ..."

"What if she's only come back for the pool?" Genesis whispered, tears in her eyes. "Her leg must be bad, if that's why she returned."

"Hey, don't look at this as her being forced home for the pool," Tori said. "This all has to happen in its own time. You know that."

Genesis nodded, but her gaze was locked on Tori's face, as if waiting for her to make a decision.

Matt knew the decision had to be made by the two sisters, not him. But, damn it, this one *should be* his decision. Celeste was *his*. She'd run from him and what they had, but she'd been in his heart. Part of his soul. And, damn it, she should have come home a long time ago.

His world had improved so much since adding Genesis and Tori to his life, but the one person who truly belonged here still refused to have anything to do with him. Maybe that would change now.

Darbo reached out a small paw and gently brushed it down his cheek. Matt stroked the super soft fur of the tiny lemur who lived attached to his heart, but hung most of the time from his ear. "I know. She's home, and she's hurting."

But the lemur's actions also said he knew that Matt was hurting too. So hard to deal with this when everyone was caught in their own cycle of pain and hope.

So much had happened since Celeste had left. Had she

any idea of what had gone on? What was still going on? The world she'd walked away from didn't exist any longer. At least, not in a form she would recognize. The town was likely hers and her sisters, although that legal fight might still come. He was waiting on the judge's ruling now. They had deeds proving the land, for as far as they could see, belonged to the three sisters. As for Grandfather, … Celeste's old enemy was no longer the same man either. The healing pools had affected even him.

Not fully a normal peaceful man yet, Grandfather had already had enough of a change happen that there was no going back. But no one knew just how much he'd changed, so no one could trust him.

The pools were healing; the forest was healing. However, still massive electrical storms and system-wide energy outages occurred that no one could explain. Some hypotheses had been formulated. A few of those were downright scary.

Besides those events, some things had happened to Tori that even Matt wondered if their granny had set something into motion before her death. But she had died over a year ago—and had sparked a year of severe trial for the triplets. Matt could only hope that Celeste would survive hers—and that he would be the one she would turn to for help.

He loved her. Always had. Would have given his right arm to not have hurt her. But, after Granny's death, every-thing had changed for Celeste. And she had gone to pieces. The slightest things bothered her, and slights that would have normally set her off in a small way had devastated her.

Matt was a patient man to begin with, and he'd desper-ately tried to wait. To be there for her. To help her. To be the one she leaned on to get through this. But she'd been confused and overwrought, and his patience had worn thin. To her, it seemed like everyone had let her down. And perhaps that was understandable, given that fragile state she'd been in at the time.

And then Darbo had chosen Matt, and Celeste had taken it as a horrific betrayal. Matt hadn't understood. He'd so wanted Darbo to be his, understood that Celeste had dozens of other spirit animals to choose from, and had wooed Darbo away.

He hadn't realized he'd crossed a line, until Celeste had disappeared.

That's when he understood the connection between the three of them for what it was.

Darbo had gone into a deep depression. It had taken months for Matt to bring Darbo out of it again. But now, Darbo was lit up like he was on Glory juice. And his voice? … Well, Matt hadn't seen him this excited—ever. The connection between Darbo and Celeste—indeed, Celeste's spirit pet Silky as well—had been at the deepest level, and Matt had broken it. Something that had caused them all horrific pain.

Matt had no way to atone for this—especially when he couldn't see Celeste to apologize. And, besides, an apology wouldn't cut it. Not now. Even when she did see him, no way she could avoid seeing Darbo, and that wound would hurt her again.

He dropped his face to his hands and groaned.

He knew of no way to make it better.

And now, after all this time, she was back.

Would she forgive him? Or was it too late?

Book 3 is available now!

To find out more visit Dale Mayer's website.

https://geni.us/DMceleste

Author's Note

Thank you for reading Tori! If you enjoyed my book, I'd appreciate it if you'd leave a review.

Dear reader,

I love to hear from readers, and you can contact me at my website: www.dalemayer.com or at my Facebook author page. To be informed of new releases and special offers, sign up for my newsletter or follow me on BookBub. And if you are interested in joining Dale Mayer's Reader Group, here is the Facebook sign up page.
http://geni.us/DaleMayerFBGroup

Cheers,
Dale Mayer

About the Author

Dale Mayer is a *USA Today* best-selling author, best known for her SEALs military romances, her Psychic Visions series, and her Lovely Lethal Garden cozy series. Her contemporary romances are raw and full of passion and emotion (Broken But … Mending, Hathaway House series). Her thrillers will keep you guessing (Kate Morgan, By Death series), and her romantic comedies will keep you giggling (*It's a Dog's Life*, a stand-alone novella; and the Broken Protocols series, starring Charming Marvin, the cat).

Dale honors the stories that come to her—and some of them are crazy, break all the rules and cross multiple genres!

To go with her fiction, she also writes nonfiction in many different fields, with books available on résumé writing, companion gardening, and the US mortgage system. All her books are available in print and ebook format.

Connect with Dale Mayer Online

Dale's Website – www.dalemayer.com
Twitter – @DaleMayer
Facebook Page – geni.us/DaleMayerFBFanPage
Facebook Group – geni.us/DaleMayerFBGroup
BookBub – geni.us/DaleMayerBookbub
Instagram – geni.us/DaleMayerInstagram
Goodreads – geni.us/DaleMayerGoodreads
Newsletter – geni.us/DaleNews

Also by Dale Mayer

Published Adult Books:

Shadow Recon

Magnus, Book 1

Bullard's Battle

Ryland's Reach, Book 1

Cain's Cross, Book 2

Eton's Escape, Book 3

Garret's Gambit, Book 4

Kano's Keep, Book 5

Fallon's Flaw, Book 6

Quinn's Quest, Book 7

Bullard's Beauty, Book 8

Bullard's Best, Book 9

Bullard's Battle, Books 1–2

Bullard's Battle, Books 3–4

Bullard's Battle, Books 5–6

Bullard's Battle, Books 7–8

Terkel's Team

Damon's Deal, Book 1

Wade's War, Book 2

Gage's Goal, Book 3

Calum's Contact, Book 4

Rick's Road, Book 5

Scott's Summit, Book 6

Brody's Beast, Book 7

Terkel's Twist, Book 8

Terkel's Triumph, Book 9

Terkel's Guardian

Radar, Book 1

Kate Morgan

Simon Says… Hide, Book 1

Simon Says… Jump, Book 2

Simon Says… Ride, Book 3

Simon Says… Scream, Book 4

Simon Says… Run, Book 5

Simon Says… Walk, Book 6

Hathaway House

Aaron, Book 1

Brock, Book 2

Cole, Book 3

Denton, Book 4

Elliot, Book 5

Finn, Book 6

Gregory, Book 7

Heath, Book 8

Iain, Book 9

Jaden, Book 10

Keith, Book 11

Lance, Book 12

Melissa, Book 13

Nash, Book 14

Owen, Book 15

Percy, Book 16

Quinton, Book 17

Ryatt, Book 18

Spencer, Book 19

Hathaway House, Books 1–3

Hathaway House, Books 4–6

Hathaway House, Books 7–9

The K9 Files

Ethan, Book 1

Pierce, Book 2

Zane, Book 3

Blaze, Book 4

Lucas, Book 5

Parker, Book 6

Carter, Book 7

Weston, Book 8

Greyson, Book 9

Rowan, Book 10

Caleb, Book 11

Kurt, Book 12

Tucker, Book 13

Harley, Book 14

Kyron, Book 15

Jenner, Book 16

Rhys, Book 17

Landon, Book 18

Harper, Book 19

Kascius, Book 20

The K9 Files, Books 1–2

The K9 Files, Books 3–4

The K9 Files, Books 5–6

The K9 Files, Books 7–8

The K9 Files, Books 9–10

The K9 Files, Books 11–12

Lovely Lethal Gardens

Arsenic in the Azaleas, Book 1

Bones in the Begonias, Book 2

Corpse in the Carnations, Book 3

Daggers in the Dahlias, Book 4

Evidence in the Echinacea, Book 5

Footprints in the Ferns, Book 6

Gun in the Gardenias, Book 7

Handcuffs in the Heather, Book 8

Ice Pick in the Ivy, Book 9

Jewels in the Juniper, Book 10

Killer in the Kiwis, Book 11

Lifeless in the Lilies, Book 12

Murder in the Marigolds, Book 13

Nabbed in the Nasturtiums, Book 14

Offed in the Orchids, Book 15

Poison in the Pansies, Book 16

Quarry in the Quince, Book 17

Revenge in the Roses, Book 18

Silenced in the Sunflowers, Book 19

Toes up in the Tulips, Book 20

Uzi in the Urn, Book 21

Lovely Lethal Gardens, Books 1–2

Lovely Lethal Gardens, Books 3–4

Lovely Lethal Gardens, Books 5–6

Lovely Lethal Gardens, Books 7–8

Lovely Lethal Gardens, Books 9–10

Psychic Vision Series

Tuesday's Child

Hide 'n Go Seek

Maddy's Floor

Garden of Sorrow

Knock Knock…

Rare Find

Eyes to the Soul

Now You See Her

Shattered

Into the Abyss

Seeds of Malice

Eye of the Falcon

Itsy-Bitsy Spider

Unmasked

Deep Beneath

From the Ashes

Stroke of Death

Ice Maiden

Snap, Crackle…

What If…

Talking Bones

String of Tears

Inked Forever

Psychic Visions Books 1–3

Psychic Visions Books 4–6

Psychic Visions Books 7–9

By Death Series

Touched by Death

Haunted by Death

Chilled by Death

By Death Books 1–3

Broken Protocols – Romantic Comedy Series

Cat's Meow

Cat's Pajamas

Cat's Cradle

Cat's Claus

Broken Protocols 1-4

Broken and… Mending

Skin

Scars

Scales (of Justice)

Broken but… Mending 1-3

Glory

Genesis

Tori

Celeste

Glory Trilogy

Biker Blues

Morgan: Biker Blues, Volume 1

Cash: Biker Blues, Volume 2

SEALs of Honor

Mason: SEALs of Honor, Book 1

Hawk: SEALs of Honor, Book 2

Dane: SEALs of Honor, Book 3

Swede: SEALs of Honor, Book 4

Shadow: SEALs of Honor, Book 5

Cooper: SEALs of Honor, Book 6

Markus: SEALs of Honor, Book 7

Evan: SEALs of Honor, Book 8

Mason's Wish: SEALs of Honor, Book 9

Chase: SEALs of Honor, Book 10

Brett: SEALs of Honor, Book 11

Devlin: SEALs of Honor, Book 12

Easton: SEALs of Honor, Book 13

Ryder: SEALs of Honor, Book 14

Macklin: SEALs of Honor, Book 15

Corey: SEALs of Honor, Book 16

Warrick: SEALs of Honor, Book 17

Tanner: SEALs of Honor, Book 18

Heroes for Hire

Diesel, Book 13

Jerricho, Book 14

Killian, Book 15

Hatch, Book 16

Corbin, Book 17

Aiden, Book 18

The Mavericks, Books 1–2

The Mavericks, Books 3–4

The Mavericks, Books 5–6

The Mavericks, Books 7–8

The Mavericks, Books 9–10

The Mavericks, Books 11–12

Standalone Novellas

It's a Dog's Life

Riana's Revenge

Second Chances

Published Young Adult Books:

Family Blood Ties Series

Vampire in Denial

Vampire in Distress

Vampire in Design

Vampire in Deceit

Vampire in Defiance

Vampire in Conflict

Vampire in Chaos

Vampire in Crisis

Vampire in Control

Vampire in Charge

Family Blood Ties Set 1–3

Family Blood Ties Set 1–5

Family Blood Ties Set 4–6

Family Blood Ties Set 7–9

Sian's Solution, A Family Blood Ties Series Prequel
    Novelette

Design series

Dangerous Designs

Deadly Designs

Darkest Designs

Design Series Trilogy

Standalone

In Cassie's Corner

Gem Stone (a Gemma Stone Mystery)

Time Thieves

Published Non-Fiction Books:

Career Essentials

Career Essentials: The Résumé

Career Essentials: The Cover Letter

Career Essentials: The Interview

Career Essentials: 3 in 1